NIGHT DRAGON

THE DRAGON MISFITS BOOK 6

D.K. HOLMBERG

ASH PUBLISHING

Cover by Tom Edwards

Want a **free book** and to be notified when D.K. Holmberg's next novel is released, along with other news and freebies? **Sign up for his mailing list by going here**. Your email address will never be shared and you can unsubscribe at any time.

www.dkholmberg.com

1

The darkness swirled all around the inside of the forest and Jason focused on it, staring into the inky depths. In this case, it could just be the fog of night layering over everything, but it could also be something more, something unsettling. He had enough experience with the small night dragon to question why it created this shade.

He held onto the power of the other dragons. He could feel the ice and the iron dragons' power flowing through him as it often did. Jason added a hint of the forest dragon, that connection that allowed him to be able to shift reality. On top of that, he had a faint and distant sense of the storm dragon. That dragon was there, crackling energy, and the more that he focused on that sense of energy, the easier it was to know there was some way to use it. It was a new connection.

He took a step forward.

He was careful when he did so, not wanting to move too quickly, not wanting to risk the danger of the darkness. He could feel that around him, almost as if it were squeezing around him, though even now, he couldn't tell whether or not that darkness was anything other than the shadow of night. When he looked up at the sky, he saw only a cloudless night, no moon, no stars, just the blanket of black. That, as much as anything, suggested this was supernatural.

"I can feel you," Jason mumbled. His voice came out muted, quiet and soft, and it came out as if it were within a fog of energy.

It was another clue that he was right about what he had detected and how he believed the night dragon to be here. He held onto the other dragons' energy, calling that power to him, letting it surround him, swirling throughout him.

Jason started with the iron dragon, letting the heat radiate outward. It was one aspect that he knew the night dragon wouldn't be troubled by, and then he added a hint of the ice dragon's cold. By holding onto the two, the bonding pair allowed him to create a fog of his own, a cloud of water vapor that hovered over everything. Finally, he added a hint of the forest dragon. Vaguely, he noticed something different.

It was an insidious sort of sensation, something that filtered through, leaving a trailing swirling all around him. There was a part of Jason that thought it felt cold, though cold wasn't quite right. When he was connected to the iron dragon as he was, there was no real sense of cold anyway. Jason had long ago lost the fear of the endless bite of cold he had once known his entire life.

What he knew now was a sense of energy. That pressure upon him was little more than a fluttering.

Tracking through that connection, Jason could feel something more.

He took a step. Out here in the darkness, surrounded by the energy of the night, it was dangerous to take too many steps.

Especially as he had no idea where the dragon was and whether there was anything about the dragon that he needed to be more careful with. Jason had learned that the night dragon could hide from him all too easily. He took another step and braced himself.

This time, he held out the ice and iron dragon connections, pulsing it away from him. That cloud of water vapor radiated around him, creating a circle.

There was pressure upon that circle.

There.

Jason turned toward it and began to move more deliberately. There was a soft and persistent pressure upon him, and as he headed toward that sense, he moved as carefully as he thought he needed in order to detect the sense of the night dragon.

The dragon was near enough that Jason thought he could reach for him.

Gradually, he took another step, and then another.

Jason moved toward that pressure around him.

His heart hammered, racing wildly.

He paused a moment to steady himself, not wanting to get too caught up in the emotion of what he was doing. He took another step.

Now he was turning toward that energy and he could feel it crashing around him.

He turned in place, sweeping the energy of the other dragons through him. There came a small echoing. It was faint and subtle, but because he had sent the power, he could detect its echo.

He took another step.

A shadowed form loomed near him: a tree, at least as far as he could tell.

Jason ignored it and took another step.

There came a bulging of energy, a quick reaction, almost a terrified sense, but Jason held on. He took a quick step forward and exploded power and light around him.

Suddenly, the forest was awash in bright orange light, the energy of the iron dragon. It radiated all around, filling the space between the trees. A shadowed form loomed near him, trapped within a bubble of energy Jason had created.

He hurried toward the dragon, squeezing a moment longer.

The dragon struggled within that barrier, continuing to try to break free, but Jason held tightly, maintaining his connection to the dragon as long as he could. He wanted to ensure he had that dragon wrapped up with that energy. It was a test, as much for Jason as it was for the dragon.

He paused in front of the night dragon, the energy swirling within the barrier he held. "I got you this time," he said.

The struggling continued, tendrils of darkness that attempted to swirl out, slamming into the barrier, but the energy Jason maintained through his connection to the other dragons allowed him to keep the night dragon inside.

"You don't have to struggle quite so much," he said.

The dragon settled.

Finally, the dragon came fully into view.

He was small. Smaller than the other dragons, little more than the size of a large dog. His wings stretched off to either side, and though he allowed Jason to see him more clearly now, his wings took on some of the shadowed form as well, stretching out in a way that left it looking as if there were shadows streaking away from them.

The dragon rubbed up against the barrier, testing it. Wings slashed at it.

Jason had long ago learned that they were sharp and could damage his barriers. It required he hold more firmly to his barriers, clinging to them tightly enough that he would ensure the night dragon was unable shatter them and break free.

Jason crouched down in front of the dragon.

The dragon turned its face toward him. Everything

was dark. It was impossibly black. The only light was a faint flicker of light within his eyes.

"You aren't going to be able to break free this time," Jason said.

The dragon started again and shadows streamed off him, slamming toward Jason. Jason held onto the barrier, solidifying it for a moment to ensure that it held, but the dragon didn't attempt to break free again.

Jason grinned. "What else do you want to try?"

The dragon turned toward him and lowered his head.

"That's it?"

"You have succeeded," the dragon said. Even his voice was wispy, little more than a faint tremoring.

"I expected you to try more than this," Jason said.

"Why should I try more when you succeeded in holding me?"

"You can see if you can break free again."

That was the game. He would try to find the dragon, trapping him within one of the barriers, and the dragon would either try to hide or break free. Feeling the pressure from the dragon now, the way that he was no longer attempting to shatter the barrier, Jason recognized that he no longer attempted to surge free.

"The game is done," the dragon said.

Jason released his hold around the dragon. There was no point in maintaining it, as he didn't want to harm the dragon, and he certainly didn't want to scare him. He needed to maintain that hold so that he could continue to work with the dragon, trying to get a better understanding of him.

Even though he had spent time like this with the dragon, Jason still couldn't use his energy. That was the next step, a part of his desire to bond with him, to gain an understanding of the power within the night dragon. He hadn't succeeded, not yet, but he was optimistic he would do so.

"What's wrong?"

The night dragon turned away, slipping between the trees.

Now that Jason held onto the power of the iron dragon, illuminating all of the forest, he no longer struggled to see the dragon disappearing. It wasn't as if the dragon were doing anything to try to mask his disappearance, either. Though he slipped off, he didn't disappear in a way that made it difficult for Jason to see him.

Jason followed.

The dragon headed deeper into the forest, and as they went, Jason knew exactly where the dragon intended to go. He'd been here before, and knew it well.

He shifted the illusion all around him, creating another layer, making it so that there wasn't anything to be concerned about. He didn't want anyone else, even from Dragon Haven, to interfere.

Not that he thought that anybody from Dragon Haven would cause any problems for this dragon, but Jason didn't want to startle the dragon, and he wanted to have an unencumbered opportunity to continue to work with the dragon.

The night dragon glanced back at him, turning in his direction.

A burst of power came from him and struck Jason.

He squeezed a barrier around himself and waited.

The night dragon turned toward him, radiating energy again. "I would like to leave these trees," the dragon said.

He stopped in a small clearing. This was where the egg had hatched, and there were still fragments of the shell remaining. Jason had one in his pocket, his way of trying to see if he might be able to connect to the dragon in a different way, but so far that shell hadn't done anything to help Jason establish that connection. He didn't know if it would or not, but he also worried that if the shell were to be found by someone else, there was a danger to the night dragon. The other pieces of shell were within Dragon Haven, secluded in a room that Jason had sealed off with a powerful illusion.

"What do you hope to find outside of the forest?"

"Something else," the night dragon said.

Jason leaned against one of the trees, watching the night dragon. He was so different than the other dragons.

Of course, when it came to these dragons—the misfits—all of them were different from each other. While the night dragon might be small, there was no doubt in Jason's mind that he was powerful. As far as Jason could tell, the dragon had considerable energy trapped within him, and he could use his power and energy in order to reach for the kind of magic that the other dragons could not.

"The others aren't sure it's safe for you to leave yet."

"The others are afraid," the night dragon said.

"Yes," Jason said. He stepped forward and crouched down next the night dragon.

He swished his tail, the only part of him that was enormous. It was incredibly long, snaking out from him, long enough that he could wrap it all the way around the entirety of his body.

"There is someone out there who would try to control the dragons, and she has already attempted to do so with the others."

"But she has failed," the night dragon said.

"So far, she has failed," Jason agreed.

"Then she would fail with me," the night dragon said. He looked over, and those dark eyes held Jason. Power seemed to swirl into him, trapping him. "You haven't been able to hold me with only the energy of one dragon."

"I haven't," Jason agreed.

That was part of the game, their way of trying to work together to see if there was anything that Jason might be able to do to hold the dragon, and in all the times he had attempted to trap the dragon, a single connection wasn't enough. The night dragon could break free when Jason held him with the energy of the ice dragon or the iron dragon or even the forest dragon. Jason hadn't attempted to do so with the storm dragon, though his connection to that dragon was different, not nearly as potent as it was with the others. Regardless, only in mixing had he been successful in holding the night dragon.

Part of that might just be a failing of Jason's, not necessarily a sign of how powerful the night dragon could be, though he couldn't help but wonder if it truly did demonstrate the true strength of the night dragon, of the power that existed within him.

"You're right, but the person we worry about can command hundreds of dragons," he said.

"You have freed most of those dragons," the dragon said.

"I've freed as many as I can, but there remain hundreds still trapped."

"There are others that need freed."

"From her?"

Jason created an illusion, holding an image of Jessica. She stood on the far side of the clearing, her arms crossed, a dark tilt to her jaw. She had dark black hair, deep brown eyes, almost black, and pale skin. She was dressed in a dragonskin jacket and pants, much like she had the very first time he'd met her.

Despite the illusion, there was an anger and energy that filled her, and Jason couldn't help but feel as if there was something within the illusion that he needed to be careful creating. Every so often, he wondered if the illusion had more power than he suspected.

He knew illusions, especially those illusions that shifted reality the way that he had the ability to do, could call upon power that brought more energy into existence.

When it came to Jessica, he worried about giving it too much power. So far, they had defeated her, pushing her back and preventing her from probing toward Dragon Haven. For now. Eventually, he worried that would change, and when it did, he wanted to be ready to protect Dragon Haven.

"She doesn't look too powerful," the night dragon said, swishing his long tail toward her. Shadows streamed off the tail. They swirled around the illusion, shattering it.

It was a physical sensation when the illusion shattered. More than that, there came a surge of power that exploded, and it sent a shiver radiating up through him.

He tried to ignore it, trying to focus only on holding onto the illusion rather than trying to use it as an opportunity to combat the night dragon, but he couldn't help feeling as if there was something that made it difficult. He struggled with it.

The more power that streamed off the dragon, the more he could feel the change, the way that energy shattered.

"Not only from her, though," the night dragon said. It seemed to Jason that he became more confident each time they spoke.

He took a deep breath, letting it out slowly. He noticed the energy the night dragon held onto, and as he did, he tried to hold onto something different, attempting a different approach. Rather than fighting through the burst of energy the night dragon used, Jason tried to solidify the illusion in a different way, shifting it.

He allowed the shadows to slide through the illusion, but once they were through, he added a hint more of power, connecting to the illusion again. Doing so, he felt the power that he'd been holding onto shatter, but then it reformed in a way that allowed Jason to maintain it again.

The night dragon looked over at him. "Why do you hold this image?"

"Practice," Jason said.

"Why must you practice?"

"Because you continue to test me," Jason said, smiling, though he didn't feel much humor. The night dragon would be too great a prize were Jessica to claim him. Jason needed to protect him—all of the misfits—from Jessica and Lorach.

He took another step toward the dragon and reached toward him.

He hadn't touched the dragon yet, either. As much as he wanted to feel the night dragon's skin, to see what the scaled surface of his body might feel like, the dragon had avoided any contact.

Jason didn't even know if the night dragon was substantial or whether it consisted of shadows swirling around. As far as he knew, it could be either.

The night dragon continued to move, writhing around, and as Jason held onto the sense of the night dragon, he felt power flowing from him. There wasn't anything more that he could detect coming off the dragon, just a certain anger and energy that suggested his irritation with Jason.

Jason took a deep breath. "The other dragons want you to stay here," he said.

"And you?" the night dragon asked.

"I think it's necessary you stay here for now. Eventually…"

Even then, Jason wasn't sure what it would take for him to feel confident with the night dragon leaving the forest. Knowing how powerful the night dragon was, knowing just what Jessica would do to get her hands on a dragon like this, he feared that she would try to capture this dragon in particular. She would use and control him the way she had with the others.

He didn't even know if she was aware of the egg or the existence of the night dragon, though it was unlikely she knew it had hatched. Still, he wouldn't put it past her to have learned that *something* had happened. The dragons under her control may have felt some influence.

Jason took a deep breath, focusing on the power within him, trying to calm himself and to focus on the other dragon energies. "Let us resolve this."

The dragon looked over at him. "If you don't, I'm leaving," the dragon said. "There is much that must be done."

"I understand."

"You don't understand. Not yet." The dragon watched him. "Soon you'll have no choice but to understand."

Jason had a sense the dragon was done talking to him. He curled around and shadows began to bloom off him, sweeping out in a tight circle of energy.

Jason focused on the power coming off the night

dragon, but there wasn't anything he could use of that power. Though he could feel the energy coming from the night dragon, and though he was aware of that power, he couldn't draw on it.

Perhaps he never would be able to.

Reaching the power of the other dragons was different with each, but part of it came from a willingness of the dragon to grant that energy to him. When it came to the night dragon, Jason didn't think he would be allowed to use that energy. Perhaps in time, or when the night dragon finally freed himself from the forest, but until then…

Jason turned away. With each step, he solidified the illusion of the forest around the night dragon, holding it in place. Partly that was for the night dragon's protection, but partly it was to keep the night dragon here.

Jason didn't need to tell the dragon that. He already knew.

He solidified aspects of it, barriers that he layered in place, and the power of illusion that he drew from the forest dragon.

He added each of the other dragons' power to what he placed, mixing more and more energy with each step he took. By holding onto that energy, Jason created enough of a layer that it would be difficult for the night dragon to press through.

That was another advantage of their games. By holding on to the power with the night dragon, giving the dragon opportunity to test what he could do, Jason had an opportunity to determine whether or not the dragon would be able to break through this illusion.

So far, he had not.

What would happen when he could?

Worse, what would happen if he realized just what Jason did?

He tried not to think about that, focusing instead on protecting the night dragon. That was all he truly wanted to do. If he could protect the night dragon, he could ensure his safety, the way he wanted to ensure the safety of all the dragons he'd come to lovingly deem misfits.

I'm a misfit, too.

Jason had been one ever since he could remember. In the mountain village, he'd never fit in. Not really. Now that he was in Dragon Haven, Jason still didn't fit in, despite what others tried to make him believe. He knew the truth.

The dragons were the reason he stayed.

Mostly the reason. He had people in Dragon Haven he cared about, though they didn't understand him—or the dragons—as much as he wished they could. They didn't understand that Jason would do anything to keep the dragons safe.

He was the only one willing to do so.

Now that the night dragon had hatched, he could keep the night dragon from the dangers of Jessica and the people of Lorach. She wouldn't have the chance to harm him the way she had harmed so many other dragons, forcing them to serve her and the people of Lorach. He would protect him.

Jason looked back, feeling the way the night dragon pressed against the barrier, as a strange thought came to him.

Does the night dragon even need for me to keep him safe?

2

There came a buildup of power, a surge of energy in the distance, as Jason made his way back through the forest. Light began to bloom in the sky, daylight rising over the horizon, filtering through the trees. He found it easier to work with the night dragon in the darkness, partly because that seemed to be when he was most active, but also because that was when he was the most powerful.

His power fell off in the daylight. For some reason, the dragon wasn't able to summon nearly as much power then. It was almost as if he fed on the darkness.

Given Jason's experience with the other dragons, it was possible that was exactly what was happening. He knew enough about the night dragon, and enough about the power the dragon could summon, to believe the night truly did strengthen him, giving him the energy that he needed.

Heading into the outskirts of Dragon Haven, Jason

reached the street leading toward the main part of the city. It spread out around him. The roads were fairly straight, though the city gently curved toward the forest that surrounded it. Most of the buildings had domed roofs, though not all of them. Sculptures of dragons adorned the city, some of them enormous, carved out of a pale white stone. Smaller sculptures could be found within the city, as well, and many of them were made from obsidian.

He glanced toward the dragon sculptures. One of the sculptures was small, reminding him of the night dragon. The sculpture itself was a deep black obsidian, the surface smooth. Jason had attempted to test that sculpture before, probing into it with the power of the other dragons, searching for something that he might be able to detect within it, but when he had, there had been nothing there.

He lingered there a moment, probably a moment too long.

"Why are you standing here?"

Jason looked over to see his sister coming toward him. She was tall, slender, and seemed fitter than she had before. She had changed in the time that they had been here, though they all had changed.

"I'm just checking out the statue," he said.

"Really?" Kayla joined him, standing next the statue, her hands clasped behind her, and she tilted her head to the side as if she were appraising it. "I don't see anything within the statue that is all that worthwhile to look at."

"Sarah once claimed the city was home to a people

who understood the dragons far differently than we do." As he looked at the statue, he couldn't help but feel as if that were true. There was so much *detail* in each of the sculptures. "I wonder it what it was like then."

"With the city this size…"

Jason looked up. As far as he knew, Dragon Haven was home to several thousand people, though not all of them had a connection to the dragons. Few, in fact, did. Those who did helped keep the free dragons safe, though did so by hiding them from the world.

"I wish I knew what it was like when the dragons were able to fly freely," he said softly, turning his attention back to the sculpture. He held his hand above it, feeling a faint warmth coming from the sculpture.

"Some would call that dangerous," she said.

He looked up, arching a brow. "Some?"

"Not me," she added. He'd been working with her and the possibility that she could have a connection to the dragons and had begun to suspect she did, though she hadn't demonstrated it. Yet. "I just meant some people."

"Not the people who once lived here," he said. "I feel a sense of power coming off it."

Kayla leaned close to the statue. "I don't detect that," she said.

Jason smiled. "Do you think that you would?"

"Didn't you say I have the potential to connect to the dragons?"

"I'm sure you do. That *is* why I've been working with you to develop that connection."

"Not so much lately," Kayla said.

He'd been distracted, and she deserved more time from him. "We can work together soon. Once this is over."

"Will it be, though? There's always something else you need to do. Some other thing you need to keep Lorach from achieving. When will it be enough?"

It was a strange question from his sister, but she wasn't wrong. When *would* it be enough?

He stared at the sculpture and others like it on the street around him, knowing the answer. It came easily, almost as if he could see it in his mind. The connection to the dragons seemed to reverberate there, as if in agreement.

When the dragons are free again.

"We're going to draw that ability out. In time. Had Mother and Father allowed us to learn about our connection earlier, we would have known about it by now," Jason said.

"I know you haven't talked with her," Kayla started, and when Jason opened his mouth to argue, Kayla just smiled and waved her hand. "You don't have to pretend as if you have. She's told me. She also told me about why they ended up there."

Jason watched his sister. It was a question that he hadn't an answer to. He wondered, though, and knew that he had no choice but to do so. How could he not wonder why his family had ended up in the coldest part of the world, a place that had been so impossible to survive?

"It was how they were able to get away," Kayla said. "At

least, that's what Mother said. Getting away from the Dragon Souls required committing to something else."

He frowned at her. "What do you mean that they had to commit to something else?"

She shrugged. "I mean, they had to commit to watching for signs of dragons."

Jason didn't know what to say. It was something he would need to ask his mother about if he ever had the opportunity, but did it even matter? At this point, the only thing that really mattered was what he had ended up doing.

Getting away from his mountaintop village. Away from the cold. Away from the snow.

And he had ended up getting closer to the dragons.

"I know you don't want to talk to her about it."

"It has nothing to do with what I want to talk to her about," he said carefully. "It has more to do with how they hid that from us."

"Because they left," Kayla said. "They couldn't tell us anything. They weren't permitted to."

He doubted that was the entirety of the truth, but maybe it was true enough.

He breathed out heavily and shook his head.

"You got away, anyway," Kayla said, her voice dropping. "Now that mother is better, I don't have anything. Not like you do."

Now, their mother had recovered, at least enough that she no longer needed Kayla the same way that she once had. Did Kayla miss working with their mother? Maybe she wanted to feel important—and working with the dragons would give her that.

Which was what he needed to do.

Find some way to give her responsibility.

He smiled at his sister and held onto the power of the dragons, summoning their power through his connection. He probed the dragon sculpture again, feeling a hint of energy that came from the dragons, echoing within him.

"Do you feel anything when I do that?" he asked.

"What is it you're doing?" Kayla asked.

"I'm trying to see if there's anything within the sculpture that might react to the dragons," Jason said.

"What exactly do you expect to be able to feel?" she asked, her hand waving above the surface of the dragon for a moment.

He shook his head. "That's just it. I don't know if there's anything I'm going to be able to feel. There's a sense of something from within the sculpture, some energy that strikes me as familiar, though…"

He didn't know. More than that, he had no idea as to the purpose of the sculpture at all. The only thing that he knew was that the sculpture demonstrated considerable skill in its detailed construction.

"What are you doing up so early anyway?" Kayla asked.

"I was taking a walk," he said.

There were only a few who knew about the night dragon, and Jason tried to keep that limited to those who really should know. Unfortunately, his sister wasn't one of them.

She flicked her gaze to the sky, then back to him. "So early?"

"I was checking on something."

She turned back, looking toward the forest, frowning. "You don't have to be the only to do that. Others are willing. Able. You can let them."

It was something that his sister still didn't understand, something that Jason wasn't entirely sure how to explain. Maybe he couldn't explain, anyway.

He smiled at her, knowing he couldn't let others be the ones to protect the dragons.

It was *his* responsibility. He was the misfit who had pushed so hard on behalf of the dragons. It was him and him alone.

If he didn't do this, there wouldn't be anyone willing to do so.

"Let's meet later to work on your connection to the dragons," he said.

"You would do that?"

"You're my sister. Of course I would do that."

Jason hadn't attempted to see if she could reach to any of the dragon misfits yet. If she'd been working with the Dragon Haven dragons, or even the freed dragons, it was possible there wouldn't be anything within any of those dragons he would be able to help her reach, but the misfits were different. Not only was the power different, but the way that someone could connect to them was different.

She smiled and wrapped him in a quick hug. "Thank you." She raced off, a lightness to her step.

It pleased him to see his sister like that. There had been too long where she'd been dour and sad, and seeing her like this, moving with such happiness within her, filled him with a similar happiness.

He turned, heading into the building that housed his family, along with several others. The building itself was fairly standard for Dragon Haven, with a domed roof, long walls, and windows that let light in throughout it. Carvings of dragons adorned the outside of the building, and many other dragon carvings lined the hall inside, some of them in the stone, but most along the doorways. They gave an aura to the entirety of the building, a feel for the way the people of this place valued the dragons, and forcing him once again to reflect on what it might be like for the dragons to fly freely.

He hurried through the halls. Lanterns lit the way, casting a bright light that washed along the hallways.

His boots thudded off the hard stone and he made an effort to mute the sound, using a hint of the forest dragon power with which to do so. It was unnecessary, though he didn't like to announce his passing quite so loudly.

He reached the end of the hall and paused in front of one of the doorways, knocking briefly. For a moment, there was nothing. He knocked again, waiting, but again, there was nothing.

Jason continued to hesitate and pushed out with a hint of the sense of the ice and iron dragons, using that combination to create a burst of power that he pressed through the doorway.

Using power in that way, he could feel whether there was somebody in the room on the other side. It was empty.

Strange. He would've expected Sarah to be there at this time of day, but there was no sense of her. Turning and heading back down the hall, he paused at the branch point leading to the main part of the building.

Voices caught his attention and Jason headed in that direction, hurrying toward them. When he reached the wide double doors leading into what he had once considered a throne room, he found Sarah speaking quietly with several of the Dragon Guard.

Jason stood in the doorway, listening. He wasn't concerned about eavesdropping, knowing she wouldn't be concerned about his presence, but he was curious as to the nature of the conversation.

"They have to be somewhere," Sarah said.

"I'm sorry, but we haven't been able to find anything of them."

Jason understood what they were talking about. And he understood just why Sarah would be so passionate as she spoke.

Her parents.

They had disappeared, and in the days since the night dragon had hatched, there had been an attempt to try to find them, but none had succeeded. They had to be somewhere, but as they continued looking, it seemed almost as if Olar and Cherise had completely disappeared.

"I'm not sure I can give you the answer you want, then," Sarah said.

"You understand that with them gone—"

"They will return," Sarah said.

The Dragon Guard tensed.

Jason looked over at the Dragon Guard, studying him.

He was probably ten years older than Jason, with dark, close-cropped hair, a wide chin, and a muscular body. He was dressed in dragonskin, much like most of the Dragon Guard, and a curved blade hung at his side.

He felt a sense of energy radiating off the Dragon Guard, the kind of power that Jason had come to attribute to them, though he wasn't sure if there was something more to the Dragon Guard that he should be able to detect at this point.

Finally, the man leaned forward, bowing briefly before heading out of the room.

Sarah leaned down, resting her head on the table, shaking it slowly. Her blonde hair dangled in front of her face and her crystal blue eyes stared straight ahead. She was lovely, but looked as if she were irritated.

Jason cleared his throat and she looked up. She wiped tears from her eyes.

"No sign of them?" Jason asked, his gaze going back toward the spot the Dragon Guard had occupied.

"There's been none. I don't know why they would have disappeared. Or if Lorren did something to them."

As much as it pained him to admit, that was the most

likely answer. "Do you think they might have detected something they would have gone after?"

"My parents wouldn't have abandoned the city like that," she said.

Jason didn't know her parents all that well, but wasn't sure he would consider that abandoning anything. They had been confident in their desire and willingness to do anything that was necessary to protect Dragon Haven, and yet, in the time that Jason had been here, he hadn't seen them leave the city once. The fact that they had done so, or had been abducted and taken from here, was startling.

"We have to find them," she said. Her eyes looked as if they wanted to burrow into him, demanding him to help.

"There are others looking," Jason said.

"I know there are others looking, but *we* have to find them."

Jason had had this discussion with her before, and it hadn't gone any better than this one was going. "What do you think that you and I might be able to do that's more than the Dragon Guard can do?"

"What can you and I do? The better question is what can *you* do, Jason Dreshen? You're the one who managed to break into Lorach, and you managed to save dozens—no, *hundreds*—of dragons, rescuing them from the Dragon Souls. What can you do?"

"You know why I can't leave," he said softly.

"I know why you *won't* leave," she said.

"Henry agrees."

"Henry." She shook her head, looking back down at the table.

Jason realized a stack of papers rested in front of her, and couldn't help but wonder if there was something on them. Perhaps it was something that detailed what had happened to her parents. Or perhaps it was something to do with the ruling of Dragon Haven.

When it came to understanding just what they needed to know about how to lead in Dragon Haven, he didn't have much of an idea about what was involved. The only thing he knew was that Cherise and Olar had done so effectively for many years.

"Henry feels we're doing everything that we need to do," Jason said.

"Henry is doing everything he needs to do. The Dragon Guard are doing everything that they need to do. And what I need is my friend to do everything he can do," she said.

Jason sighed. "I can send the dragons looking."

Of course, he had already done that. He'd asked the ice and the iron dragons to search, hunting for signs of Cherise and Olar. There had been nothing. The forest dragon wouldn't look. She rarely left her forest, and when she did, she wasn't one to go searching for someone like this. That wasn't a task he could request of her.

If only his connection to the storm dragon were stronger. The storm dragon might be able to investigate in a way that the other dragons wouldn't manage quite as effectively. Only, he didn't know if the storm dragon would even be willing to do so.

What he didn't want to tell her was his real hesitation. He risked the dragons by sending them out. If anyone from Lorach came upon the misfit dragons, there was a real risk that they would be taken, trained, and forced to serve.

"Sarah…"

He took a step toward her and pulled a chair out from the table, taking a seat next to her. He rested a hand on her arm and she looked up, meeting his eyes. She didn't bother to hide the tears streaming down her face.

"I just want to find them," she whispered.

"I understand. I'm willing to do whatever I can to help," he said.

Even as he said it, he knew that there were limits to what he could do to help, limits to the nature of what he might be able to offer, limits to just how far he could protect her.

She looked at him for a long moment before taking a deep breath and nodding.

"My parents always told me that I would have to lead, but they also believed one day they would be the ones to overthrow the Arnson family." She shook her head. "We've been exiled for so long that it's hard to imagine a time might eventually come when Lorach could be overthrown."

"Well, you *are* royalty."

She looked up and seemed to miss him teasing her.

"Not directly," Sarah said. "And until we managed to overthrow Lorach, I'm nothing more than an exile. The same as you."

She was more than him, but Jason wasn't about to push her on the issue. He had come to Dragon Haven as an outsider, a misfit, and in many ways, he remained that. He might've been accepted, at least for the most part, but he didn't really fit in here.

There were times when Jason wasn't entirely sure if he fit in anywhere.

His connection to the dragons was different enough that he did not know.

"What do you have there?" he asked, nodding to the pages.

"Movement," she said.

"What kind of movement?"

"For the most part, it is movement of the people of Lorach. They continue to move along the edge of the forest, though it seems as if your illusions have held."

Jason smiled tightly. It took considerable effort to place those illusions, so he appreciated that they managed to hold. He worried what would happen if they failed. He doubted he'd be able to replace them very easily.

"I've freed as many dragons as I can over the last few days," he said. "We continue to weaken them. Each dragon we free from them diminishes them." And saves the dragon, he didn't need to add. There was a time when Sarah would have been as much an advocate for the dragons as him. With her parents missing, that had changed, like so much else had changed.

She nodded again. "I know."

"What else do you want me to do?"

She took a deep breath, resting her hands on the table. "I don't know. The last time the dragons of Lorach moved, we think it was because they uncovered the egg. Or they went to hatch an egg. Or… I don't know." She shook her head, staring at the page. "This time, I don't really know why they continue to move. I don't know what they intend to find."

"Maybe they aren't trying to find anything," Jason suggested.

"They have to be after something," Sarah said. "The way they're moving suggests enough activity that they have uncovered something." She pulled the page out and Jason stared at it, realizing that it looked something like a map. There were crosses and arrows and strange lines squiggling all over. Sarah pointed to one section. "Here' the edge of the forest. It looks like they continue to sweep along the edge, heading back and forth, almost as if they're searching for something."

"For us," Jason said.

"Maybe, but what if they're looking for something else?"

"What else do you think they might be after? *We're* hidden here," he said.

"We are, but think about what Lorren was doing." She tapped on the page. "This is where he'd been hiding."

"Not so much hiding, as…" Jason realized what she was getting at.

Lorren had been in the same place not long before his death. He hadn't been hiding. Lorren didn't fear the Dragon Souls. He had been willing to take the fight to them, willing to attack. Then again, Lorren had been after both the egg and the misfits. Maybe not the night dragon—not at first—but when he'd learned of it, he had wanted it as well.

If the people of Lorach, the Dragon Souls, were out there now, had they uncovered something?

He studied the page but he wasn't able to determine just what was written there. It was too strange, too difficult to make much out. "I can go and see what's there."

She held his gaze, not bothering to hide the hurt in her eyes. "You would do that, but you wouldn't search for my parents?"

"I'm not sure being gone for long stretches of time searching for your parents is the safest thing, not with the—"

"The dragon. I know."

"It's not only him." His protestation sounded weak, even to him. "And you understand just how unique this dragon is."

"I understand how unique all of the dragons you have a connection to are. There isn't anything you are willing to do to sacrifice them."

"This isn't about sacrificing them or not. This is about trying to ensure that the people of Lorach—and Jessica in particular—don't gain the dragons to use. We can't have them getting those dragons, using them against us, and finding a way to harm us."

So far, they had only managed to influence the storm dragon, but even that had nearly been devastating. Therin had nearly killed the iron dragon, though had not corrupted him. Jason worried what would happen if they were to find a way to use their magic differently and harm his friends. He couldn't imagine trying to battle dragons he now considered friends.

What would happen if he were to have to try to combat the ice or the iron or the forest dragon? He certainly wouldn't take the tactic Lorren had taken. He had wanted to destroy the dragons rather than allow the Dragon Souls to gain access to them.

"I'm willing to do whatever you need me to do to see if there's anything that we can uncover here," Jason said, tracing his finger along the border. "I could do that and return the same day." He looked up, meeting Sarah's eyes. "Anything else, and I don't know if I could return in the same day."

"Why do you need to return each day?"

"Because the night dragon continues to push on the illusion I've formed. In time, I worry he's going to be able to break free of it."

"Aren't you testing him to ensure he can't?"

"I am testing him, but I still don't know if there's going to be a point in time when he's going to be too strong for me to be able to do anything to keep him confined within the forest."

Even in that, Jason didn't like that he was confining the dragon, holding him in place. Eventually, he wanted the night dragon to be able to fly freely, the same way the other dragons did. Only, he had no idea what else would happen then with that dragon. Perhaps nothing. Perhaps trying to give the dragon an opportunity to fly freely was a mistake.

Am I the one controlling him now?

All of them?

The dragon misfits didn't *have* to stay here. They did so because of him, but would it be so bad if they left? They could be safe, not having to fear what Lorach might do to them. They could fly freely.

He had to push those thoughts out of his mind.

"We will find them," he said, resting his hand on Sarah's. "Whatever happened to your parents, we will find them."

"And if we don't?"

He needed to pick his words carefully. "If we don't, Dragon Haven will continue."

He thought that was her concern, though he didn't know if that was it or not. It was more about the safety of her parents, about worrying about what had happened to them and whether there was anything she could do to bring them back.

"I know Dragon Haven will continue. I'm not worried about that. There are enough people here, and dragons, that the city will survive. Thrive, even. It's been a long time since we've had this many dragons freed within the city." She looked at Jason, locking eyes with him. "All of that is because of you. That's why I wondered if there's anything that you might be able to do to help my parents, and to see if we might be able to help rescue them."

"If we know where to look, then I would be willing to do anything to rescue them," he said, and he meant it.

Searching for her parents was something that he didn't know if he was be best suited for, but rescuing them did fit him. Not only did it fit him, but it fit the strengths he now possessed.

"You mean that?"

"I do," he said.

She breathed in heavily, stared at the page, and then nodded. "See what you can find along the border here," she said. "And continue to free as many of the dragons as you can."

"I will." He hesitated, thinking she might suggest that she would come with him, but in the days since her parents had disappeared, Sarah hadn't tried to come with him.

Of course, by default, she had begun to rule in Dragon Haven.

She was royalty here. The idea of it had amused him at first, enough that he teased her about it, but he had also realized very quickly that she wasn't willing to tolerate any sort of teasing like that. Given that her parents had disappeared, Jason understood.

He got up, nodded, and then leaned down, wrapping her in a quick hug.

Sarah stiffened for a moment before relaxing and breathing out.

Jason thought about something he might be able to say to her, anything he might be able to offer to appease her, but there were no words that he could say, nothing that he could do, that would reassure her.

There was nothing.

Instead, he held her for a moment, his arms around her, and they stayed like that until she pulled away and turned her attention back to the papers in front of her.

3

The iron dragon surged with heat. Power undulated beneath him, flowing from head to toe, surging through him. There was a sense of it radiating down his length. The power of the iron dragon was unique amongst the dragon misfits. While not summoning all the heat that he could, he seemed to draw only a little bit of power, leaving his body looking like gleaming silver metal. When calling upon the power of fire, heat surged through him and energy filled him, leaving him glowing, practically molten metal.

Jason maintained their connection, holding on to the power and the bond that he shared with the iron dragon, feeling it as it flowed through the dragon. He looked out through the dragon's eyes, staring down at the landscape. The dragon saw everything below him in bursts of color. Heat and energy and a brightness and vibrancy bound the dragon to everything below him.

In this case, Jason made out the brightness along with the dragon, staring at the shifting landscape below them. There came the energy of the heat rolling off the dragon. Some of that energy came in the form of a soft glowing light, and some of it came in the form of contours rolling across the landscape.

"Are you seeing anything?" he asked the iron dragon.

"I see what you see," the iron dragon said.

"I don't see anything, but I'm not as comfortable looking through your eyes."

"Yet you do it easily," the iron dragon said.

Jason smiled to himself. The iron dragon allowed him to reach for that connection and borrow it, surging through it, but he still enjoyed the idea that he could taunt Jason about the lack of ability on his part.

"There *is* something down there," Jason said.

"There is something," the dragon said.

As Jason stared, he tried to determine if what he detected was anything useful, but he wasn't able to tell. As he stared into the distance, looking from this vantage, he searched for movement.

They had taken to hunting in this way.

When they left Dragon Haven, they searched for Dragon Soul dragons, and he was prepared for the possibility that he might need to add ice and iron together, healing those dragons, but partly that was a matter of searching for movement, something that would give him a way of finding the dragons that had to exist down there. Jason hadn't seen anything yet.

"Why do you think they've been trailing along that border?"

The iron dragon was troubled, and Jason could feel it through their connection. He had shared with the iron dragon, along with the ice and forest dragon, what Sarah had shared with him.

None of them had known quite why the Dragon Souls would have been searching along the border. None of them had any idea whether there was anything there that they needed to be concerned about, or whether there was anything that Lorach would have discovered.

"I cannot tell."

Jason looked with the iron dragon, straining for whatever reason the Dragon Souls might have for being out here, but even as he stared, he could come up with nothing. There was no answer, no sign of what they were after, just the presence of the Dragon Souls.

The iron dragon turned, shifting course, when a flurry of winged movement caught both his and Jason's attention at the same time. It was like a flurry of birds in the distance, though Jason knew that was not the case. No birds moved like that. No birds radiated the energy that these did. No birds circled the way these did.

Dragons.

There had to be nearly a dozen of them.

He focused on the sense of the dragons, pushing out with a connection to the ice and iron dragons, radiating that power out from him. He tapped on the iron dragon's side, motioning for him to turn.

"Are you sure?" the iron dragon asked.

"You don't think we can handle a dozen Dragon Souls?"

"I can," the iron dragon roared.

There was a hint of the anger and rage that still boiled within the iron dragon, anger at his initial captivity upon his hatching. Jason tried to soothe him, but there wasn't much he could do to soothe the iron dragon when it came to his past. The iron dragon had experienced far more than Jason could fully understand, and there was a limit to just what he might be able to do to counter the dragon's feelings about his initial captivity.

All he could do was ensure it didn't happen again. By protecting the iron dragon, working with him, and helping to stop the Dragon Souls from attacking, Jason did everything that he could to offer the iron dragon what he needed.

He started to push, using the power of the ice and the iron dragons, but he met resistance. He summoned more power, but the dozen dragons loomed nearer.

He tapped on the iron dragon's side and they streaked higher into the sky, heading up and up. As they went, he felt the others following. They trailed after them, now chasing him.

Jason continued to push, using the connection to the ice and the iron dragons, letting power flow. He used a burst of energy, a surge of power that exploded out from him, trying to overcome the resistance he detected.

When he had battled with the dragons before, Jason had managed to overwhelm the resistance to him. This was something else. This was a different kind of resistance, a different kind of strength, and Jason couldn't overwhelm it.

Here he'd believed he was strong enough to do so.

Too arrogant.

That was his fault. Especially when it came to the dragons these days.

He had to find some way to stop the Dragon Souls. They were preventing him from healing these dragons.

He twisted, turning to look behind him, but he couldn't see anything that clearly. As he strained into the distance, he didn't make out anything that suggested the Dragon Souls were doing anything unique. The only thing he could feel was the power radiating off the Dragon Souls, the energy that existed as they were holding onto the power that kept him from healing the dragons.

How many Dragon Souls would it require to do that?

Jason didn't know, though he had some experience with the Dragon Souls pushing against him.

Jason braced himself.

The dozen dragons were getting close enough that they would begin to attack. Stranger, several of the dragons seemed to be carrying something with their forelegs. Long lengths of gleaming pale white bone.

Dragon bone?

Something struck the iron dragon. The dragon roared,

power building from within him. His sides began to glow with the molten metal kind of heat, and he surged even faster.

Another burst of power struck, blasting into the dragon.

Jason focused on the ice dragon flying high overhead.

"We're going to need your help," he said.

He stared at the nearest of the dragons, focusing on him. A burst of power erupted from the sky. Ice lightning streaked down, crashing into the dragon—and the Dragon Soul riding him. The power from the ice dragon erupted over him, bursting with the kind of power that exploded. The dragon roared and another burst of ice lightning struck, this one slamming into the dragon again.

Jason hurriedly added a healing type of power, washing iron and ice dragon energy together, sweeping it through that dragon.

There was resistance, but as he continued to push, he overwhelmed it.

The healing washed over the dragon—and he roared, shaking. The bone the dragon had been holding fell to the ground as five riders were thrown free.

Five?

That was too many. Far more than they ever would have sent before.

At least Jason understood how the Dragon Souls had managed to prevent him from overpowering them. If they all had a dragon pearl, all of them drawing upon the energy of the dragon—

Jason was thrown forward, almost off the dragon itself.

He gripped the iron dragon, slamming his iron glove down, forming a connection between himself and the dragon. By doing so, he maintained his grip on the dragon, though he wondered if he would be able to hold for much longer. He tried, struggling to right himself, but wasn't able to get himself back on top of the dragon.

Jason tried to move, shifting in a way that would allow him to slide back onto the dragon, but even as he tried, he couldn't find a way to turn. He borrowed from the iron dragon's energy and burst it through him, shifting in a way that allowed him to reposition himself.

When he shimmied up the side of the dragon, he lay there for a moment.

They soared through the sky, eleven dragons still chasing them. If there were even three Dragon Souls on each one, that might be more than they would be able to overpower. Jason clung to the dragon and twisted so he could look down, trying to see whether there was anything he might be able to make out, but he still couldn't see anything very clearly in the distance. He held on, gripping tightly, holding onto the energy within the iron dragon.

He focused on the nearest of the enslaved dragons.

He sent that image through to the ice dragon. A burst of lightning shot down.

That's not ice lightning.

Thunder rumbled distantly, and Jason looked up.

The storm dragon had come.

While the storm dragon had helped him before, Jason had no idea why the dragon had come now or what he had done to summon that assistance. Only that the dragon had responded.

Lightning from the storm dragon struck the enslaved dragon and Jason followed it with a healing wave of ice and iron dragon energy. As that washed over the targeted dragon, he could feel it fighting the influence of the Dragon Souls. It shook, sending four Dragon Souls free. Much like the last dragon, this one released what he carried, dropping the bone.

The Dragon Souls fell, screaming as they did.

That left ten dragons.

If the ice and the iron dragon along with the storm dragon were there, then they could succeed. All it would take would be for them to continue to push, to hold onto the power within them, to find some way to use that energy—

Another attack struck, and Jason was thrown off the iron dragon.

He fell.

For a moment, panic flooded through him, but it was quickly replaced with an understanding of what he needed to do.

Jason wasn't helpless.

There was a time when he would have feared falling like this, a time when he would have believed he would've died, but now he understood he had power within him, and with that power, he could summon energy and draw it through him to find safety.

Jason drew upon that energy and sent it flowing out.

Ice and iron.

It burst from him, an explosion of power that went up and away, and Jason used it to shoot into the sky. The iron dragon swooped, dropping below him, and caught Jason.

He slapped the iron dragon glove down, connecting to the dragon and gripping tightly. Holding on to the iron dragon in that way, Jason turned, twisting so that he could look behind him, and he stared, searching for anything that might be there.

He didn't see anything else.

Where had they gone?

He continued to call upon the energy of the iron dragon, and then he focused above. Holding onto energy of the ice dragon, the power exploded down, bursting around him. That energy exploded near him. Another burst of power came. This one came from the storm dragon. It was followed by a heavy rumbling and energy that crackled in the sky.

Jason gripped the iron dragon and they turned.

There were still ten dragons out there, but where were they?

He connected to the ice dragon and looked down through his eyesight. As he did, he didn't see anything more than what he'd already seen. He searched in the distance, struggling against the emptiness of the sky.

What were they doing? Better yet, *how* were they doing

it? Somehow, the dragons had disappeared. They were after something. Carrying the dragon bones suggested Jessica had a new plan—but what was it?

Now she had the dragons hiding.

Illusion.

That was what had to be, but he wouldn't have expected the Dragon Souls to be so skilled with illusion that they could hide from him.

Jason maintained his connection to the other dragons, but he added to it that of the forest dragon. While fighting with dragons, he hadn't attempted to fully use that power of the forest dragon before, but now that he realized what was taking place, he realized he needed to do so. By holding onto the power of illusion, Jason *shifted* everything.

A shimmering shattered the illusion.

They had surrounded him.

The ice dragon exploded energy, and it struck one of the other dragons. It was followed by an attack by the storm dragon. Over and again, power streamed from the sky, coming down from above, slamming into these dragons. The ice and the storm dragon beat power upon the dragons, upon the Dragon Souls, and they used that energy to shatter the illusion. Not only that, but they used that power to knock through the captive dragons' resistance.

Jason sent energy through the Dragon Soul dragons, combining the power of the ice and the iron dragons, sending it sweeping through them.

Jason targeted the nearest of the dragons and healed it. The dragon roared, shaking as it threw the Dragon Souls off. The bone the dragon carried dropped to the ground.

He turned, looking for the other attackers, but he didn't see any others.

Where were the other dragons?

An illusion must've formed again.

Jason hurriedly began to focus on the energy of the illusion, holding onto the forest dragon's power, letting her power fill him. As he did, he could feel the source brightly within him, the source of magic surging up through him, enough strength within it that he could use it in order to be able to withstand the next illusion, which was forming right now.

He shattered that illusion.

It wasn't that it was difficult to fully hold on to, though he strained, pushing outward with as much force as he could, trying to ensure what he might be able to detect would overwhelm the sense of power that was there.

A burst of ice lightning came streaking down again.

It was followed by a burst from the storm dragon.

The combination of the two continued, each one streaking high from overhead, shattering the illusion, raining down upon it with a surge of power, the illusion shattering and dragons getting struck, over and over again.

Jason clung to the iron dragon's back.

The Dragon Souls used incredible power as they blasted at him. Their magic beat upon him, their energy cascading outward, slamming into him, building up with an intensity as it hammered, one after another with a steady, rhythmic nature.

The power that flowed through him was considerable, hot and fiery, filled with his rage and anger. That rage amplified what was happening to Jason.

The iron dragon roared, power filling him, anger at the idea that something could happen to Jason, that somehow they would dare to attack him.

A burst of iron dragon magic exploded from Jason.

Regular dragons burned hot, but the iron dragon was the molten metal of a forge, burning bright and hot and blazing even brighter than anything else. As Jason pushed it away, sending it streaking outward, it slammed into the nearest of the attackers.

Heat washed outward. It burned through the dragons.

Dragons were hot and fiery, and the dragons could withstand that heat.

The Dragon Souls could not.

As he freed dragons, he could feel the way they swung the Dragon Souls free, shaking them off in a violent explosion. This was not about saving the Dragon Souls. Jason didn't know if it was even possible to save them. At this point, the only thing Jason wanted to do was save the dragons.

Suddenly, more ice lightning streaked down from the sky, joining with the heat Jason radiated, and an enormous explosion of steam and mist and power filled him.

All of that energy radiated outward, exploding into the air.

Jason could feel the other dragons better than he had before, and he pushed.

The resistance faded. Finally, the dragons were freed.

The sky filled with the rage and roaring of the dragons.

They shook the Dragon Souls free and flew off.

As the fog cleared, Jason and the iron dragon flew alone.

Somewhere distantly, he could feel the energy of the ice dragon, but though the storm dragon had helped, Jason wasn't aware of him, not the same way as he was with the ice dragon. Eventually, he wondered if he might be able to find that connection, and he might be able to better understand the storm dragon in a way that he currently didn't, but for now, he was thankful that he had what connection he did. That connection had saved him, if only for now.

I'd nearly failed.

That worried him.

Had I not had the help of all the misfits...

Not all, but nearly so.

They circled, continuing to fly, heading in the same direction, but there was no other sign of more dragons. There was no sign of the bones they'd been carrying.

What was Jessica doing?

The dragon continued flying, searching over the

ground, and Jason clung to him. Surges of energy flooded through him, though for a moment, he wasn't entirely sure of the source of that energy or whether there was anything within it that he was supposed to find other than what he already had. He found no evidence of Lorach being involved, but feared that it would not be long before he came across something that would implicate them.

Why had they been traveling with the dragon bones?

The ice dragon roared.

Jason frowned, connecting to him and using the dragon's sight, and realized something. There were bones down below.

The dragon dove.

They were on the border of Lorach, with a dense, grassy plain stretching in front of him, a forest behind him.

As he approached, he continued staring through the dragon's eyes, and recognized what he saw. Remains of a dragon.

It was a small dragon.

He jumped from the iron dragon's back and hurried toward the remains, swishing through the grass, using power from the iron dragon to smooth down the grasses until he reached the remains.

His breath caught.

Not just any dragon, but a misfit dragon.

It was the small misfit dragon that Jessica had tried—and he had thought succeeded—to hatch. This was what Jessica had been after.

He looked back at the ice dragon. "Did you know?"

"I did not," the dragon rumbled.

"But she had hatched it."

He had seen her hatch it. A dragon misfit.

Which meant that she wouldn't be able to control it nearly as well as she would have been able to control the others.

And because of that, she might not have been able to bring it back to Lorach.

He ran his hands along the dragon's side, focusing on the power within it, and was tempted to use illusion to see what the dragon might've looked like, but instead, he pressed out with heat, letting the power of the iron dragon flow through him. Flames engulfed the remains of this dragon.

The hot rage and anger of the iron dragon still filled him with a sense of something familiar. And within that sense, Jason knew a different sort of purpose. It was the purpose of the dragons.

He breathed it in for a moment before letting it out.

He didn't need to hang onto that anger. All he needed was to release it, to let it flow out and to spread away from him, heading toward the sense of the other dragons. He didn't want to embrace the rage and anger, not wanting to be bound up in that violence. There was no point in doing so.

Letting out a deep breath, he looked over at the iron dragon, and he focused on the power from the dragon and tapped on the iron dragon's side. They needed to find the bones—and why the dragons had been carrying them.

"It's time for us to understand what they were after."

4

Jason reached Dragon Haven, and he stood on the outskirts of the settlement. The city itself was massive, far more extensive than the number of people that filled it would require. There were times when he was left wondering what it might have been like when the city contained as many people as what must have filled it at its peak. How vast must Dragon Haven have been at that time?

He breathed in. The air smelled of the forest, along with the dampness of earth. Overhead the shimmering illusion held in place, protecting Dragon Haven.

The city had been protected from the very first moment that he had learned to place illusions. If it were up to Jason, he would maintain those connections and prevent Lorach from reaching him or the city.

It was as much a home as any place could be.

Even though it was, there was part of Jason that still didn't feel as if the city was *home.*

It was strange to think that way, and stranger still he understood precisely why he did. Though he had been welcomed here, not only by Sarah but also by her parents and Henry and William and the others he'd met, there was a faction that did not welcome him. A faction, including the Dragon Guards, made him feel like he was still an outsider. That made him feel as if he were still a misfit.

Would that ever go away?

He wanted to protect Dragon Haven, but he also understood it was more than just protecting Dragon Haven. Jason wanted to protect the dragons.

When he had first come here, he had assumed that was what the people of Dragon Haven had wanted as well and had believed that they had shared values in that, but the more he had learned about these people, the more he had come to wonder if that was true or not.

He smiled to himself and started into the city, taking one of the main roads, before he veered off.

He needed to return to Dragon Haven, but there was something else he needed to do first.

He needed answers.

And he needed to check in on his small dragon charge.

He veered through the trees, ducking underneath branches that strained to brush at his face, focusing on the energy he could feel from the small night dragon. As he got closer to the dragon, he could practically feel the shadows starting to coalesce around him, as if some energy to them tried to wrap around him, to consume him. It was almost as if some power built up and around to squeeze upon him.

At first, he thought that maybe it was nothing more than his own illusion, but the closer he came, the more he realized this was not just the illusion he'd placed.

This was an illusion the night dragon had layered onto it.

It augmented it, adding even more power.

How much had the night dragon grown in just the last few days?

The night dragon had already proven he was incredibly powerful, and with each passing day, Jason had come to see and feel how powerful the night dragon would become. He was a mixture of other dragons, and that mixture made him into something more, something powerful, something incredible.

He passed through a darkened section of the forest, so dark that it pushed out all the daylight as if crushing it.

Jason paused. "You can reveal yourself."

There was no response.

Strangely, coming into this part of the forest, he not only could feel the dragon around him, but it squeezed in such a way he could not feel anything else. It was almost as if the dragon prevented him from feeling any other connection. The sense of the ice and iron and forest dragons faded from him. The awareness of the dragons in Dragon Haven faded. It left Jason with nothing more than the energy that surrounded him. At least he could still feel that.

"You can step forward," he said, this time more firmly.

He turned his focus inward, squeezing his iron dragon glove, reforming that connection, and heat surged in his hand, binding a connection back to the iron dragon. Cold flared within him, as if the ice dragon forced that connection between the two of them. Distantly, he was even aware of the forest dragon, as if whatever the night dragon attempted could not separate him from those primary connections he'd made.

"You're getting stronger," the night dragon said, slithering forward.

Jason cocked his head, regarding him while suppressing a smile. The dragon looked small, but the shadows around the dragon made it difficult for him to appreciate any scale or sense of size. He was left with the same question that he had other times. How large would this dragon eventually become?

"I should be the one saying that about you."

The dragon slipped between the trees, shadows trailing after him. "How long do you intend to hold me here?"

Jason shook his head. "Am I even holding you any longer?"

The night dragon paused and looked over to him, darkness filling his eyes. "No."

Jason breathed out. "It's dangerous beyond the forest."

"So I understand."

"What's that supposed to mean?"

"I saw what you saw," the dragon said.

"And what was that?"

An image came flickering into view before him, but it was one that took a moment for Jason to process and understand just what it was the dragon showed him.

A bone.

"How did you see that?"

"I saw what you saw," the dragon said.

Jason let out a frustrated sigh. Maybe the dragon could help. "I don't know what the bone means. I don't know what Lorach is after." He looked over to the night dragon. It felt strange asking such a young dragon for advice, but the dragon was precocious, and given his connection to so many of the other dragons, he couldn't help but feel as if the night dragon might have him an understanding of things he shouldn't have had otherwise.

"I don't know, either," the dragon said.

"Why would they want bones?"

The dragon slipped between more trees, forcing Jason to turn with him, to follow and watch him. "There is power in bones."

"Power?"

"Heat. Other power, depending upon the dragon." Shadows swirled out from him again before settling. The darkness was almost absolute, compressing down upon Jason in a way that made it difficult for him to see much of anything other than the night dragon. "Power. Would they want that kind of power?"

Jason shook his head. "I don't know. I wouldn't put it past Lorach to use that kind of power to their advantage, but why would they need to? They have dragon pearls. They have dragons. They have—"

"This is a different kind of power."

"How different?"

The dragon slipped between other trees, shadows trailing, and when he stopped again, he seemed larger.

Was he feeding?

Jason had no idea what this dragon would feed upon, but he doubted that he hunted the same way that the other dragons did. Maybe the dragon fed on the darkness itself.

"There are others who can use a different power."

"You mean there are others who can use the power of the dragon remains?"

"Other power."

Could that be what Lorach was after?

He wouldn't put it past Jessica. Jason didn't really know what she might be capable of, other than using dragons, and all their parts, to draw upon as much power as she thought she would need to attack—and defeat—Dragon Haven.

"I will keep searching," Jason said.

"I fear the time is short."

Jason started to smile. "Why?"

"I don't know." He tipped his head back, almost as if sniffing at the air, and the shadows circled around him. "There is a change. I can feel it. Can you?"

Jason watched the night dragon, but whatever the night dragon detected, he did not.

As he looked at the night dragon, he couldn't help but feel as if there was something quite strange with this dragon. It was the same way he had felt every time that he had been around the dragon, and though he'd playfully attempted to partake in games with the dragon, there was still part of him that was left wondering just how powerful the dragon might be.

What Jason knew with certainty was that the dragon was far more powerful than the other dragons. Even in his small form, he'd proven he was an incredibly powerful dragon, and he grew with that power with each passing day, coming to understand all aspects of his own connections, to the point where Jason wondered how powerful he would become.

"A change," the dragon said again.

Jason nodded. "I understand."

Darkness slipped around the trees, making his way toward him, and he watched Jason. There was something off-putting about how the dragon moved, something that unsettled Jason, but he wasn't going to tell the night dragon that. Unfortunately for him, he had the feeling that the night dragon already knew.

"You must go."

Jason hesitated. He looked around him before turning his attention back to the night dragon. "I will go, but you need to stay. At least until I figure out just what Lorach is up to. What they are after. You need to stay."

The night dragon slipped around the trees again before facing Jason. "You must go."

Jason started out of the forest, and for a moment, it was almost as if the night dragon slipped after him, chasing him, but then the shadows began to retreat, and he stepped free of the darkness, finally making his way out of the forest, to stand at the edge of Dragon Haven once again.

He could see the dragon yard in the distance, and there were half a dozen dragons of different sizes in there. Several of the dragon sensitive people of Dragon Haven were there, working with those dragons. William was among them, his hair wild and distinct, though he stayed close as to the small red dragon that he had always seemed connected to.

Kayla was there, as well. He watched her for a moment and could see William grinning at her, laughing as he spoke to Kayla, every so often sweeping his attention back to the other dragon and then turning his attention back to Kayla.

"They've become friendly."

Jason spun to see his mother standing next to him.

How had she approached so quietly?

Of course, she was a Dragon Soul, or had been, so maybe he shouldn't put it past her to be able to sneak up on him in such a way.

"Good. He can help her," Jason said.

"Does he have enough knowledge to help?"

Jason shrugged. "Probably not." He turned to his

mother and frowned at her. She looked healthier than she had when they had first come to Dragon Haven. When he had brought her from the village, she'd been wasting away. Her illness had consumed her and nearly took her from Kayla and Jason altogether. Her golden hair had grown more vibrant, and there was a brightness to her pale eyes that had not been there before.

How had he never noticed before?

Now he realized what she was doing, he could see through the faint traces of illusion, and he recognized the silver beneath.

"You don't have to hide who you are here in Dragon Haven," he said.

"I'm not hiding," she said. She looked down, though, and he knew that he had gotten to the truth of it.

"You're still ashamed."

"It's not ashamed. It's fear." She shook her head before finally looking up at him. "We should've told you."

"Yes," Jason said. "And you still haven't told me why you went there."

Kayla had alluded to it, though it hadn't been enough for him to know the full reason.

"It was what we had to do," she said.

"You had to?"

"We had to be far enough away from Lorach. Far enough that we wouldn't be found. Far enough that you wouldn't be found." She looked across the dragon yard and locked her gaze on to Kayla. "So that she wouldn't be found."

"You were more concerned about her than about me."

His mother looked over. "I wasn't sure what potential you might have. You always took after your father, but never enough that I believed you would have the necessary potential to be a Dragon Soul. You had dragon sight, which was both a blessing and a curse, especially there."

Jason snorted. "It was never a blessing."

She frowned at him, cocking one eye. "Wasn't it? When you were hunting, did your dragon sight not help you find movement? Did it not allow you to find your target more easily?"

"I suppose it did," he said.

"And did it not give you an advantage of being able to see things that others could not?"

Jason rarely focused on his dragon sight these days. Now that he could focus through the dragons themselves, he could borrow from their eyesight, which gave him a very different advantage, and one he used as often as he thought necessary for him to be able to make out details he wouldn't be able to see otherwise.

With the ice dragon, Jason could use his eyesight to see the crystalline structure in the world, movement through the ice dragon's enhanced eyes, and understand things he wouldn't know otherwise. With the iron dragon, Jason made out aspects of the world in shades of orange and red, heat signatures he had come to understand as reflections of different levels of intensities of heat. That wasn't altogether so different than what Jason's dragon sight could do.

"None of that matters," he said.

"I suppose not."

"You could work with the dragons," Jason said. He nodded to Kayla. "You could even work with her. She's been looking for her place in Dragon Haven." He left unsaid that Kayla had been looking for her place ever since their mother had recovered. He didn't need to remind her, as he suspected his mother knew. And he wondered whether or not she even cared.

"I abandoned that connection long ago. There is no reason for it to return."

"If you have a connection to the dragons, then you never really abandoned it."

"I did." She looked down. "Besides, Kayla has others who can teach her in ways I cannot. My way of reaching the dragons is not the way those in this place would appreciate."

He snorted. "You could talk to Henry."

"I suppose that I could."

"He's made the adjustment from Dragon Soul to a functional member of Dragon Haven."

"I will see what I can do," she said.

"Besides, when it comes to dealing with Lorach, we might need everyone capable of reaching for the dragon connection to work together."

There was a moment of concern that flickered in her eyes, but she nodded. "Perhaps."

"Or you can stay here. Others will protect you."

She looked up then. "You will protect us. Your father

would've been proud of you, Jason."

It wasn't the first time that she'd said that, and even hearing it now didn't make it any better or easier for him. All it did was make him more irritated that he had never learned about his connection in time to learn from his father.

Having that connection would've made things easier for him when he was younger. He wouldn't have had to struggle.

But then, would he have ever been able to form the connection he had?

Without feeling how he did, without suffering the way he had, Jason may not have come to know other dragons. He may never have wanted to work with the ice dragon, or come to understand what it would take for him to bond to the iron dragon, or…

He pushed those thoughts away.

"Have you ever seen Lorach using dragon bones for anything?"

His mother wrinkled her brow. "The bones? Other than as decoration, the bones don't have much use. They can put off some warmth, that much is true, but they are difficult to carve. Only the most skilled artisans can use them, so perhaps it's for artistic purposes."

That didn't strike him as likely. Not when it came to Lorach.

He'd seen dragon bone swords, knives, and other decorations, but that wouldn't be reason enough for the Dragon Souls to have gone searching for bones.

"This is different," he said. "I'm not entirely sure what Lorach was up to, but I suspect they were after something."

"I have faith that you will figure out what is going on," she said, waving her hand.

His mother wasn't going to be helpful with that, either.

She turned her attention back to Kayla. "She does have a connection to them, doesn't she?"

Jason followed the direction of her gaze, looking over to the dragon yard. Kayla had crouched in front of a small dragon, and she held her hand out. Even from here, Jason could feel how that connection had formed, the way that the dragon received her. There was enough of a bond between the two of them, enough of a connection that he could feel it, and he recognized just what it was that Kayla was doing. Even if she didn't.

He smiled to himself.

"She does have a connection," he said.

"Will you work with her?"

"When I have time," Jason said.

"I suppose that will have to do."

"It will have to do," he said. "I have other things that I am responsible for." And perhaps that was what he needed to get back to. It was long past time for him to return, to search for Sarah's parents, and for him to figure out what it was that Lorach was up to.

Because he knew they were up to something. They were always up to something.

Then there was what the night dragon had said.

Time is running short.

Jason had no idea how much the night dragon actually knew, but there still was something unusual about what he experienced, something unusual about the energy within him, that left Jason thinking that perhaps he knew more than he should.

He looked over to his mother, but she had already moved on, heading over to the dragon yard and watching Kayla.

Perhaps his father would have been proud of Jason, but his mother was obviously proud of his sister.

Without Kayla, his mother wouldn't even be here any longer. She wouldn't have survived the time in the mountains without Kayla's care, so he understood. It didn't make it any easier for him, though.

He tore his gaze away, focused on the ice dragon.

"Are you ready to search?"

The dragon circled overhead, and through the ice dragon, Jason was aware of the cold, a familiar sensation to him, even now when he was in Dragon Haven. It didn't worry him, or even bother him. It was merely familiar.

Within his mind, he felt a roar of approval.

The dragon was ready. Eager, even.

He had to be ready, as well.

He looked over to the heart of Dragon Haven. Sarah needed him to find her parents. And he needed to find what Lorach was after.

Before other dragons were hurt.

5

The search along the border of the forest in Lorach yielded nothing. No sign of any dragon remains or the bones the dragons had been carrying. Jason continued flying with the iron dragon, streaking over the ground but staying high overhead, but even as he looked, he didn't see anything useful. There was no sense of energy down below, either.

There was no doubt in his mind that Jessica and her Dragon Souls had been after something here. He could not imagine that she would've sent so many dragons out here for just bones though. He probed with the energy coming from the iron dragon, adding the power of the ice dragon, mingling the two and sweeping it across the landscape. There was nothing. Every so often, he mixed in the sense of the forest dragon as well, thinking that if he were to be able to add that sense to what he was doing, he might find more answers, but every time he tried to do so, he didn't uncover anything new.

The last time that he had seen Jessica, she'd tried to give power to a misfit egg, and he'd thought she'd succeeded until seeing the remains of the dragon. He had searched since destroying Lorren, pushing Jessica back, but had not found anything.

Why had they come with dragon bones now?

Answers were needed.

Not only about what sort of misfits had Jessica managed to hatch, but also about the misfits that Lorren had been working with. Jason was going to need to go after them, to try to understand what Lorren had been doing with them, and he was going to need to find some way to offer them a connection to others who would protect them. He didn't have any idea if they would listen. Those dragons had protected Lorren, and more than that, they had stayed with him. They had wanted to be with him, to protect him. This despite what Lorren had done to them.

And he still had not seen any sign of Sarah's parents. All of this fed into each other. Jason was certain of it, but he had no idea how.

He tapped on the iron dragon's side and they came to land near a wide, flowing river. Water burbled nearby, and as Jason focused on the sense of the river, he didn't detect anything more than that burbling. If only he could reach the river dragon.

"Do you feel anything here?"

The iron dragon sniffed the air and slithered along the ground, heat radiating along his sides. "No," he finally said, circling around and facing Jason.

Focusing on the energy of the ice dragon high overhead, he called to the dragon, summoning him. The ice dragon answered, roaring with a loud rumbling sound, and began to descend from high overhead. Awareness of the ice dragon drifted through the bond between them, the cold radiating up from someplace deep within him.

The ice dragon came hurtling out of the sky, coming to land on the ground near him. He breathed in, his icy sides glistening, spikes protruding outward.

"I needed you closer. I can't quite find anything," he said.

The dragon moved closer to him and a cold fog drifted from the dragon, sweeping away. "Nothing more than what was here before."

"What do you mean what was here before? I don't know that there was anything here before," Jason said.

"I can feel it," the ice dragon said. "It comes from someplace deep within the ground, connected to this land."

Jason closed his eyes, wanting to know if there was any reason Jessica might have found this place valuable. Knowing what he did of Lorach, knowing how they used the land, he couldn't help but feel as if there was something important about this place.

He detected a twinge. It was faint, subtle, but the more that he paid attention to it, the more certain he was that it was there. Distantly, there was another sensation that he continued to detect. At first, he thought that it was something that was only in his mind, but the more that he felt it crackling within him and the energy bubbling up from someplace deep inside him, the more certain he was that it was there. That it was real.

The storm dragon.

It was unusual for Jason to feel anything when it came to the storm dragon. Unusual that he would even notice the dragon in that way.

Still, the storm dragon had responded to his request before. The storm dragon had helped him with the night dragon egg and had helped him defeat Lorren.

He needed to bond to the storm dragon the way that he had the others, and needed to get to know him somehow.

He could feel something else sizzling up within him. It was there, deep within him. It rumbled.

Jason rumbled.

Had he somehow bonded to the storm dragon?

If he could use that power, he might be able to find a better way to understand the magic within this land, whatever it was Jessica had done and the way she intended to use this land against the people of Dragon Haven.

He let the energy of the storm dragon sizzle up from deep within him.

The rumbling began to build within him again. That rumbling started slowly, softly in the back of his mind, and it built forward. Jason thought that he could call to it, but every time he tried to, it faded again.

He opened his eyes, looking over at the two dragons that were on the ground with them, but neither of them were paying much attention to him.

He doubted either of them would know what he needed in order to reach the power of the storm dragon. For that matter, he doubted either of them would be interested in helping him. It involved him finding his own connection, finding some other way to reach through that power and grasping it, pulling it to him.

He tried again.

More and more power came to him, but it came to him from the other two dragons—three, really. Even the forest dragon granted enough power to him he could detect her energy, and it flowed within him too.

He turned to the ice dragon. "We need answers," he said. "Something happened to Sarah's parents."

"We have searched," the ice dragon said.

It sounded to Jason as if they'd abandoned the search, as well. Jason could not.

"If you don't want to search for them, then we need to better understand just what Jessica's people were doing out here."

"They were hunting for bones," the ice dragon said.

"I know that, but *why*?"

There was one consideration. They had learned how to create misfits, and he wouldn't put it past Jessica to use that knowledge against him, but would they have done so this close to Dragon Haven? What if there was something to the dragon bones that the Dragon Souls could use against Dragon Haven?

"What if there's something else they intend to do?"

Jason tried to think about the connections he had. The dragons that he was connected to might not be enough for whatever was coming if Jessica moved with more force. They had the dragons of Dragon Haven, both those that had never been captured and those Jason had freed, along with the misfits, but that might not be enough against the might Jessica could bring against them.

There are other dragons.

Jason didn't know if those other dragons would answer him. Given that he had been the one to kill Lorren, it was possible the mist dragons and the earth dragons wouldn't respond to him.

How would he even find those other misfits?

He didn't know where to start. Even when he found them, he worried about their response to him. Given what he had done, the way that he had been involved with the person who had helped bring them into the world, he couldn't help but wonder if they would not respond to him. Stopping Lorach—especially if they continued to develop resistance to his attacks—would require more than just *his* misfits.

He looked over at the iron dragon. "I'm going to travel with the ice dragon. Can you return to Dragon Haven and make sure the night dragon is safe?"

The iron dragon radiated a hint of heat, and he

rumbled with energy. It was frustration. Jason thought he understood the iron dragon's frustration. He wanted to be a part of what Jason did and wanted to be useful, but in this case, since he wanted to start by heading to the cold and northern mountains, he didn't think that the iron dragon would be able to offer much assistance.

"It's not that I don't want you with me. It's more about whether or not you'd be able to withstand the cold."

The iron dragon rumbled again, his frustration evident.

Jason hadn't spent any time looking in the north, searching for the key to what Lorren had done with his dragons. It was long past time that he make that attempt. As much as the iron dragon might be angry with him for wanting to head to the north without him, this was something Jason thought he needed to do.

He also thought the iron dragon might be able to offer a level of protection that the other dragons wouldn't be able to do. The iron dragon could ensure that the night dragon remained safe and stable. That was part of what Jason needed.

He tried to convey all of that through the connection they shared, and he thought that he was effective in doing so, but he didn't know for certain. As the iron dragon slithered off, heading through the trees before launching himself in the air, Jason wasn't sure if he had conveyed what he wanted to the dragon. He couldn't tell anything other than the dragon's frustration.

Jason breathed out heavily and then turned, focusing on the ice dragon.

It wasn't all that warm here, though it was warm enough that moisture glistened on the side of the ice dragon. He radiated energy, and within that energy came the power of the dragon, filling the clearing around him with a fog of moisture that drifted off his sides.

Jason climbed onto his back and the ice dragon shook for a moment, droplets of water freezing in the air, and then he launched into the sky.

"Where's the storm dragon?"

"He comes when he is needed," the ice dragon said.

"Are you able to reach him?"

"When he is needed," the ice dragon said.

"How does he know when he is needed?"

"He comes."

Jason started to laugh but he had the sense that the ice dragon didn't share in his amusement. It was almost as if the ice dragon didn't understand what Jason was getting at, nor did he understand why that would amuse him so much.

He motioned to the ice dragon to veer off, and as they flew, Jason could feel the energy of the ice dragon as they headed off to the north. There was a power to the dragon, a surge of energy, and it flowed out from him, cold radiating away from him in the same sort of fog that Jason had become accustomed to. Within that fog was the power of this dragon, and within the fog was the connection to the cold high overhead.

When Jason focused on that sense, he could feel a connection to the energy high overhead. That was new for him. When he had connected to the ice dragon before, he had felt as if he were connecting to his power, but this time, what he detected was something else, something different. It felt almost as if he were connecting not to the ice dragon so much as he was connecting to the source of his own power.

Jason thought about the way the cold radiated toward him, the energy within it, and he thought about whether there was something that he might be able to glean from it. If he could access that cold power, he might be able to draw upon it directly.

"Do you think that I would be able to access that?"

The ice dragon shook the ends of his wings. Icicles shook free from them, shooting off in either direction.

They parted a cloud and the ice dragon continued to fly faster and faster. He was an incredibly powerful and fast dragon, and the more that he raced forward, the easier it was for Jason to feel that energy within him.

"It's possible that you would be able to," the ice dragon said.

"Just possible?"

"You aren't a dragon."

Jason smiled. "No, but I do wonder if maybe I would be able to use some aspect of your power."

"You use an aspect of my power when you connect through me."

"What I'm thinking about might be different," Jason

said, closing his eyes for a moment. He reached across the distance, feeling the cold high overhead. There was something about it that was familiar, stirring deep within him. He could feel the energy sweeping around, the power of the cold of the north, all of it mixing together, forming a cloud of energy that washed over him. Jason held onto that sense, thinking that if he could reach across that distance, maybe he could call to the cold and maybe he could recharge with the energy of the upper atmosphere. Maybe he would even be able to call upon ice lightning. If he could do that, he thought he would have an advantage.

They swooped off to the side, and Jason put those thoughts away.

If he were able to reach for the power of the dragons, the source from where they drew their energy, he might be able to use it directly, and he would no longer have to fear weakening the dragons as he called to them. Each time he called upon that energy, Jason could feel some aspect of them shifting, almost as if their power were fading as he dragged on it.

The ice dragon headed toward the north.

When they reached above the clouds, the energy of the ice dragon still flowed from him, powerful and free, filling Jason with it. Every so often, Jason could feel the ice dragon making a connection to the cold around him. It was something that he felt distinctly. It was almost as if he were *meant* to feel it.

Could I use that?

As he focused on that sense, he thought about the

energy that was there, and he thought about whether there was something he might be able to master within that connection. Jason could feel something within it, almost as if he should be able to draw upon that power.

Even though he'd tried to push that thought away, thinking about the power that was out there, he still hadn't fully abandoned it. The sense of that energy, the power he could detect, remained within him, something more.

He shifted the connection to that of the iron dragon. He could feel something through the iron dragon glove, the power he had, the heat radiating from him, and through that connection, he was aware of something more, an energy that burned within him. Within that energy, Jason recognized the source of that heat, the power that burst within him, and he was aware of just how much power he could call upon.

Still, there was something else within it. It took him a moment to realize what it was: frustration. The iron dragon remain frustrated by what Jason asked of him. Not only that, but he remained frustrated by feeling as if he were separated from what they were doing.

Maybe that was a mistake.

As far as he knew, he had done what he thought was right, but the iron dragon wouldn't have an opportunity to choose for himself. These days, it seemed to Jason that more and more, he irritated the dragons. As much as he wanted to work on their behalf, trying to help them, trying to ensure that they were safe, there were times when he felt as if the only thing he did was manage to annoy them.

He'd become overly protective. All he wanted was to let them be free, but what if in doing so, he had controlled them in his own way?

"Would the dragons prefer to be left alone?"

The ice dragon didn't answer right away, and Jason thought that was more than enough of an answer.

They streaked toward the north, and through the openings in the clouds, mountains rose up around them. The cold and white-capped mountain peaks created a separation between this land and the one that was beyond, a separation difficult for most dragons to cross. The only dragon Jason knew who was able to do so was the ice dragon. The regular dragons, those from Dragon Haven and those from Lorach, struggled with the cold and the energy present here, and Jason knew they wouldn't be able to travel quite so far. The cold seemed to push back, as if it were trying to prevent them from passing into it.

"There are times when the connection to your kind is difficult," the ice dragon finally said. "There are times when the connection is rewarding."

"What times are those?"

"Such as when I feel how you feel about the dragons," the ice dragon said.

"I want to do whatever I can to help free as many of the dragons as I can," Jason said.

"I know. That is why I help."

"I don't know that I'm doing that good of a job with

it, though. Even knowing what to do and everything that I can do to help the dragon, I still feel as if it's a struggle."

Jason looked out into the distance. He could feel the energy of everything moving past him, the swirling sky, the power that surrounded them, coming through the ice dragon to him. He breathed it in, letting that energy connect to him through the dragon. Even in that, Jason realized what he was doing.

He was borrowing from the dragons.

Maybe that was a mistake. Everything he did, all the power that he used, borrowed from the dragons. More than that, everything that he had done had involved the dragons. Perhaps it was time that ended.

The dragons needed to have freedom, and they didn't need people like Jason or the others from Lorach or Dragon Haven to continue to use their power.

How was he going to be able to ensure that didn't happen?

He didn't know. Perhaps there was no way for him to ensure the safety of the dragons and to ensure they weren't used. When this was over, though. When Lorach was defeated. When Jessica no longer used the Dragon Souls to attack.

Then the dragons could be free. They could be free of human influence.

He wondered if they would embrace that or not.

Feeling the energy coming off the iron dragon, the power and the frustration coming from him, Jason couldn't help but feel as if that might be exactly what they wanted.

Then there was what he felt from the ice dragon. There was the power freely given, flowing through him, and he recognized that perhaps he didn't feel quite the same way. He was but one dragon, and Jason wondered how many others were like the iron dragon, feeling that frustration. How many of the dragons of Lorach, and of the free dragons now in Dragon Haven, felt that same way?

Probably far more than Jason had ever known.

Here he had been using that power, drawing upon it freely, letting it flow through him, and perhaps that was his mistake. He shouldn't be calling upon it, letting it fill him. Jason needed to be far more careful with the way that he called upon that energy, no longer borrowing it but trying to find a way to power on his own.

They headed over the mountaintops. He pushed those thoughts away, as well. It was time to focus on the reason that he'd come.

"Let's see what we can find of Lorren and his dragons."

6

They had been flying for the better part of an hour, circling high over the mountaintops, drifting throughout the various locations within the mountains, but every place they went, Jason felt nothing other than the sense of cold. He thought he might be able to find the mist dragons, but even if he couldn't find them—or the smoke dragons, he realized—he thought that he might be able to detect something of the earth dragons, but there had been no sense of either of them.

"Where do you think the dragons have gone?"

"Someplace where they thought they could be safe," the ice dragon said.

"We should have trailed them so that we could know where they went," he said.

"Do you think that would have allowed them to be safe?"

Jason shook his head. He didn't really know, not

anymore. When it came to the dragons, when it came to what they had been going through, he wondered if there was any real safety when they were in contact with people.

As he felt the power of the ice dragon, he pushed it out, using that to sweep along the mountainside, searching for anything unusual. So far, he detected nothing.

As he flew, Jason's frustration began to build.

It was a different source of frustration than what the dragons felt. In this case, Jason was frustrated because he knew there should be something out here, something he should be able to detect, but even as they traveled, he couldn't find the earth, mist, and smoke dragons. He breathed out a frustrated sigh, holding on to the energy within him, thinking about that power and thinking about whether there truly was some method he might be able to use to find them. So far, he had come up with nothing.

Jason looked into the distance. Snow covered the mountains and every so often, a hint of wind swirled up, kicking around and raising the snow, making it difficult for him to see anything. It was as if the snow and ice all swirled around in a powerful pattern, and there was something about it that reminded him very much of his home.

It had been a long time since he had been back to the village. They had placed ballista at the top of the mountain, prepared for the possibility of a dragon attack, but the dragons wouldn't have traveled that far.

At least, not most dragons.

Of course, the mountain village was on the very southern edge of where Lorach might be able to reach. His village had been isolated by the way they had been situated.

He sat up.

"What is it?" the ice dragon asked.

"What if my village never hunted dragons?"

That had been the traditional belief, and it was what Jason had believed growing up, but as he thought about it, and as he thought about the purpose of the ballista, he wondered if that were it at all.

"I thought your village had those weapons in place so they could shoot dragons out of the sky."

"That's what I had always been taught," Jason said.

If only there were some record of the people of his village. He could remember the stories that he'd been told as a child, stories that all depicted the danger of the dragons, stories that affected the fear of his people. Having experienced dragons as he had, Jason understood that fear and understood there wasn't anything his people would be able to do against the might of dragons. Their ballista would have been useless against a dragon.

As Jason stared into the distance, he wondered if perhaps there might be a different reason for the ballista and the protections that the village had around it. What if there was a possibility the village had been designed to prevent the dragons from going any *farther* rather than hunting them?

It seemed unlikely, especially given what he had seen,

but there were so many things when it came to the dragons that were unlikely that Jason longer knew if this was just one of them or whether it was simply his imagination.

He continued searching for anything that might suggest the power of the other misfit dragons. A distant rumbling came, and for a moment, Jason wondered if that rumbling represented one of the earth dragons, but as he listened to it more closely, focusing on that energy, he realized it was the storm dragon. Thunder rumbled, but nothing more.

"Has he been following us?"

The ice dragon shook and shards of ice streaked away from him. "He has been there," the ice dragon said.

"Why?"

"He questions," the ice dragon said.

"And what does he question?"

"His place," the ice dragon said.

The words struck home. It was the same thing Jason had started to question.

Jason held onto his sense of the storm dragon, feeling that energy between them and wondering if there might be something that he could offer, some explanation that might be able to help the storm dragon.

When it came to working with the dragons, trying to help them, he had continued to believe there was something that he might be able to do, but perhaps he should stop thinking in that way. The dragons needed to find their own way, needed to find something of themselves in order to be truly free.

The sense that he had from the iron dragon was that the dragons wanted to be free, that they wanted to be separated from the people who had worked with them, and they no longer wanted to fear the dangers of men—and in particular, Dragon Souls—controlling them.

Jason wasn't going to be able to find that for them. He was only going to be able to work on their behalf, not work *for* them.

They turned, heading farther north.

A rumbling came again and he turned, thinking that it was nothing more than the storm dragon again, but there was some aspect to it that was different than what he had detected from the storm dragon.

Earth dragon.

Jason smiled to himself and tapped on the ice dragon's side.

They veered toward the distant rumbling.

That power built within Jason, calling to him.

Surprisingly, the earth dragon seemed to be deep below them.

Perhaps not surprisingly. Jason understood the dragon had the ability to slither beneath the ground, hiding from anyone searching for him.

"Do you detect the earth dragon?" Jason asked.

"He's down there, but I can't see him."

"We couldn't see him before, either," Jason said. "He

came up from below, making it difficult for us—and our dragons."

The earth dragon had a way of adjusting the way the earth moved. Feeling the power of the earth dragon now, he wondered at the intent behind it. He doubted the dragon intended to attack. That didn't seem to be the reason for the presence, and Jason had seen that the dragon had been willing to help before, but there would have to be a reason for him being here now.

The ice dragon began to dive, feeling the energy from Jason and so knowing which way he wanted them to go, and together they began to descend.

They burst through the cloud on their descent. When they did, the landscape spread out below them. Mostly it was icy and snowy, with swirls of snow streaking toward him, crashing into his face.

Not completely, though.

He created a barrier around himself, shielding himself from the wind.

He didn't have to shield himself from the cold. The ice dragon did that well enough, offering him the protection that their connection granted, but then there was something else with it, not just the connection that the ice dragon offered, but there was the heat the iron dragon granted as well.

The energy of the ice dragon granted him the strength that he needed in order to create a separation between himself and the cold, and by using that, Jason pushed back the ice swirling around him. He recognized the trembling in the ground, feeling that energy from the earth dragon rumbling toward them.

It surprised him that he would be aware of it so high in the sky.

They landed on the slope of the mountain.

The wind continued to swirl, and the landing of the ice dragon did nothing to settle it. In fact, if nothing else, the ice dragon's landing only caused the wind to stir up even more, creating a burst of power.

There was more rumbling from deep beneath the earth.

Connecting to the cold and the ice, he pulled upon power and sent it through the ground beneath him, letting the ice claim the energy. Gradually, the sense of the rumbling persisted, increasing in intensity, and he focused on it as that began to build.

By holding power and energy, he tried to determine where the earth dragon roamed. He couldn't tell, only that the sense of the earth dragon was there.

Jason didn't want to draw on too much energy as he focused, but in this land, surrounded by the cold as he was, the ice dragon didn't suffer. There was no way for Jason to take too much power away from him here. The ice dragon gifted power to him, now pushing it toward Jason, who pushed it out beneath him.

There.

Jason held onto that energy as he probed, pulling at the snow.

That wasn't going to work. He needed to pull on the ice dragon.

He anchored to the ice dragon, holding onto his connection to power, and he used that to find a way to wrap outward, embracing the power deep beneath the ground, and he pulled on it. Gradually, the rumbling started to intensify.

The earth dragon struggled against the ice.

"What are you doing?" the ice dragon asked.

"I can feel the earth dragon beneath the ground. I have to help him break free. I have to pull more."

He left unsaid what would happen and what he worried might happen to the dragon.

"Then do it."

Jason pulled, letting that energy flow, drawing on the sense of the dragon, but also drawing on something else there. The ground beneath his feet began to shake and tremble. Finally, he wrapped the power of the ice dragon around the sense of the other energy deep beneath him.

The ice dragon trembled, his wings spread out.

Wind swirled around him. There was a tremulous sort of energy around the ice dragon.

He needed to call that power up from the earth. Jason needed to speak with him to know just what Lorren had done, mostly so they could better understand the nature of his kind of attack on the other dragons.

Jason wrapped the power around the earth dragon and continued to pull, drawing that up from the ground.

Gradually, the earth started to shake and tremble and a

section of snow shifted underneath his feet. Jason braced himself, holding on to the power in the ice dragon, and it allowed him to float. He hovered above the ground, pulling upon the ice, the cold, everything all around him.

Jason continued to call on that power, letting it explode through him.

He needed to anchor to that energy to ease the earth dragon free of the ice.

Finally, the ground split. He pulled something free.

It was an earth dragon larger than the ones he remembered seeing with Lorren. The earth dragon was solid, almost impossibly so. His leathery hide looked to be made of gray colored rock, and he had a squished face, stunted wings that Jason suspected did not even work, and a long, thick tail. Everything about him seemed to rumble as if he used that tremoring for him to penetrate through the earth itself.

This one struggled against his grip, but Jason clutched him in the ice and cold, and he trapped him there, holding him in place so that the earth dragon couldn't escape him. He didn't want to harm the earth dragon, and he wished there was some way to convey that.

"All I want is a chance to speak to you," he said.

The earth dragon continued to struggle against him, and Jason squeezed, holding onto him with the cold. By wrapping that cold and that energy around the earth dragon, Jason thought he might be able to find a way to help the dragon, but what he needed to do was to settle him.

Could I offer a healing to the dragon?

Jason didn't know if it was going to be enough, or if what he had just done already made it so that the dragon wouldn't trust him. Either way, he had to try to continue to squeeze, and he added more energy to what he did.

Energy flowed out from him, and it stretched through the barrier he had around the earth dragon, drawn from the cold, from the ice dragon, and even from high overhead. He tried to soothe the earth dragon, but he didn't know if he did or if he only made the situation worse. The earth dragon continued to struggle against him, and Jason forced more power out.

"I need to know what Lorren did with the other dragons," he said.

The earth dragon turned toward him and the struggling started to ease.

"I don't want to harm the dragons." He knew how it must seem to the earth dragon, and convinced himself that what he had been doing was on behalf of the dragons, not intending to harm him. "All I want to know is what Lorren did."

He tried to make his way toward the dragon, but there was a power radiating off the earth dragon, something that pushed toward Jason, a sense of energy that squeezed at him. Jason struggled against it, continuing to battle that energy, focusing on the power that was there within the dragon.

He fought against it, straining as he did, feeling his own energy as it flowed out from him, toward the dragon, and outward. Jason held onto that power within him, and he focused. The energy coming off him was different than he had been drawing before, and he didn't know if it was something that the ice dragon had started to grant him, a different way of connecting.

He recognized the power that flowed around him. It was power that came from all around, power that came from the energy of the cold, from the air around him, from everything that struck him as home.

Familiar.

He took a step toward the earth dragon, wrapping the energy of the cold and the north all around the dragon as he did. He held him in place even as the earth dragon struggled to try to descend back underground. By holding onto the energy that he did, the earth dragon was unable to escape.

"I'm not trying to hurt you," Jason said, knowing that it might seem like he was.

The earth dragon turned toward him and rumbled. The energy coming off him was enormous, a burst of power that trembled within him, causing the snow to shake.

Jason turned to the snow, and by borrowing the cold and the energy he felt all around him, he smoothed it back out. He turned toward the earth dragon. He had to convince the dragon to work with him, not force him.

Somehow.

Jason took a step toward him, letting the power that he held onto fill him, and as he did, he led that energy radiate outward toward the earth dragon so that he could share with him what he wanted. *Not command him.* Jason was not a dragon soul who would control him. He wanted to work together with the dragons.

"I need to know more about Lorren. I need to visit with the others."

Would the earth dragon answer?

Even if he did, Jason wasn't sure that the earth dragon would be willing to offer up what Jason needed. He needed the answers, and he needed to better understand just what Lorren had done when he'd been working with the other dragons, including the way he'd been tormenting them.

The ice dragon was an extension of water. That seemed to be the key. Jason could use that, and he could use the heat that he felt within him, heat that he was borrowing from the iron dragon.

Jason took a deep breath and turned to the dragon, holding his hands out. "All I want is an opportunity to speak with you. I want to better understand just what Lorren had done."

He continued to release his hold on the dragon.

The ground started to tremble, releasing energy coming from the dragon, but Jason did nothing to counter it. The only thing that happened was that the ice dragon used the ground, using power within him in order to try to calm things.

Jason held his attention on the earth dragon, letting that awareness and the power that he felt continue to flow into him. He held onto power, letting it wash into the dragon. Jason recognized there was something more that he might be able to do, and he released power, unleashing it into the dragon for a moment.

No evidence of control.

Not that Jason had expected Lorren to have controlled the dragons. His understanding of the way that Lorren worked, the help that he offered them and the way that he worked with the dragons, was such that he didn't think that Lorren had done anything to control them. Not the way that the Dragon Souls had attempted to control dragons.

Finally, Jason released all of his power.

He stood on the snow and faced the earth dragon.

There was incredible power coming off that dragon, a sense of energy, a sense of strength, and it connected from someplace deep. Jason could practically feel it. It was almost as if the dragon tried to connect to the bones of the earth, to a place trapped beneath him.

"I just need answers. Nothing more than that. Lorach is continuing their attack, but I don't understand what they're doing and what we can do. All of us. Somehow, we have to stop Lorach. That's the only way the dragons will finally be free."

Even if he were to stop another dozen dragons, or more than that. He didn't know if it was going to be enough. Having seen the way that Lorach was able to attack, the energy that the people within the Dragon Souls possessed, the way that they were able to bring more and more Dragon Souls to bear, Jason didn't know if he was going to be able to withstand them.

The last time, he had managed to get lucky, but that was because he had all of these dragons working on his behalf. What would happen if the dragons stopped assisting him? What would happen if the storm dragon hadn't arrived?

Jason knew what would have happened. He wouldn't have succeeded.

There would not have been enough strength within him to stop those dragons. He would have been defeated, destroyed. It was why he needed the help of any of the dragons who might be able to offer him any assistance.

That included the earth dragons. That included the mist dragons.

"Help us."

The earth dragon rumbled again, the rumbling taking on words. "Follow."

7

Far below him, he could see the earth dragon, and as they traveled, Jason tried to understand what the earth dragon was trying to show him, but there wasn't anything obvious.

The ice dragon didn't seem to have any idea, either, but he didn't object to the travel. Jason would not have expected the ice dragon to object, though. The ice dragon was willing to go along with all of this, wanting to know what they were doing and if there was anything that they needed to do to help the earth dragon.

Finally, the rumbling stopped.

They were near a small valley with a stream running through it.

The ice dragon descended rapidly, dropping to the ground, and the earth rumbled enough to reveal the presence of the earth dragon.

As he appeared, Jason climbed off the ice dragon. "What is this?" he asked.

"This is where you need to be," he said. The earth dragon had a deep, strange way of rumbling, and there was an energy in the way that he did it, an energy that called to Jason, and within that energy was something else.

"What do I need to see?"

"Him."

Jason made his way around the stream, glancing over at the earth dragon, though his head barely protruded above the rocky ground. The stream spilled down the mountainside with a burbling. Jason paused for a moment, taking a drink of the cold water, detecting a familiar coppery taste to it. It reminded him of the stream that he had drunk from when he was in his home, back in the cold north.

As he stood, he saw a small alcove that looked to have been carved into the rock near the stream.

Jason frowned as he approached.

It was carved.

Not only that, but he found three small white fragments. They were tiny, little larger than the palm of his hand, and all dragon bone.

He lifted the first, feeling heat radiating within it, and wondered why that should be, but there was nothing within the bone that he recognized.

"Somebody placed these here," he said, looking over at the ice dragon before turning his attention to the earth dragon. "Is that why you brought me here? Is this a place that people from Lorach came?"

"Not Lorach."

Jason grabbed for the other bones. It was probably a finger bone, though it was difficult for him to know. There was heat within it, and it seemed to create a gentle haze that surrounded the bone. "If it wasn't Lorach, then who?" He looked up and his heart hammered. "Lorren?"

The dragon rumbled.

"That's why you wanted me to see this. You wanted me to see where Lorren had been."

"Come."

The dragon disappeared, though there was a faint rumbling that came from him. Jason recognized it and could feel it pulling him.

He turned to the dragon and hurried over to the ice dragon, pocketing the bones.

"Should we follow?"

"He needs to show you something," the dragon said.

"I realize that he does, but what is he trying to show me?"

"I do not know."

Jason held onto power and as the ice dragon took to the air, they followed the earth dragon.

They ascended over the mountains and then reached a small stream.

From there, they followed it until the landscape shifted again, becoming something altogether different. It was a sweeping grassy hillside. A few trees dotted the horizon.

They were just on the border of Lorach, near enough that he recognized it, even if he didn't recognize why they would be here.

The earth dragon rumbled again, drawing him down.

They descended, and he found the earth dragon near a small copse of trees. As before, he barely showed himself, revealing little more than his face. Jason headed forward, trying to gauge what the earth dragon wanted him to see, but could not find anything.

"What is here?"

"Him," the earth dragon rumbled again.

Him.

"Lorren?"

Was this all about the earth dragon showing him different places where Lorren had been?

He headed through the trees, making his way slowly, and this time, rather than going blindly, he started to focus on the energy within him.

He could feel the cold coming off the ice dragon, and recognized that there was something different about it, almost as if in this place, the ice dragon struggled.

Of course he would, though. In this place, the ice dragon's connection to the cold did not work nearly as well as he needed.

Jason summoned the connection between himself and the ice dragon, stretching outward, wondering if perhaps he might be able to press that connection far enough to reach beyond, and strained to the distant north to help the ice dragon, only to realize that he didn't even need to. The ice dragon didn't need his help in that.

Jason pushed power out again. This time, he swept it out through the trees.

It was a combination of the ice and the iron dragon's power, but as he was in a copse of trees, he also chose the forest dragon, letting that energy flow out and away from him.

As he did, he felt something changing.

There was some aspect of the ground that shifted, and then he met a resistance.

Dragon resistance.

He hurried forward, moving carefully, holding onto the connection he shared with the dragons, and looked over to see the ice dragon slide forward.

He didn't move nearly as comfortably through the trees as the iron dragon did. The iron dragon was able to somehow slide forward, using his heat to practically glide along, but the ice dragon still managed. As Jason followed, he realized there was a different energy coming off him, almost as if he were uncertain.

Not only uncertain, but unsettled. All of this troubled the ice dragon in some way.

"What do you think is here?" Jason asked.

The dragon rumbled softly. "I do not know."

Distantly, he could feel the earth dragon, though he had not seen him again.

"Do you think this some sort of trap Lorren set?" Jason asked.

He felt into his pocket, feeling for the dragon bones that he had gathered from the last place they had visited, but had a hard time thinking that there would be some sort of trap.

He could feel the warmth coming from the dragon bones and recognized that there was something else like it nearby. That was what he was supposed to find.

It was the dragon bones.

He held onto the smaller one, the one that was most like a finger, and let the heat radiate through it, flowing into him. It wasn't enough that he could feel it. It felt as if there was some part of that bone he needed to utilize.

The trees were close together, close enough that the ice dragon couldn't go any farther.

"You can stay there," Jason said. "I can find what's here."

"You should not do this alone," the dragon said.

"Who said I was doing it alone?"

He was faintly aware of the dragon rumbling, the steadiness that was coming from someplace deep beneath the ground, and near enough that he could feel it.

He trailed through the trees, and then he saw something.

It was nestled in the combined roots of two large trees and he strode forward, reaching the trunk, glancing back to see the ice dragon straining to get between the trees. If Jason didn't do anything, the dragon would attempt to push his way through, and might even try to blast his way through the trees. He would knock down the trees and leave a path for others to follow and know that they had been here.

"You can wait there," he said and turned to the earth dragon. "You brought me here. What is it that you wanted me to see?"

"Come," the rumbling of the dragon said.

His voice was low, producing a deep and painful sort of rumbling, and as it echoed out, Jason realized that there was more than just an uncertainty from the dragon. There was more than just the energy within the dragon. There was something else.

And it was that something else that he needed to help find.

The dragon rumbled, guiding him forward.

And as he did, he led Jason toward the massive trunk of the tree, and from there…

Jason crouched down. He could feel heat radiating. There was warmth, only a bit, and nothing more than that.

Dragon bones. He was certain of it, though why?

He held out his hand, probing, reaching into the tree, trying to feel for something that was here, to understand just what Lorren would've been after, but even as he stretched forward, Jason couldn't feel anything more.

"What is it?" he asked softly, trying to get the earth dragon to share more with him.

Only, the dragon did not.

There was only a faint rumbling. He reached forward

and came across something warm. As he grabbed it, he realized that it was another bone.

It was different than the others. Longer. At first, Jason had even believed that the bone was not even a bone but a branch. Warmth radiated off it, making it clear what it was, though it looked discolored.

He pulled it forward and rested it on his lap.

The heat coming off it was diminished a little bit, certainly diminished compared to what he had felt from the other bones.

Why would that be?

He needed the earth dragon's help.

"What is going on here?" he asked.

"Him," the earth dragon rumbled.

"Him? You've showed me two places now, and in both places, there are bones."

"There are," the dragon rumbled.

"Why do you need me to see this?"

"For you to understand," the earth dragon said.

"This is something Lorren had been after, but what was it?"

The earth dragon rumbled, but there was no further answer.

That was what Jason needed to know. He needed to understand what Lorren had been looking for. That was the only way he was going to find it.

He probed the bone.

Something about it felt off, though Jason wasn't entirely sure what it was. He could feel the heat radiating off it and he recognized that there was some energy there, though he had no idea what it was or why he should feel it.

He needed the ice dragon.

He crawled through the trees, feeling the earth dragon trailing after him, saying nothing. When he reached the ice dragon, the moisture dripping off him revealed just how much he struggled.

"Can you feel anything through this?" Jason asked, holding the bone out to the ice dragon.

The ice dragon rumbled softly, and there was a bit of energy that came off him. "It has been burned," the ice dragon said.

Jason held onto the bone, turning it from side to side, feeling for the energy within it.

Burned? Maybe that's why it feels off.

He looked behind him. This had to be a place of Lorren's, only why would it be here?

He got to his knees, holding onto the bone, trying to feel for the energy within it, but recognizing that there was still something off about it.

"Why did you want mc to find this?"

"Him," the earth dragon said.

"I understand that it's him. I understand he was doing something with dragons, trying to create other misfits. What was it?"

"Him," the earth dragon said again.

Jason tapped the bone against his hand and turned it from side to side, feeling the energy within it and wishing that there was something different that he could do with it, something different that he could feel from it, but every passing moment gave him no further answers.

"You brought me out here for a reason. You brought me to the other place for a reason. You wanted me to know that Lorren had places like this?" He looked down and dropped the bone.

As soon as he did, the ground rumbled even more.

Jason grabbed it and held onto the bone again.

"Fine. I won't drop the bone, but you do need to tell me why I need to hold onto it. You need me to know what you intend."

"Him," the earth dragon said again.

Jason let out a sigh of frustration but realized that maybe that was a mistake.

The earth dragon was trying to reach out to him, and because of that, he needed to reach out to the earth dragon and to see if there was some way for them to connect.

When he had done it before, he had used illusion, and he did that now.

He held an illusion, creating a vast meadow with a sun shining down and a gentle breeze. The earth dragon rumbled for a moment until the illusion took hold.

Jason shifted it the way that he often did when working with illusions. It wasn't difficult, as the earth dragon didn't struggle against him, not trying to fight past what he was doing. Instead, the earth dragon seemed to welcome the illusion. Jason kept the ice dragon out of this although distantly, he was aware of the ice dragon pressing inward, trying to pry his way into the illusion, but he didn't want that imposition. He needed for the earth dragon to have enough of a separation he felt comfortable revealing to Jason his reason for having come here.

"You brought me here," he said, standing in a meadow with flowers of dozens of different colors sweeping around him. He didn't have enough control over the illusion to create the aromas coming from the flowers, though he suspected he could if he were to work with the illusion longer. Holding it this firmly, and shifting into a way that created something more real, was challenging enough. "You wanted me to see this, though why? What is it that Lorren had here that you needed me to know?" He summoned the image of the bone, and something about it caused the illusion to shimmer.

That was odd.

It was almost as if the bone itself were corrupted, and introducing it to the illusion corrupted the illusion.

"Is that it? Did you want me to know that Lorren was somehow poisoning dragon bones?" He shrugged. "Does that even matter? The bones are useful, but at the same time, the bones cannot harm us."

The dragon rumbled and the flowers in the meadow trembled as if reacting to the way that the earth dragon shook.

"If you need me to understand more, then help me understand."

Jason reached out, pressing his hand toward the dragon, and when he did, there came a bit of resistance.

"Tell me what you need from me."

"Him," the earth dragon said, this time more softly.

Jason realized that the dragon was telling him more than he had realized before.

It wasn't just him. It was something else. It was a rumble of knowledge, a rumble of the dragon trying to give him something more, attempting to share what he needed to know. The problem was that Jason didn't know what it was. Jason couldn't detect anything more within it.

"You can't tell me. I see. Something is still compelling you."

Any influence that was on the dragon should have been lifted the moment that Lorren was gone, but perhaps his influence had lingered.

"He's gone."

"Him," the earth dragon said, this time with more urgency.

That was what he needed. That was what he wanted. Somehow, he had to find an understanding. The dragon needed it from him.

Jason reached out and touched the earth dragon.

There was a tremor underneath his skin, almost as if the dragon were filled with energy he was trying to fight against, or as if the dragon were struggling against something that Jason did.

He held his hand in place, waiting, knowing that he

had to do something more for this dragon, only not knowing what it was.

"I can help," he whispered.

The dragon turned to look at him. The earth dragon was so unusual compared to some of the other misfits, blocky, filled with power, and with small, stubby wings that wouldn't be able to split the sky and fly. Still, there was an energy within the dragon that Jason could feel. An energy that carried through him, and it was an energy that Jason recognized would be powerful.

"Let me help you."

A surge came off the dragon.

"Him," the earth dragon said.

Jason recognized it. It was a request to follow.

But follow him where?

8

Jason stayed atop the ice dragon, and they headed steadily north.

It wasn't at all where he expected the earth dragon would've led him. He thought that by following the other dragon, they would've headed south, to less snowy and cold lands, not at all in this direction. Only, the earth dragon continued to rumble through the ground.

It seemed to Jason that the earth dragon wanted to augment the sound he traveled with, making it so Jason could more easily follow him. The ice dragon did so, having no difficulty maintaining the same pace as the other dragon.

Jason shouldn't be traveling this way. There were other things he needed to be doing. Understanding Lorach's plan. Finding Sarah's parents.

This felt like something the dragons needed from him.

How could he refuse?

Gradually, the snowcapped mountains began to fade.

Jason had gone this way before, though it had been a while. Beyond the mountains was a strange, bleak land, a place of heat, and it was a place in which the ice dragon wouldn't be able to last for long. Perhaps if Jason would've brought the iron dragon, but he didn't know if the iron dragon would have been able to manage the cold.

It was the same reason Jason didn't think the other dragons had traveled this far. This land was protected, separated, and by taking the ice dragon, Jason had an opportunity to travel where the other dragons wouldn't be able to go. Finally, they passed the last of the snowcapped mountains.

The earth dragon roared in the distance.

It was a steady trembling, an energy that came up from deep within the ground, and it rumbled with a sense that seemed to urge him onward. Jason could feel the way the dragon called to him, summoning him, trying to compel him to follow.

He felt not only that of the earth dragon, but there was something else. It was a familiar sense. The mist dragons.

Jason looked down at the ground, but he didn't see any sign of the mist dragons. The mist dragons had been difficult to track before, and in this land, he wasn't sure if he would be able to do it more easily. As they descended, the ground took on a haze. It was the power of the mist dragons.

That wasn't all that it was, though. Smoke drifted in.

A memory of what Lorren had said to him came to

him then. Lorren had suggested he had some way of creating smoke dragons. He had claimed the smoke dragons weren't that powerful, but Jason could feel energy within them. They might not be all that powerful, but they had their own unique kind of power.

The ice dragon came to land amidst the mist and the smoke.

He tapped on the ice dragon's side as he slipped from his back. "Are you going to be okay here?" There was heat in the air, and he could feel the energy and he worried about what it might do to the ice dragon.

The ice dragon rumbled, power radiating from him. "I can manage," he said.

Jason smiled at the confidence, but he could feel how the ice dragon was pulling upon energy, the way he summoned it from the distant mountains, but even more than that, he could feel the way he summoned it from high overhead. Jason thought he could connect to it in a way that would allow him to call upon some of that power as well.

Strange that he would feel that flow of power so distinctly now.

Always before, he had felt the flow of power coming from the connection he shared with the ice dragon, but in this case, the flow of power he detected came from not only the ice dragon, but it also came from somewhere overhead.

Jason turned to the rumbling sound around him. It began to intensify.

He didn't think that he was in any danger, but he had come here to the stronghold of these misfits, dragons that had been commanded by Lorren, dragons that had been willing to fight and harm other dragons.

He looked over at the ice dragon. "Maybe you'd better stay in the air."

"Are you sure?"

Jason focused on the earth dragon, on the power coming off the mist dragons. There was more than one here. He knew there had to be at least three, and there could be even more than that. Lorren had claimed to have hatched a number of dragons, but Jason didn't really know how many mist dragons that Lorren had managed to hatch. He had no idea how many smoke dragons, either. All of those could be a danger to him.

"As sure as I can be. I'd rather have you be in a position where you can offer assistance if it were needed rather than risk you."

The ice dragon took to the air.

Jason strode forward, into the mist.

As he did, he drew upon the cold from high overhead. The connection between him and the ice dragon was strong. Only, the longer he held onto the power of the cold, the harder it began to be. The smoke dragons were swirling around him.

Strangely, he felt as if the smoke dragons were trying to create a sort of separation to the power he had over the cold and ice.

Jason resisted, pushing against them, to see if he might

be able to prevent them from using their power to harm him. He added a hint of heat, drawing through the distant sense of the iron dragon. He hoped the iron dragon didn't mind, and worried that the way they had left each other had made the iron dragon upset that Jason would even dare borrow from him, but the power came to him freely.

The only dragon that he didn't have the kind of connection to that he wished that he did was the storm dragon. *That's not quite true.* If Jason had the power of the night dragon, he thought he might be able to use that as well.

He turned, focusing on the power that was around him.

Earth and mist and smoke.

"Reveal yourself," Jason said, standing in the midst of all of it, holding his hands out to the side. He released his hold on the power within him, trying not to grip cold too strongly, not wanting to do anything that would anger the dragons here. "I've come before you willingly. All I want is to have the opportunity to talk, and to see if there's anything Lorren might have shared with you about how he created dragons of your kind."

Perhaps that wasn't the way that he should best address them, but Jason didn't know what else he needed to do. He could feel that energy within them, and he could feel the way that the power continued to radiate out from him, and he held onto it, trying to see if there might be something more that he could do by pushing out, using the power within him to try to understand it. Even as he did, he didn't find anything more.

The sense of the dragons rumbled again, coming near him.

Jason could feel one, maybe two earth dragons.

He counted the mist dragons as well. Three of them. That he could tell. There might be more, though the sense of them was tenuous and difficult to fully detect.

"Please work with me," Jason said. "I know you haven't been controlled by the Dragon Souls, and that's why I've come to you. I need your help. We face the danger of Lorach, but I don't want to attack them the way Lorren did."

That was the critical piece.

Jason looked around, but it was difficult to see much of anything. He had a sense of a bleak landscape, the same landscape that he had seen from high overhead, even though he wasn't able to make out much else about it. He could feel the energy of this land, he could feel the power that was within it, and he recognized there was dragon power here.

Were there other dragons that he had yet to see?

As Jason focused on that energy, he tried to see if there might be a dragon pearl or even a dragon or, worse—what if there was a Dragon Soul?

Jason didn't think that was the case.

The rumbling continued around him. The mist swirled, a steady sort of movement to it. Smoke and the haze within danced around him.

All of it was disconcerting, and it made it difficult for Jason to focus, to pay attention to anything other than that strange energy he detected all around him.

There was little doubt in his mind that these were powerful dragons. Even the smoke dragon released a sense of vast energy. Lorren had misled him.

Of course Lorren would have misled him.

Lorren wouldn't have wanted to admit the kind of power that he had access to.

Jason recognized the energy within the smoke dragon, and it came to him as something familiar. Within the smoke was a sense of irritation. Rage.

It reminded him of the iron dragon.

Jason smiled to himself.

Perhaps the iron dragon *should* have come.

Then again, the iron dragon wouldn't have been able to make it here.

Heading through the cold would've been stressful for him, and Jason had already traveled with the iron dragon enough times through the cold that he realized there were limits to how far and how well the iron dragon could fly against those conditions.

"We could talk. I have worked with other dragons much like you."

"There are no other dragons like us," a voice said.

This was strange, twisted, and higher-pitched.

Could it be a female dragon?

Had Lorren had a female dragon, Jason would have expected that he would have done anything to protect it.

Of course.

That explained far more than anything else he had seen so far.

Lorren had been protecting her.

"Who are you?" Jason asked.

He focused on the power within him, and he tried to focus on the energy that he detected all around him. There was that of the earth dragons, that of the mist dragons, even that of the smoke dragons, but what he felt on top of that was something else.

He didn't even know what it was, only that what he detected felt different.

It was unique.

A misfit, that much was certain, especially given what he knew about Lorren and the type of dragons he kept. He stayed in place, holding onto the power of the ice dragon, feeling the irritation from the iron dragon, and using that to probe.

"I am the queen," she said.

"The queen of what?"

"The queen of dragons."

A shape appeared in front of him.

Jason hesitated, feeling uncertain, but there was a dark shadow that loomed out of the fog and the haze and the mist. The dragon that came toward him was enormous. Jason had never seen anything quite like her. As he stared, he couldn't help but feel a trembling within him.

"The queen?"

"The queen of the dragons."

Power radiated out from her. It was the kind of power that Jason had never felt before, the kind of power he recognized as definitely dragonlike, but he couldn't tell if this was a typical dragon—or if this was a misfit.

The shadow loomed even larger, standing tall, and massive wings spread out to either side, and then she reared up.

The mist around her lifted. It had been enormous, the mist incredible, and yet, as she lifted up, Jason was aware of just how powerful she was. He could feel the energy radiating off her. Somehow, she been masking that power and that energy, and somehow she'd been hiding from him.

Now that she reared up in front of him, she seemed almost as if she wanted to make him fully aware of that power within her. It was almost as if she wanted him to know that she was there, and that she was powerful.

Heat began to radiate from her, wafting away in a cloud of power and energy. Jason stood back, looking up at her.

The sense of her was immense, enormous, and incredible. As he stared at her, feeling the power coming off her, he couldn't help but wonder if perhaps he had made a mistake in coming here.

He probed gently, using ice and iron, mixing them together, and he pushed. For the first time when attempting to use that connection on a dragon, he felt something pushed back. This was different than the resistance he felt from the Dragon Souls. This was something actively pushing against him. It was something that strained to rebuff him. This was something refusing his touch.

It was power.

The power of this dragon pressed upon him. She *wanted* him to feel it. She wanted him aware of what she did and wanted him to know her, to know the energy she possessed. She wanted him to fear.

For the first time in a long time around the dragons, Jason did know fear.

She reared up again, heat and fire radiating along her skin and scales, flames fluctuating, filling her in the same way that they did around the iron dragon, pulsating out from her. Then she wrapped her wings toward him, engulfing him.

Jason barely had a chance to react.

He created a barrier, wrapping ice and iron and forest around him before begging to whatever distant connection he had to the storm dragon, crying out, pleading with him for a hint of power, something that would grant him enough of a connection so that he could resist what was happening, though Jason didn't know if it was going to be enough. Pressure built around him.

The queen of the dragons grasped him and pulled her toward him.

Jason struggled, pushing against the power of this queen dragon, feeling the energy within her. He didn't know if there was going to be anything he could even do against the power she possessed, the way she wrapped her wings around him, but he had to do something. He could feel her energy as she squeezed, trying to suffocate him.

What purpose would she have in attempting to squeeze him?

Jason drew upon the power of the ice dragon, exploding that outward.

That power burst away from him, enough of it that it freed him briefly from her grasp. Jason could feel the energy within her, the way she continued to batter at him. That power held him in a way he hadn't felt before, but he strained, trying to get himself free of her grasp.

He had to use something different.

Power surged within him, coming up slowly. Jason realized its source. Distantly, the awareness of the storm dragon came to him, a power of energy that began to build, rising up within him.

Jason burst it outward.

It crashed into the dragon queen's wings, slamming into them.

He didn't hesitate as he released that energy, letting it strike her, not at all concerned about what it might do to her or whether he might harm her. With the way she attacked, he wanted nothing more than to use every bit of power he possessed, every bit he could call upon, to avoid her doing something more to him.

He'd come willingly, straining to find whether there was something more that he might be able to understand, but there was nothing else here for him. It was a mistake. After visiting the other places where they had seen evidence of Lorren, he hadn't expected the earth dragon to have led him here to such danger.

Jason burst power outward again, drawing on the energy of the storm dragon, letting that power slam out from him, using everything in his might in order to overwhelm the way the dragon attacked him.

He mixed the power of the other dragons in with what he drew through the storm dragon. By wrapping each of those energies together, power exploded away from him.

It burst, striking the dragon queen.

Jason maintained that connection, forcing more power from him. As the four dragons' power continued to mingle, their power exploding, Jason erupted with that energy.

Finally, the grip around him eased.

The dragon queen's wings spread apart, freeing him.

Debris filled the clearing.

Distantly, he was aware of something else, the sense of other dragons, that of the other misfits he knew were around him. Jason could feel that power and energy coming off them, that of the smoke dragons, that of the earth dragons, that of the mist dragons. All of it was enough that he could make out the sense coming off them.

Surprisingly, the sense coming from the dragon queen was different. Less.

He couldn't tell if there was anything more that the dragon queen would do.

She loomed in front of them.

She was massive. Enormous. Powerful. Jason could feel

that energy coming from her, but he wasn't able to pinpoint just what it was about her energy that felt so different. He maintained power within himself, holding onto it, feeling for the energy radiating from the queen dragon.

As he did, he recognized some aspect about it.

Strangely, there was something almost familiar about her power. Jason focused on that power and felt something within him, along with it, that seemed to echo with him.

Why should she be so familiar to me?

"I came here to understand you dragons, not to fight," he said.

He maintained his connection to the energy within him, the power from the other dragons, letting that stretch away from him, sweeping toward her.

"I'm not like the others. I'm not like the Dragon Souls of Lorach. All I want is to try to help the dragons."

As he said it, he created an illusion. He used the energy of the forest dragon in order to do so, creating something that was almost real, a sense of the dragon and a sense of her power, binding it together in a way that granted the dragons an understanding of just what he'd done and how he'd done it. He tried to gift them an understanding of him and what he intended. The image formed, though it didn't form in a way that he fully intended.

The dragon queen spread her wings again and Jason braced for her attack.

Thankfully, she didn't.

Power built from her and Jason readied for what she might do, the way she might use that power, but her wings simply spread out. The energy coming off her swirled. It was a strange combination of powers.

It was a mixture.

Jason hadn't been aware of that before, but now that he was, he could feel how the powers she possessed all combined together, all lingering in a way that bound them together.

A mixture of energy. A combination of earth and smoke and mist and… he couldn't detect what else. How was such a thing possible?

He mixed the powers of the other dragons again, creating a combination of energy.

She watched him, power radiating from her, the energy of the combination of elements coming from the ice and iron and the other dragons bonded together, forming something unique. Powerful.

Something very much like the night dragon.

Jason hadn't considered that before, but with the realization, he recognized that had to be what it was.

"He made you, didn't he?" Jason asked, looking at the dragon queen. "You're here because of Lorren."

The other dragons were touched by her energy.

Either that, or *she* was touched by *their* energy.

With the night dragon, there was considerable energy within the dragon itself. The other dragons had seemed to feed it, giving it the strength necessary in order for the dragon to grow, to develop, and to become the powerful creature that he was.

"Do you know about Lorach?" Jason asked.

He created another illusion, this time using everything in his power in order to focus on the nature of that illusion, trying to hold it so that he could create the image of Lorach, the image of what had happened, and the image of what risk the dragons were in.

As he did, he held that image, though he did so in a tightly controlled fashion. He didn't intend to create anything that would frighten the dragons. The only thing he wanted was to give the impression of what he had experienced and the understanding of what he knew.

Using a hint of illusion, he added even more power, calling those dragons into the illusion. It was slow. Subtle. And he did so as carefully and cautiously as he could in order to ensure the dragons saw what he saw, that they were aware of Lorach, the dragons they created, even the Dragon Souls. He created them in such a way that they looked as if they were off in the distance, beyond the mountains, but near enough that the dragons would recognize just what he wanted to show them. Jason held that image tightly, holding it within his mind and giving it to the dragons.

Somewhere distantly, the earth rumbled.

He pushed more energy into the illusion, creating enough that he could call the queen dragon into the illusion in a way that wrapped everything up tightly, binding the dragon in such a way that she knew what he was showing her.

More power rumbled within him.

Jason held onto that power, letting it flow out from him.

Within the illusion, he created dozens upon dozens of dragons. He demonstrated the capital city. The dragon pens. Even the slaves locked at the edge of the city.

All of those were things he'd seen, and because of that, Jason could re-create them far more easily than he could if they were not something that he'd seen. It made it so that he was able to show that power, to hold onto it in a way that was real to the dragons.

"Enough," the dragon queen roared.

With a surge of energy, the illusion shattered.

Jason had known that she was powerful, but the way she shattered his illusion with little more than a thought revealed just how powerful she was.

"I'm trying to demonstrate what we face. What the dragons face." He recreated a Dragon Soul riding on a dragon, controlling it. Even the bone, like he'd seen before. That seemed significant.

The dragon queen reacted, pushing against him.

Jason pushed a hint of energy through it, giving enough that he could feel the power flowing from him. He maintained his connections, holding onto the power, and he pushed again, creating more of an illusion.

He felt something off within the dragon queen.

Energy built, rising up from within her. Not only from

within her, but from within the dragons. By stealing that connection, he understood something that he hadn't seen before.

The power that was within her wasn't her power.

That was why he hadn't been able to uncover the sense of her before.

It was power, but it was *borrowed* power.

It was no different than the way he connected to power.

With an understanding flowing into him, he knew what he faced.

Strangely, it wasn't at all what he had first thought.

Jason built that energy, letting more flow, connecting to it so that he could fully understand just what he detected. Holding onto that power, he recognized something else. There was a source of it flowing near him, a source of power all around him. And that source of power seemed to fill him.

That was what he had to understand.

Jason gripped that energy, wrapping himself within it.

It was strange, but it was also distinct.

It was all too similar to what he had flowing within him.

By holding onto that power and energy, Jason recognized the dragon queen for what she was. He sent a surge of power out from him, blasting toward her.

He targeted the illusion she maintained.

When it shattered, a young woman stood before him.

9

Jason could scarcely breathe.

He stared at the woman, feeling the power within him but also recognizing something similar within her. She held onto her connection to the dragons, but she bound it within whatever strange connection she had, using it to create an illusion of power, an illusion of the dragon, and she used that in order to give off the appearance of the dragon queen.

Jason continued to hold onto power of the different dragons, and he watched the woman in front of him. She had to be about the same age as him, maybe even a year or two younger.

She had black hair, and there was something about its darkness that reminded him of the dragon she'd created in the illusion. Of course it would, though. She had likely done the same thing that Jason did when he created illusions, using something familiar in order to create a sense of reality. By holding onto an illusion that had elements of reality within it, she was better able to maintain it. Her freckled skin was pale, and it reflected some of the power that he held onto, making it appear as if it almost glowed.

"Who are you?" he asked.

She started to build an illusion again, and this time, Jason was prepared for it.

He could feel the way that she called upon the energy, using that of the mist dragons. By using them, she borrowed the same sort of energy that he had seen Lorren use. Knowing how she created the illusion allowed him to counter it more effectively.

Jason shifted the power within him, taking whatever image she created and twisting it. By holding onto that energy, twisting it away, Jason prevented her from doing anything more than what she'd already done. He continued to turn it, holding onto that power, and he waited. There was a sense of energy coming from her, but it wasn't the kind of energy that suggested anything unusual.

"You must have known Lorren," Jason said.

She looked down, seeming to realize that she no longer had the appearance of the dragon. "How did you do that?"

"Lorren wasn't the only one who knew how to create illusions," Jason said. "And unfortunately, Lorren wasn't strong enough to be able to withstand my control over them."

She glared at him. "Are you the one who killed him?"

He wasn't sure how to answer without angering her. He had been there and been a part of Lorren's death. "I didn't kill him."

"Someone did. The dragons tell me he died fighting."

"The dragons killed him," Jason said.

She shook her head. Her dark hair swirled from side to side as she did. "Dragons wouldn't have killed him. Lorren fought on behalf of the dragons."

"Lorren *attacked* the dragons. If he would have fought on behalf of the dragons, he might have been able to live, but unfortunately..."

She started to shift again, the power of the illusion that she drew through the mist dragons enormous. Jason maintained his own connection, holding onto the power within him, and turned the nature of her illusion against her.

Her illusion failed.

"That isn't going to work against me again," Jason said.

"Why are you here?"

"Your earth dragon brought me here after showing me other places Lorren had been," he said.

And because it had brought him here, Jason had to wonder if there was something to this place. The earth dragon would have had a reason to have brought Jason here. There must've been some reason, something the earth dragon would've thought they would have been able to accomplish, and whether or not it had something to do with something Jason might be able to do on behalf of the dragons or whether it was simply to try to get vengeance for what had happened to Lorren, he didn't know.

"The dragon would not have brought you here."

"Unfortunately, the dragon did."

"How were you able to travel here?"

Jason called upon the cold, the energy of the ice dragon, and he set it swirling around him. By holding onto that, letting it fill him with power, it swirled outward, flowing out and around him. It built powerfully. Ice began to glisten along the surface of his skin.

Strangely, it didn't seem as if all of that power came from the ice dragon. For the first time, it seemed almost as if some of that energy came from *him*. As he held onto that energy, he sensed something that struck him as similar to the energy that was in the north, the power that connected him to the mountains, that was filling him, and similar to a sense of energy that drew him closer to the power that existed out in the world.

Am I somehow drawing upon that?

Jason had no idea whether or not what he drew upon was something that he needed to use or better understand, or whether it was something more. He focused on that power and tried to call it, letting it flow from him, through the ice dragon, and even from the north.

The girl borrowed energy from the other dragons and sent it sweeping against Jason. He ignored the pressure against him, focusing only on the power within him. As he did, he could feel some aspect of the energy she held onto, the way she called upon that power, squeezing it out from her. By holding onto that energy within him, he recognized there was something more to the way that she held onto her power.

"You don't need to keep attacking," Jason said.

There had to be some reason the earth dragon had brought him here.

Jason turned toward the earth dragon. The dragon queen tried to hold onto power, using it in a way that would prevent him from seeing anything, though he could feel the power that was there, the energy around him, and he could feel the connection she tried to use to create another illusion that would make it difficult for him to make anything out. By studying that energy, that power that was out there, he focused, feeling for the power.

That energy persisted, the source of it flowing everywhere, and he held onto that connection. He turned toward the earth dragon and summoned that power, letting it flow to him.

"Why did you bring me here?" he asked the earth dragon.

The ground rumbled through the ground once again.

Jason ignored the rumbling. It almost sounded like some sort of a threat, though the kind of threat the dragon tried to use was such that he attempted to dissuade Jason from causing problems with the dragon queen, though that wasn't at all anything that Jason was interested in doing. He wanted to know more about why the earth dragon had brought him here.

He looked over at the earth dragon again, focusing on

the power within him, feeling that energy flowing from deep within the ground, through the connection he shared with the other dragons.

"He wouldn't have brought you here," the dragon queen said.

"He would and he did. Why?"

She continued to use the mist, trying to turn it into an illusion.

It now took little thought on Jason's behalf to shatter her illusion. He recognized what she did and the way she turned it. As he looked around, he realized something.

The dragons were in this strange and desolate land. Isolated.

When he had seen Lorren, there hadn't been the impression that he'd been cut off from the other dragons, only that he had chosen to avoid Lorach. He wondered if all of the dragons would have been capable of traveling to Lorach.

As he focused on the power he detected from not only the earth dragon but the smoke and mist dragons, he couldn't help but wonder whether or not there was something to that connection, and to the mountains themselves, that created a barrier.

Not just to the smoke dragons.

To the dragon queen.

"Where is your home?" Of all the places he'd seen, this one was different. More isolated. Desolate.

"Why? So you can go there and destroy it as well?"

"So that we can understand each other."

She attempted to pull power again, but now that he was aware of what she did, Jason knew how to counter it fairly easily. In fact, he found it far more effective to ignore the nature of the energy she pulled upon and the way that she summoned that power through the ground and from the other dragons.

It was energy he could use, energy he could counter.

"What are you—"

He didn't get the opportunity to finish. The earth dragon started to rumble again, and he listened. This time, there was something within the rumbling that he understood. He could feel the energy within that rumbling, but there was more than that.

Words.

He turned to the earth dragon, focusing on it, feeling the connection between them, and trying to gain an understanding of what the earth dragon was trying to say.

The rumbling began to make sense. There was a communication. A conversation.

He heard the earth dragon and the dragon queen speaking.

He hadn't even been aware she was saying anything.

Could she have been talking this whole time? If she had, then she was doing so by the earth, communicating through something different. As he listened, Jason began to recognize the argument between them.

"He can help," the earth dragon said.

It seemed to Jason that there was a sense of irritation within the dragon, a sense of exacerbation, as if they'd had this argument before.

"He's the one responsible for what happened to Father."

"Father?"

Jason couldn't help himself and realized he revealed his awareness of their conversation. He knew he shouldn't have said anything, but couldn't help it.

She turned to him, crossing her arms over her chest. "You shouldn't be able to listen."

"Because I'm not connected to an earth dragon?"

"Yes."

He shrugged. "I can't tell you anything about that, only that it seems like the dragon wants me to listen."

As he said it, he realized it was the truth. The connection that he had, the understanding that he now possessed, seemed to come as much from the dragon as from anything else. By holding onto that connection and understanding, he recognized just what the dragon did, the way that he connected to Jason.

He remembered the time when he had first felt this dragon. Jason didn't even know if it was the very same dragon or if this was a different one. The only thing that he did know was that he had felt something coming from the dragon that reminded him of this. Perhaps he had connected in some way to the earth dragon.

He nodded to the earth dragon. "You wanted me to come because you were worried about her."

The earth dragon rumbled.

"Why are you worried about her? She seems quite capable."

Unless the Dragon Souls had made it this far.

He didn't think so, though. The mountains served as a natural defense, preventing almost anyone from heading beyond them. He had no idea whether or not dragons would even want to come this way or if the Dragon Souls would be willing to accept that hesitation on the dragons' part.

Only, they had been after dragon misfits. There had been what Jessica had done, how *she* had created a misfit. And even if it hadn't survived, they had wanted more.

As he looked around, noticing the landscape, the bleakness out here, he had to wonder: Was this why Therin had wanted to find different dragons?

He wouldn't have been able to reach here by traveling with one of his Dragon Soul dragons. They were powerful, and they could fly great distances, but Jason had seen limits to them.

Of course, the ice dragon had a different type of limitation.

Jason focused on the energy around him.

"Lorach isn't the only danger," she said.

"What other danger is there?"

"More than Lorach," she said.

Her gaze drifted to the sky and Jason followed it, wondering what else she might know, but she said nothing more. The earth dragon continued to rumble, connecting to her, through her, and in doing so, shared something Jason understood.

He laughed.

"Why are you laughing?" she snapped.

"Only because I think I understand why I'm able to understand you and the earth dragon."

"Because he has permitted," she said. "He has betrayed me."

"Nope. I think he has connected to you, but the reason I'm able to understand the earth dragon is because of you."

"Me?"

He shrugged. "I think it's you. You're putting off energy, and you're connecting to the dragon." He thought about what he detected when he was near the Dragon Souls, along with what he detected from those within Dragon Haven. "What are you suffering from here?" he asked.

Jason focused on what he could see through the ice dragon's eyesight, using that to augment what he could make out, especially now that he had this woman in front of him. The landscape around him was all flat earth, and there was no longer any smoke hanging that obscured his ability to see anything. The ground was bleak, and he saw no sign of city or villages or any other evidence of life.

Why would she have been here?

The ice dragon continued to circle, making ever larger arcs as he did, allowing Jason to try to see beyond what he had managed to see so far. With each sweeping arc, he could barely make out the changing ground beneath him. Distantly, Jason thought he caught sight of a forest and perhaps even a city's first vestiges, but he couldn't tell.

He had to turn his attention back to the girl.

She stared at him for a long moment before shaking her head. "You wouldn't care."

"Are you under attack?"

"No."

"Then why did you react the way you did with me?"

"Because it was necessary," she said.

"It wasn't necessary. I didn't come here to fight."

The earth dragon didn't seem as if he had drawn Jason here for a fight, either.

As he looked at the earth dragon, and as he felt the power coming from him, he couldn't help but feel as if there was something more that he needed to understand. He focused on that power, feeling it within him. The earth dragon began to rumble with a different frequency.

Strangely, that frequency came up from the ground, through his boots, and Jason could feel it. Gradually, words became a part of what he felt.

The earth dragon spoke to *him*.

He had done so before, but the way that he did now was different.

Jason watched the dragon queen, but it didn't seem as if she heard what the dragon said to him. It was separate. It was meant only for him. If that were the case, then he had to listen.

"We are alone."

"That's why you came for me?"

"When Lorren lived, we were not alone. He kept us safe from Lorach."

Safe? That didn't sound like what Jason had seen Lorren doing with the dragons. "He used you to attack in Lorach."

"He gave us the choice."

"Did he?"

"He gave us the choice," he said. "And he searched for the answer."

"What answer?"

"The answer to after."

Jason frowned. There was something he didn't quite understand. Yet.

He focused on the energy he felt coming from the earth dragon, and he listened to the rumbling. He watched the dragon queen as he did, feeling the power coming off her. "Are you keeping her from hearing?"

"I am keeping you bound to me."

"Bound?"

The idea of having the dragon bound to him suggested something else.

Given his experience with the other dragons, and what he knew of his connections with them, he couldn't help but wonder if perhaps there was something more. Some other reason.

If that were the case, then…

He focused on the power beneath him, the energy of

the ground, the energy of the rumbling that he detected. As he did, he could feel more and more power bubbling up deep beneath him. It started slowly. It was a strange and heavy connection, one that he recognized, but only because he had almost been buried by the earth.

He wondered if he would have the same understanding of it had that not happened.

Jason slowly started to draw on that connection.

Gradually, it came to him.

Earth.

The earth dragon had chosen to connect to him in a way that he hadn't before.

It was different than what he experienced with other dragons. In this case, he felt the way that power was there, the surge of the energy, and the burst of power that exploded between them. Could he find something similar with the mist dragons and the smoke dragons?

They all watched, the energy swirling around him, the power filling him. Jason held onto that, focusing on what he could make out and on the power that was there. It came to him slowly, but it built all around him.

"Why?"

"Because it's needed," the earth dragon rumbled.

The dragon queen turned to him, stepping toward him. Power began to swirl away from her. "What did you do?"

Jason shook his head. "It's nothing that I did. The dragon chose to let me connect to him."

"He wouldn't have chosen. You did this. You forced this."

Jason shook his head and held that connection through him, feeling it rumbling deep beneath his feet. What would it mean if the earth dragon granted him power?

How could he use that against Lorach?

He'd already seen the way that Lorren had used that power, but Jason had no interest in doing something similar. He refused to attack in the same way as Lorren.

"It seems your dragon wanted me to connect to his power, so…"

What would happen if I were to mix it with the power of the other dragons?

He had seen what happened when he added the energy of the other dragons together, and had noticed the connections and that power, the way that they had worked together, but he didn't know if there was anything that he could do differently with that power if he were to mingle it.

"Why?" she snapped, turning to the earth dragon. "Why would you betray me like that?"

"I was there," the dragon said, a heavy rumbling coming from him.

"You were where?" she demanded.

"I was there when he helped the dragons."

"I know you were there. You were there when he killed Lorren."

"Not Father?" Jason asked.

"He had her call him Father," the earth dragon said.

That was strange. Why would Lorren have done that if he wasn't her father?

"Lorren killed other dragons. He left me no choice," Jason said.

She turned to him. Anger clouded her face, but it was not only anger on her face. It was in the power she held onto, drawing from the other dragons. Only, even as she drew on that power, he had a sense of something different. It seemed to him that the earth dragon pushed against her connection, which he resisted.

The earth dragon didn't want her to use his power against Jason.

Interesting.

From what he'd seen, especially with the forest dragon, the dragons had control over who used their power. Jason couldn't imagine the other dragons willingly allowing Lorren to use their power, to draw upon it and steal that energy, harming other dragons, but what he had seen suggested that they had.

Unless they hadn't known.

"You didn't know the dragons could be freed," Jason said to the earth dragon.

The dragon rumbled again.

"Have you been controlled, yourself?"

The dragon rumbled, and within it, Jason heard a hint of a message, something that suggested the energy of the dragon, though he wasn't able to tell anything from it. The only thing he could determine from the way the dragon communicated with him was that there was some energy.

"I didn't know," the dragon said.

"Had you known, would you have allowed him to use you?"

The dragon rumbled again. "No," he said.

Jason nodded. It was different than the Dragon Soul dragons. With those dragons, they didn't have much choice as to how they were used. They were forced to serve, forced to work with the other dragons, and they didn't have any choice in the matter.

In the case of these dragons, they loaned their energy intentionally. They gave it freely. And they could withdraw it just as freely.

By holding onto that energy, Jason could feel the power coming off the dragon, and he was aware of how it could wax and wane, how the energy between himself and the dragon connected, but it was something the dragon controlled; there was a way that the dragon could strip that power back from him once again. It was the same thing he had experienced with the iron dragon

"The dragons can be saved?" the dragon queen asked. "We don't have to run from Lorach?"

Jason looked over at her. For the first time, other than when he had stripped away her illusion, he sensed hesitation from her. The isolation.

She'd been hiding from Lorach. The same as Dragon Haven. And she'd been doing it alone. Her only companions were the dragons—and Lorren. Now that he was gone, she had only the dragons.

"They can."

"He said it wasn't possible. That he had found another way."

Jason wondered what other way Lorren might have discovered. "Most didn't believe it was possible."

"Did you show him?"

She took a step toward him before hesitating.

"I showed him," Jason said. "I demonstrated how the dragons could be saved. I did everything that I could in order for him to know that there was no reason to continue to attack the way that he did."

"If he knew they could be saved, he wouldn't have kept doing it."

"I'm sorry."

"He wouldn't have," she said.

Jason watched her, and he understood the way that she felt.

Given his experience with Lorren, Jason had felt something similar. There had been concern on his part about why he would have attacked, why he would've used the power that he possessed to cause harm to the dragons, and why he wouldn't have been willing to listen to Jason to see if there was something that could be done to protect them. Given what Jason had shown him, Lorren should have not done what he had done.

"I showed him the dragons that were freed," he said.

"How many dragons?"

"Hundreds," he said.

"If you freed hundreds of dragons, then you would have decimated Lorach. We wouldn't have to hide."

Jason smiled sadly. "Were that only the case. Lorach has hundreds upon hundreds of dragons. Many more Dragon Souls. Now that Lorren is gone, they have concentrated the Dragon Souls with the remaining dragons, making it increasingly difficult to free the rest of the dragons."

"Which must've been why he was willing to do what he did," she said.

"I didn't get the sense that he cared all that much. He tried to harm the dragons as much as he tried to harm the Dragon Souls. He didn't seem to care one way or the other."

"That's not true," she said.

"I can show you."

The earth dragon rumbled.

"You don't think she should go?"

"She will be separated from the others."

Jason frowned, looking around. "Then it proves she would trust me."

"What proves that I would trust you?" she asked.

"You want to know more about what he did and the dragons I've freed. I could show you."

Someone who had the control of several other different kinds of dragon misfits, could be dangerous. Jason knew that, especially given what he had felt from her and the type of power he had detected coming off her.

If she were to use it against him, and against the other dragons, he potentially opened himself up to danger.

At the same time, she had potential. She could act in a way that would be similar to what Lorren might have once been able to offer, only with her control, and with the power he detected from her, he had to believe that she might be able to do something more.

She might actually be able to help.

She watched him, saying nothing. Jason didn't have anything that he could say to her, either. He needed her to agree.

If she came along with him, heading to Dragon Haven, there would be a separation. She wouldn't have the connection to the mist dragons, or to the smoke dragons. The only dragons she would have any connection to would be the earth dragons, and given what Jason had detected, the power coming from this earth dragon and the way he sent it to him, he had a sense the earth dragon preferred to ensure she did not misuse that power.

"Why would you do that?"

"Because you need to know the truth," he said.

"You would separate me from the others?"

"I wouldn't do it. The mountains would. I'm not going to force you to go to Lorach." He thought that was what she feared. "But there's something you should see. You don't have to be alone here anymore."

As Jason looked over the mountain, he focused on the power that was there, feeling the cold and the energy, and a strange connection to it. It was the same sort of connection he felt when he reached through the ice dragon, an energy that suggested he might be able to draw upon even more than he had believed before.

He waited, watching her, uncertain how she might answer.

Finally, she nodded. “I will come with you.”

10

Jason felt as if he had to travel this way. Rather than choosing his direction, there was something that guided him, a rumbling that came from the earth dragon, a distant sort of sound that shook him, drawing up through him. The dragon queen sat behind him, barely willing to touch him, though he had a feeling she was tense.

He'd been away from Dragon Haven for too long; at least that was the way that it was starting to feel. He still had no idea what happened to Sarah's parents, and he'd promised her that he would search, offering her some answer.

What if there was no answer?

He had to push those thoughts away. They had been gone long enough he had begun to suspect they wouldn't return, or if they uncovered what happened to them, they would not care for it. It was also possible they had been captured by Lorach, though how?

The timing didn't fit. Unfortunately, though Jason wouldn't tell Sarah this, he was more concerned about the timing with their disappearance tying to Lorren. He had been around Dragon Haven near the time they had disappeared.

Still, even though he needed to return, something about what he was doing now felt important. There might be a way that Jason could see what was happening in Dragon Haven.

He closed his eyes briefly, focusing on the iron dragon. A sense of that dragon was there, though it was faint. He solidified the connection between the two of them and only saw trees around him. The iron dragon was hiding, or hunting, or…

None of that mattered. He couldn't use the dragon to go into Dragon Haven and speak to Sarah, anyway.

"How long have you been out here?" Jason asked the woman.

She looked over to him. "Not long."

"Which is why you were surprised when the earth dragon brought me to you."

She furrowed her brow, and her dark hair whipped around her with the wind streaming. "He should not have. We have been hunted."

"Hunted by Lorach?"

Her mouth pressed into a tight line. "Lorach. Worse."

"What's worse than Lorach?"

She shook her head. "There are many things worse than Lorach."

Jason looked down, borrowing from the ice dragon's eyesight but didn't see anything else. "Such as?" She wouldn't speak unless he prodded her, and he felt as if he needed to keep her talking.

"Those who would take the dragons from us," she said.

"I don't intend to take the dragons from you."

"You don't intend it, but you might."

Jason needed to get through her, somehow. "I don't have any intention of doing that. I work with the dragons, not against them." They flew for a little while, and he looked over to her. "Where have you been before this?"

"I have been through Vistel, Hamthen, Loth, Jol…"

Jason knew none of those places.

"Are those cities or countries?"

She eyed him. "How is it that you know so little?"

"I never left my home for most of my life," he said. "It's not been until recently that I had a chance to do so. Without a dragon, it was a little hard."

And that was an understatement. Even with a dragon, it had been hard to leave his homeland.

"Every place we went to was the same. They either hunted the dragons, or they wanted to force them to serve, or they used aspects of them." She shook her head, and she looked down at the ice dragon, though Jason couldn't quite read the expression in her eyes. Was it anger, or was it something else?

"I'm not like that."

"But you came for me. My dragons."

Jason resisted the urge to let out a frustrated sigh. It wasn't going to accomplish anything at this point. All it was going to do was turn her away and he needed her help, he suspected. At this point, more than anything else, he believed that he would need to work with her so that he could understand what she knew and what he could do to work with her.

"The earth dragon wants us to follow. Shouldn't that be enough?"

"It is enough for now. How did you force him to work with you?"

"I didn't force him to work with me," Jason said. "He came for me."

And it was all about him finding the dragon queen. Jason was certain of it, though he had no idea why the earth dragon would want him to find the dragon queen other than a desire for him to get to know the power that she possessed.

Somehow, he questioned what power that might be.

"He came for you because you forced him," she said.

The rumbling continued to echo, but it was different than it had been before. There was less of an intensity to it, almost as if they were heading the wrong way.

The ice dragon veered off, heading in the direction that the earth dragon guided.

"These make any sense to you?" Jason asked, reaching into his pocket and pulling out the smaller bone fragments that he had taken when he had first gone chasing after the earth dragon.

The dragon queen took them, holding them and frowning. "Where did you find these?"

"The earth dragon showed them to me."

He watched her, but she didn't give any sort of reaction.

The trembling of the earth began to build, and they started to descend.

They were in the mountains. It wasn't the cold northern mountains like Jason had known his whole life, but a tree-lined mountain. The earth dragon rumbled from a rocky portion that was more barren than others, and the ice dragon headed toward it before hovering in front of the rocky section.

"This is as far as I can go," the ice dragon said.

"Are we supposed to go somewhere else?"

"It seems he wants you to go closer," the ice dragon said.

Jason could feel the trembling of the earth dragon. He had no idea what exactly it meant, but realized that the ice dragon was right. The earth dragon did want them to go somewhere. He wanted them to head toward this section of rock.

He stood and climbed forward on the dragon's head, and then jumped.

It carried him to the rocky slope and he started to slide, but the earth dragon shifted something. He created a small ledge and Jason stopped sliding.

The dragon queen jumped and landed next to him, though she didn't slide.

She looked up at him, her dark eyes brimmed with suspicion.

"If you try to harm me, the earth dragon will protect me."

"I'm sure that he will," Jason said.

"If you try—"

Jason chuckled. "The dragon brought us both here," he said. "I'm not going to try to harm you, and I think that the earth dragon realizes that. He wants us to come here."

He climbed up the rock wall, following the rumbling that the earth dragon guided him toward, and found a small opening in the mountain. A cave.

He crawled into it.

It was narrow at first, but it opened up immediately as soon as he was inside. He drew upon the power of the iron dragon and his glove started to glow, illuminating the inside of the cave.

It was far more massive than he would've expected.

The dragon queen came behind him, and she frowned as she looked at his glowing glove. "What are you doing with that?"

"This is the dragon pearl that one of the dragons gave me. It turned into a glove."

She frowned at it and Jason held it away from her so that he didn't burn her. He didn't know if he could harm her, but with the power radiating from it, it was distinctly possible that he could emanate enough heat that he could actually cause some problem for her.

They headed down the tunnel, making their way deeper into the depths of the cave, and the farther they went, the more that Jason wondered why the earth dragon would guide him here.

He saw no evidence that anybody had been through here.

"Why would he have brought us here?" he asked, looking over at the dragon queen.

"I do not know."

The tone in her voice had shifted; she was no longer nearly as agitated as she had been before, which he appreciated. He didn't want to deal with a frustrated woman, and certainly not a woman frustrated at him.

They headed along the tunnel and he began to feel something in the distance.

Not just the rumbling, not as he had found before, but there was a warmth.

"Do you feel that?" he asked, looking back at the dragon queen.

She frowned at him and headed forward, pushing past him until she could squeeze in front of him.

Jason smiled to himself.

This was somebody he would have appreciated knowing long before now.

"How did you and Lorren end up together?" he asked. They had some connection together, and whether or not it was familial, he wanted to know.

"He found me," she said softly, hurrying into the cavern.

The tunnel was far longer than he would've expected, and wide enough to be easy for them to walk next to each other. It felt like they were heading all the way through the mountain.

The warmth in the distance continued to increase, gaining more and more heat the farther they went, and as they traveled, he wondered why the earth dragon would call him here.

"Where did he find you?"

She looked back and shook her head. "He never said."

"Why not?"

"It didn't matter. He found me. Saved me. And said that had he not brought me with him, I would have been killed."

"Why?"

She glowered at him for a moment, but then the irritation in her gaze softened just a little bit. "You have already mentioned why."

"Lorach?" Jason asked.

She nodded, then turned away, hurrying into the darkness.

He held out the iron dragon glove, letting the power flow from him, the energy glowing, and he tried to keep up with her. He felt like she was moving too quickly for him, though.

"Why would you have been in danger from Lorach?"

She shook her head. "He never said."

Her dragon connection. That had to be it.

Had he stayed in his homeland, he probably would've died. At least, he would have before learning of his connection to the dragons. Once he had connected to the ice dragon and had his help hunting, Jason had been given an advantage that he wouldn't have otherwise.

What would have happened had his parents never left Lorach?

He would've been a Dragon Soul. At least, he would've had that potential.

Would that mean I would have tried to control the dragons?

He tried to push those thoughts out of his mind, but it was difficult to do so.

"Is it because you have a connection to the dragons?"

That might be it. And it certainly would be enough of a reason for him to have done it, especially knowing what Jason had come to know about the people of Lorach and the way that they would take those who had any connection to a dragon and controlled it.

"He never said," she said again.

"Did he teach you to use your connection, or did you have it already?"

"He taught me," she said, her voice going softer. "He wanted me to understand the dragons. He taught me about my connections."

"Which dragon did you connect to first?"

She looked back at him and slowed, no longer hurrying through the cavern. "Earth," she said.

"That's why it upset you that I had connected to the earth dragon."

She nodded.

Jason could still feel the tremor in the earth dragon, and he realized that there was some sort of connection that had formed, though he didn't understand why that connection had formed. Maybe the connection had been there from the time he had first connected to the dragon, back when he had used that power to stop Lorren.

"Mine was ice," he said, looking over his shoulder, back toward the end of the tunnel. Jason was aware of the ice dragon, though he had returned to the sky, to the cold, and had welcomed the swirling energy that was high overhead. "I found him near my homeland."

"How did a dragon like that survive?"

"That's a great question. I think Lorren had a hand in creating him, somehow."

"Lorren would not have."

"You know where Lorren had been before?"

She frowned. "No."

"Could he have been involved in any of this?"

"I don't know," she said.

"I don't know, either," Jason said. He shrugged. "I believed it was a man from Lorach named Therin, but even that, I'm not entirely sure."

Her brow furrowed at the mention of Therin.

She knew him.

Of course she would, though. Jason had suspected that she would have known that name, especially as Lorren had been the one to have taught Therin, and he suspected that Lorren would have mentioned Therin to others.

"Did he warn you about Therin?"

"He spoke of him," she said softly. "He called him a traitor."

"I think he was," Jason said. "He's gone now."

"As is Lorren."

Jason nodded. "He is."

"Because of you."

"Because of me." There was no point in denying it, especially as he had been the one to have destroyed Lorren, but he needed for her to understand.

"Did he ever talk to you about what he did with the dragons?"

"He freed the dragons," she said.

She turned away and hurried into the cavern, toward the rumbling of the earth dragon, leaving Jason looking after her.

He tried to find where she was going and tried to catch up to her, but could not.

The heat radiating around him called to him, and Jason hurried forward until he could catch up with that heat.

As soon as he did, he stopped.

Bones.

There were a dozen different bones in here. All of them were different sizes, shapes, and all of them came from dragons.

Each of the bones had a different energy, and it seemed to Jason that someone had tried to arrange the bones into something resembling a dragon, though not completely.

"What is this?" Jason whispered.

"Lorren was here," she said, looking around before settling her hand on one of the bones. "This was his place."

He frowned, looking at her. "How do you know?"

"He…" She shook her head but then the ground rumbled and she frowned. He had a distinct sense that she was talking to the earth dragon, and then that sound faded, the trembling faded, and she turned back to him. "He wanted to find bones like this."

"He wanted to find bones?"

She nodded. "Lorren believed the bones brought power."

Jason stopped at one of the bones and stretched a hand out, feeling the heat radiating off it. The same way Lorach had been gathering bones. "I'm sure that he's right about that," he said. "There is something in the bones. You can feel it even now. There's warmth, and it seems to me that there is an energy that's there, even if I don't really know the purpose behind it, or whether there's anything that can be done about it."

"Nothing can be done about the energy. The bones are just that. Bones."

The ground rumbled and she looked down at it again, as if she were speaking to the earth dragon, before she looked up at Jason.

"There are a lot of bones here for somebody who wants to protect the dragons," Jason said.

"He collected them," she said.

"Collected them, or killed the dragons?"

She glowered at him.

"The earth dragon wanted you to see this place."

"To let me know how close he got," she said.

"What if that's not it?"

"What do you think it is?" she snapped.

Jason shrugged. "I don't know."

He could feel something else, though. He was drawn deeper into the cavern, and the farther that he went, the easier it was to feel something radiating nearby, and he followed that sense, letting it guide him, and he stopped.

A smaller tunnel opened up.

Jason crouched down in order to move through it, and he crawled forward.

The tunnel led through the mountain, and the farther that he went, the easier it was to feel the change here.

Finally, he stopped.

It dropped off from here.

There was something different here, though. Energy, though he wasn't entirely sure what the energy was. It radiated from down below.

"Where did you go?" the dragon queen snapped.

"I feel something up here," he said, twisting so that he could look at her. "I don't know what it is, so I can't tell you what Lorren was doing up here, but it feels like something."

He held his hand out and the glowing of his glove

reverberated, heat radiating off his hand, and he looked down.

And his breath caught.

Hundreds of bones.

All of them were darkened, corrupted the same way as the bone that he had found in the copse of trees had been.

"What do you see?" the dragon queen asked.

"Nothing," Jason said.

He didn't need for her to see this.

He started to move, but she forced her way up alongside him. She smelled of heat, strangely of mint, and there was a pleasant warmth that radiated off her, and the ground trembled between them, and…

Jason forced those thoughts away.

"What is that?" she whispered.

"You shouldn't see this."

Lorren was gone. There was an edge to her, and he didn't want to sharpen it any more than it had already been sharpened.

"You would keep me from what the earth dragon would reveal?"

Jason sighed. "There are bones. A lot of them. I don't know what purpose he had for them, but they are all corrupted in some way."

"Corrupted?"

He pulled out the corrupted bone that he had in his cloak and handed it to her.

She studied it, and some flowing of power streaked out

from her, going into the bone, before it retreated. She dropped the bone down into the pit.

"No," she whispered.

"I don't know what it means. I don't even know what it's for."

"How are there so many?"

Jason shook his head. "I suspect this is where Lorren brought the dragon bones."

But why here?

He looked out into the other cavern, though he couldn't see it. He could feel something radiating from those bones, the heat and warmth that was out there, but there would have to have been some reason that Lorren would've wanted to come here with them. Some reason that he had decided that this needed to be the place to leave the bones. Some reason that he had come here in the first place.

"He really did it, didn't he?" She looked up at him, and her eyes were rimmed with a bit of redness.

Jason nodded. "I'm sorry."

"He thought he could save them."

"I don't know why he thought he could save them. I don't know what he was trying to do here, only that whatever it is was unpleasant."

He could feel the earth dragon as he rumbled. It was a rumbling that tried to guide Jason away. The earth dragon wanted nothing to do with this place.

He backed out into the main part of the cavern and the

dragon queen followed him, taking a seat in the middle of it.

Jason sat across from her.

She fidgeted with her dress, twisting the fabric in her hands. "He'd been training me," she whispered.

"None of what you saw changes that."

"He said that he wanted to protect the dragons."

"Again, none of what you saw changes that."

"How can it not? How can it not when what I see tells me that he was harming the dragons for an experiment, not to save them?"

"That's what you brought away from it?"

"Should I not have?"

Jason shrugged. "I don't even know what to tell you about what he was doing there, or the power that was there. All I can tell you is that this is a place of Lorren's."

"A place of Lorren's," she said, shaking her head. "And it's a place of violence. A place of darkness. A place that he should not have created."

"There was some good that came of what he did," Jason said.

She frowned at him.

"The dragons that you connect to. Those are tied to what Lorren did. The dragons that I connect to. Those are tied to what he did, as well."

"Now you want to praise him?"

"Not praise him," Jason said. He wasn't entirely sure why he felt the urge to console her, but he did. "I'm just saying he was imperfect. And we can't blame him for everything, but we can try to understand what he intended." Maybe that was true about *his* parents.

Strange that he would have that realization out here.

And it was more than just trying to understand Lorren. It was a matter of trying to know that Lorren had a complicated past, an acknowledged connection to the dragons, and it was something that bonded him to the dragons in a way that made things difficult.

And it was that difficulty that Jason thought he should try to understand.

He smiled at her. "Why don't you tell me about Lorren?"

"It doesn't matter now."

"It does. All of it matters. He was important to you. And what you know of Lorren might help me know what he understood about the dragons."

She looked up at him, and for a moment, Jason worried that she was going to argue with him, but she shook her head. "He cared about the dragons. Regardless of what you saw there, he cared about the dragons."

"In his own way," Jason said, nodding. "I don't claim to understand it, but I don't deny that he did care about the dragons in his own way."

"He trained me," she said again.

"I understand."

"You don't intend to hurt them?"

"I would hurt no dragon," Jason said.

"None?" she asked, arching a brow.

"Not if I can avoid it. The dragons deserve our help.

Our protection. They need it because there are enough people who intend to do harm to them."

All he wanted was for the dragons to fly free.

But they could not until he defeated Lorach.

She nodded, twisting the fabric of her dress. "I was young when he came for me. He told me that he brought me from my village when Lorach attacked. I had a connection to the dragons, he said, and one that he needed to help me understand."

Jason held out the iron dragon glove, radiating heat from it and letting the warmth fill the inside of the cavern, and he let her talk.

For the most part, she rambled, talking about her childhood after she went with Lorren, that she didn't remember much of it from before then, and she told him about Lorren, about her understanding of the dragons, and about how he had helped her learn about the misfits.

She talked until she grew tired, and eventually she lay down, falling asleep.

Jason sat by her, watching, and knew that he would have to help her, somehow.

It had always been about helping the dragons.

Now he also wanted to help the dragon queen.

11

The earth dragon guided them to several other places that Therin had used. Each one was a pit much like the last, though not all of them were buried in the mountains. Each one contained large collections of dragon bones, all of them corrupted. After a while, Jason knew that he could no longer keep looking at them. The different locations didn't help him know anything about *how* Lorren made smoke or earth or mist dragons. They hadn't seen anything that would explain those to him.

He had been gone for several days and began to wonder what was going on in Dragon Haven in his absence. Hopefully, Lorach hadn't attacked, but they had been up to something before his departure. All of this felt important to Jason, but at the same time, he couldn't shake the feeling that by coming here, by leaving the people and places he had known, he was somehow putting those he cared about in danger.

He pushed those thoughts out of mind, having no choice but to do so.

I need to be here.

But what was going on with Kayla? His mother?

Sarah.

His thoughts went back to her, knowing that she was the one he had promised to help, and yet he had abandoned his search for her parents. Regardless of whether he believed anything could be done for them, he had still abandoned her search.

And then there was the night dragon.

Jason could feel nothing from that distant dragon, but he hoped he remained hidden within the forest. Even hidden, the night dragon would continue to grow, his power progressing.

What would happen the next time Jason encountered him?

He might be even more powerful. Maybe *too* powerful.

He *had* been gone too long.

"Enough," he said.

The earth dragon rumbled.

It was time for them to get back.

He had been traveling for the better part of several days now, traveling with the dragons and the dragon queen, and getting to know her a little bit better.

She still had not told him her name.

He'd asked, but she had avoided answering, telling him only that Lorren had told her that names mattered and she should not share.

The cold air swirled around him. He rode atop the ice dragon, the dragon queen sitting in front of him. She had to have another name, but for some reason, he almost enjoyed referring to her as the dragon queen. She gripped the dragon carefully, gloves on her hands protecting her from the cold, something Jason did not need.

"How can this dragon withstand this?" she asked above the wind.

"He is a creature of the snow and the north," Jason said.

Winds screamed around them, snow sending flurries up all around him as well. The cold whipped at him, pulling at his dragonskin, pulling at his hair, and threatening to toss him free of the dragon.

Even if it were to happen, Jason thought he would be safe. He had enough of a connection to the dragon that he thought the ice dragon would come diving for him, seeking to rescue him.

In the distance, Jason noticed the changing landscape. Mountains rose in undulating peaks, some of them taller than others, with one particular mountain rising higher than the rest. Snow swirled around, the nature of it slamming into him, making it difficult for him to make much else out.

"Where are you taking me?"

"I'm taking you to see Lorach, then I'm taking you to see the other dragons."

"Not to Dragon Haven?"

"Not yet," he said.

Eventually, he would need to take her to Dragon

Haven, if only so she could understand what he needed to do, the way he rescued the dragons, protecting them, but he wanted to ensure that when he did, he provided the necessary protection to the dragons so that they were alert enough to ensure they weren't influenced by anything that she might be able to do. He didn't know if she would be able to do anything to harm them, though he doubted she could.

"How many dragons remain in Lorach?"

"I don't know. I haven't been able to get close enough."

"But you tried?"

"I intend to free all of them. Lorach needs to be defeated. At least, the Dragon Souls of Lorach need to be defeated. We need to ensure the dragons are allowed to fly freely, no longer controlled by the Dragon Souls."

"Why do you care?" She turned, unmindful of the wind, somehow gripping the dragon with her legs in a way that squeezed him.

It surprised Jason, but even more surprising was how comfortable she seemed atop the ice dragon. He sensed an amusement coming from the ice dragon, almost as if he were pleased by this turn of events.

"I didn't always. When I was younger, I hated dragons. I was taught to hate them. There were other dragons that were dangerous, and my people were taught to believe that the dragons would attack. We believed that the dragons were our enemies."

"You don't believe that anymore?"

"When I first met him, I understood the dragons weren't anything for us to fear."

"They can be feared. The dragons are still powerful."

"Powerful, but the dragons don't want to harm us. I think if they were given the opportunity, they wouldn't even have attacked us before."

He felt the power coming off the ice dragon and a sense of connection, a communication with the dragon that sent him an understanding.

The dragon turned to the side, tilting his wings, catching the air in such a way that Jason felt the power coming off him. As the ice dragon flew, Jason clutched more tightly to him, holding his knees pinned against the dragon's sides.

The dragon queen didn't struggle.

She held tightly to him, using her legs to keep astride the dragon, holding onto him, facing away from the dusting of the wind. "Lorren told me that the dragons enjoyed attacking."

"Perhaps they do," he said. "They are dragons. I think what they don't care for is being controlled."

Jason wondered what it would take for her to begin to understand the nature of what she and Lorren had done with the dragons, how they had been used. They might not have controlled the dragons the same way Lorach had, but there was still a measure of control in the way that they worked with the dragons. She might not want to believe that, but the way she used the dragons was truly similar.

Jason held onto the power within himself, focusing within that energy, and he connected to the ice dragon. As they flew through the mountains, the wind whipping around, snow swirling, connecting to him, he couldn't help but feel the power that existed there.

There seemed to be some aspect of it that he thought he might be able to better understand, but even as he focused on it, he couldn't tell if there was something more.

Power, but it was a strange kind of power.

He nodded to the dragon queen and she turned around, looking away from him.

The dragon continued to fly, heading high through the air, sweeping over the landscape. In the distance, Jason could begin to feel something changing. It was the warmth of this land, the energy of this place, and as they flew, streaking toward the sense of the dragons in the distance, Jason could feel that energy all around him.

They banked, heading toward the ground.

When they landed, Jason focused on the power of the ice dragon, and he looked all around. They landed in a forest, on the edge where the trees began to thin. From here, he could look out, and he was able to make out the changing landscape. A rolling hillside swept in front of him.

In the distance, he felt the power of other dragons. They were the dragons of Lorach. Jason could feel the energy of those dragons, and he was all too aware of how those dragons could be used against them. There came the energy coming off them, that of the Dragon Souls holding onto that power. Jason felt it radiating in the distance.

"Why did you land us here?" the dragon queen asked.

"Because there's something here."

She headed away from the ice dragon, toward the edge of the forest, seemingly unconcerned. It surprised Jason that she would be so confident about everything taking place around her.

Power began to build from her. Jason noticed the energy she held and the way that it swirled away from her, heading out into the distance. Even though she was separated from the other dragons, she still maintained something of a connection to them, and she used that power to draw it through her and radiate it out over the landscape. The sense of that power swirled away from her, sweeping out and toward the other dragons. Jason focused on what she was doing, realizing she attempted to probe for them.

What she did was something different, though.

She borrowed the energy of the earth dragon as she probed. Now that he had some strange connection to the earth dragon, such that he was still aware of that dragon as it rumbled beneath the ground, Jason thought he could use the same technique she did. He began to connect to the dragon. It rumbled from someplace deep within him, connecting to the earth dragon in a way that he hadn't expected. By holding onto that connection, Jason recognized how that dragon allowed him to probe beyond where he stood. That energy radiated outward, sweeping into the distance.

And he felt the other dragons. Strange that he should be able to detect them so easily. Unless they were not flying.

He looked over at the dragon queen. “Can you feel it?”

“Of course I can,” she snapped. “And I don’t like that you can.”

“Your dragon allowed me to do so.”

“The dragon should not have.” She took a step forward and a continued sense of power streaked away from her, heading out into the distance. It radiated away from her, an energy Jason could feel from within him. “What is it?” the dragon queen asked. There was less of the confidence in her voice than there had been before.

“Those are Dragon Souls and their dragons.”

“Where?” she asked.

“From what I can tell, they aren’t that far from us,” Jason said. “But I worry they are close enough they will come our way.”

Attacking Dragon Souls by himself was hard enough, but if he had to worry about the dragon queen and how she might react, he feared what would happen.

“I thought you said you could manage those dragons,” she said.

“I can manage them, but as I’ve told you, as I heal the dragons and make it so they can’t be influenced anymore, the fight becomes more difficult. More and more of the dragons become controlled by multiple Dragon Souls at one time. When that happens, there isn’t anything I can do to protect them beyond what I already have.”

"Then you have to remove them as a threat," she said.

"That's not how I work with the dragons," Jason said.

"Maybe you give the dragons too much credit."

The ice dragon began to rumble with energy.

Jason raised a hand, trying to calm him. If he didn't, the ice dragon would shoot icicles at her. He suspected she had a way of deflecting them, but he didn't want to run the risk of it just yet.

"You should be more careful with the kind of things you say. The ice dragon doesn't take too kindly to some of your comments."

She looked over, seemingly noticing the icicles that had formed on the ice dragon's wings, the way that they started to protrude, elongating. All it would take would be for the ice dragon to shake, and Jason had plenty of experience with the ice dragon sending his icicles shooting into the distance, streaking at his target.

If his target was the dragon queen, then Jason might have to intervene. He wanted to help her. Despite everything else, Jason thought that he needed to try to help her.

He created an illusion. He thought that would be the easiest way to reach her, and by holding onto the illusion, creating the image of the other dragons he detected out there, he held that sense of energy away from him, focusing on the power he knew to be drifting into the distance. By latching onto that, he could feel the energy of the other dragons. All he had to do was shift the illusion and some aspect of it would become real.

In this case, all he wanted was to show her what he detected.

By holding onto the connection to the earth dragon, Jason did detect something deep beneath the ground, though he wasn't at all sure what he felt. It was tied to some of those distant dragons, but it was also tied to the Dragon Souls. His combination of connections to the dragons allowed him to be able to feel those powers flowing away, connecting in such a way that he could feel the various dragon energies combining so that he could detect the Dragon Souls.

The illusion formed and he created seven distinct dragons.

Something about the illusion took on a life of its own and Jason barely had to add any element to it. Power flowed from him, swirling into the illusion, created by the nature of what he detected more so than what he pushed out from him. He felt that energy flowing away from him and he held onto it in such a way that it allowed him to continue to maintain his hold over the image.

"Those dragons are out there?" the dragon queen asked.

"I think so. I can feel something of them, though not everything about them. I'm using what I can detect to create something more."

She headed toward the illusion and traced her hand toward it.

He expected that she would disrupt it, but nothing happened.

Partly that came from how strongly he held onto the illusion, but partly it came from how he was able to feel the other dragons that he pushed into the illusion from where he was. Those dragons were near enough that he could feel them, and he could feel their energy. He stepped toward her, holding onto the power of the illusion, using everything in his power to maintain it. As he did, he could feel the energy coming off him. And he could feel how it echoed with the sense of those distant dragons. By holding onto that sense, Jason recognized that there were these seven dragons, but there was more to it.

Somehow, through his connection to the earth dragon, he felt something else. At first, he didn't know what it was, but he began to recognize it. The power of Dragon Souls.

There were a dozen. Maybe two times that.

Enough that Jason wouldn't be able to neutralize them very easily. It would take considerable effort on his part, and with the dragon queen along with him, Jason didn't know if the two of them would be able to withstand the Dragon Souls.

Still, she needed to see the dragons could be saved. Wasn't that what he had brought her here for?

"Come on," he said.

"Where now?"

"We're going to free those dragons."

"I thought you were afraid."

Had he said that?

Jason didn't think that he had, and even if he were afraid, he doubted that he would admit that to her. "I think we can do it, but you're going to have to let me do most of it. If you do anything, you run the risk of harming the dragons, and I'm not willing to let you do that."

"I am too separated from my dragons here to be able to do much of anything," she said.

Jason studied her. Even separated from the dragons himself, he still had access to their power. He suspected the same thing was true for her, regardless of the distance. They might be on the other side of the mountains, far enough away that the dragons themselves couldn't join her, but she could access their power anyway, much like he could borrow the power of the forest dragon from anywhere.

Jason could even feel the earth dragon as he approached. There was energy within him, and the earth dragon forced his way through the ground, coming quickly toward them.

He worried that he would be opening himself up to the wrong kind of danger if he brought her, but he had to trust, too. He had asked her to trust, which meant he had to.

They climbed onto the ice dragon, who let out a sense of irritation. It came from her comment, and Jason understood.

"She's not going to do anything to harm the dragons," he said.

"If she does, I will toss her," the ice dragon said.

Jason smiled and looked over at the dragon queen. "Did you hear that?"

"I heard," she said.

"Just work with me. Don't do anything… thoughtless."

She glared at him, and then the ice dragon took to the air. Power radiated from the dragon and Jason held tightly to the ice dragon's back, clinging to the spikes.

As they gained altitude, he focused on the sense of the other dragons. Even from above, he could feel those dragons far below. The more that he focused on them, the easier it was to detect that sense of energy, the power of those dragons. Jason recognized the distant sense of the Dragon Souls, and he held onto that, feeling for it, and then they saw them.

When the dragons came into view, he realized he had been wrong. Here he thought there might be two dozen Dragon Souls, one per dragon, but that was wrong.

There were at least four per dragon. The Dragon Souls all sat two in a row on the dragon's back, and somehow there were two out on the edge of the dragon's wings.

Jason stared, but he didn't have a chance to stare for too long.

The dragons seemed to notice their presence.

Either that or the Dragon Souls seemed to notice their appearance.

Jason used the power of the ice dragon, and he quickly added that of the iron dragon, mixing the two into a stream of water energy, letting that flow out from him. It struck the first dragon—a massive black dragon he realized had five Dragon Souls on his back.

He had to act quickly.

Power flowed out from him and he pushed. There was resistance.

The Dragon Souls continued to hold, fighting what he did. Jason pushed again, sending more power out.

"I thought you could help these dragons?" the dragon queen said, shifting on the ice dragon's back.

"I can, but with this many Dragon Souls pushing against me, it gets more difficult."

"I'm going to help."

"No—"

Jason didn't have an opportunity to finish. She started to use her power.

He worried she was going to use it against the dragons, but that wasn't what she did. Instead, she focused her energy on the Dragon Souls.

She used a pulse of earth and sent one flying off the dragon.

That blast struck one of the Dragon Souls, sending them down to the ground, and suddenly the resistance began to ease.

"Do that again," Jason said.

She looked back at him but then turned her attention in front of her again, and another blast of earth exploded from her. The dragon turned, avoiding the attack.

She quickly sent another burst. This one connected.

He pushed again.

The resistance was less now that there were fewer Dragon Souls pushing against him. The more she knocked off, the easier it was. Jason radiated the energy out, letting it sweep away from him. More and more power continued to burst away from him, striking the dragon.

Then he shattered the resistance.

The dragon roared.

Jason added a hint of the forest dragon power. Illusion.

By holding onto that, he eased the dragon's recovery so that it didn't drop from the sky too precipitously. He held onto that energy and the dragon shook, still roaring as the other Dragon Souls tried to hold onto his back.

Jason sent more and more energy out from him. The dragon was safe.

But they were not. They were surrounded.

The ice dragon shook. Icicles went streaking.

Three Dragon Souls were hit by icicles and fell.

Jason turned to the nearest dragon with one less Dragon Soul.

He targeted that one, using the ice dragon, and blasted power at the Dragon Soul on the dragon's back. Jason continued to push power out, intending to attack as much as he could. He pushed more and more power out from him, exploding energy away, and he could feel that power bursting, the way that energy continued to build, and he could feel it exploding.

It struck the Dragon Soul. Jason held onto the power within him and turned it to the next Dragon Soul on the dragon's back. As he did, the ice power struck, slamming into the Dragon Soul.

The dragon queen slammed earth power away from her.

That energy struck the other dragon.

Dragons all around him began to attack, pushing energy out to try to collapse it on Jason. When he fought back, there was resistance, but it shattered. The dragon queen helped. She continued to attack the Dragon Souls, not targeting the dragons, and together they managed to push back the attack.

He strained against what the Dragon Souls were doing. One by one, Jason and the dragon queen attacked, freeing the dragons from the Dragon Soul influence.

Still, power continued to build around him.

Something was wrong.

He turned, tapping on the ice dragon's side.

"We need to go," he said.

"What's wrong?" the dragon queen asked.

Jason looked down below but didn't see anything. "I don't really know. I can feel something off, though I can't tell what it is. There is some sense of energy that continues to squeeze, and it is trying to—"

He didn't have the chance to finish. The power he detected slammed into him again, and he nearly fell. Had he not been holding onto the dragon's spikes, he might have been thrown free. Jason didn't see the source of the attack.

"Up," he said.

The ice dragon streaked upward.

The power of the dragon brought them up into the clouds, and then through. The energy of the upper atmosphere began to swirl again and Jason felt the cold, the bitter biting energy of it, and drew on it.

Up here, he could feel that cold, and he could feel the way that the ice and the storm swirled, and he recognized how that power existed. He recognized its influence upon him. He recognized that there was some aspect to it that tried to press in upon him. Not only that, but there was some aspect to it that tried to flow through him.

It was more than just his connection to the ice dragon.

It was his connection to the northern mountains.

There was that familiarity. It was an energy that existed there, an energy that flowed within him, an energy that struck him. By holding onto all of that, Jason recognized that there was some aspect to it that he could call upon, some part that he could use, and he recognized there was some power greater than what he had detected before.

It filled him, the power and energy of the mountains. That power burst everywhere around him. And Jason welcomed it. He wanted that power. He let it fill him, flowing from the mountains, from the sky, from the clouds.

The pressure continued to build, swirling around them, but Jason didn't know why he should detect it so profoundly. He looked down, borrowing from the dragon in order to see far below him. All they saw were clouds.

Jason reached through his connection to the iron dragon. The iron dragon didn't answer at first. Jason pushed again, sending a message through his connection to the iron dragon.

"Are you there?"

There didn't come any response.

He tried again, pushing outward, letting that energy flow from him.

This time, he detected something faint.

It was a stirring, but as he focused on it, connecting to the energy within his iron dragon glove, Jason noticed that stirring coming closer to him, the power of the dragon coming across the distance.

For some reason, it was more difficult than usual to connect to that power.

Normally, when he reached across the distance, connecting to the dragons, he could feel that energy flowing out, away from him. In this case, as he strained, searching for some sort of connection, he didn't find it.

He pushed again. Power exploded out from him.

There.

"What are you doing?" the dragon queen asked.

"I'm trying to uncover what happened to the iron dragon."

"You have a dragon made of iron?"

"Not exactly. Only..." He looked at her, a decision made. "Listen—if you're going to stay with me, I need your name."

"You don't need my name."

"I can't keep calling you dragon queen."

She was silent.

Jason listened for something else, another sense of power, but there was nothing. He knew that he'd felt something but couldn't tell where it had come from. Distant, but why?

What was Lorach after now?

"Janeya," she said softly. "That is my name."

"Janeya. That's a lovely name." She frowned at him. "I'm Jason…"

He felt another pressure.

This time, he knew it as a calling—and one for help.

The ice dragon felt it as well.

They turned, heading across the mountains.

"Where are you taking me?" Janeya asked. "Jason?" she pressed when he didn't answer.

The call was there. He knew it was. And that he hadn't imagined it.

"To help a friend."

12

The mountains stretched below him. They were a vast expanse of white undulating beneath him, like some massive jaw that separated one land from another, and as he passed over them, the ice dragon soaring, drawing the power of the cold and the north, Jason focused on that cold, feeling it flowing within him. There was a strange connection to it, a bond that he had never known before.

"You're doing it again," Janeya said.

"What are you talking about?"

"You're doing something with the ice dragon."

"Actually, I'm not. I feel the power of the north, and for some reason, it's flowing through me in a way it hadn't before."

"How is it you are connected to this?"

"I was raised in a land not too far from here." Jason

pointed, and he could practically feel the village in the distance. It was almost as if he were aware of the swirling wind, something about it that drew him toward his old village. "When I was younger, I lived in these mountains, struggling to survive. Much like the ice dragon, I became attached to my surroundings. I suppose you could say it shaped me much the same way it shaped the ice dragon."

Even as he thought about the power around him, Jason was aware of the energy here, the way that the power continued to build, and he held onto it, letting it flow around him, granting him an awareness of the sense of these mountains and a feeling of the place around him.

He could feel something more within it. By holding on to what he detected, that energy that existed out there, he recognized that power, and he could feel some part of him filling with that power.

Janeya looked over at him, watching. "Even now, I can feel the way you're doing that," she said.

Jason shook his head. "I'm not exactly sure what I'm doing."

"It's every time you try to draw upon the power of this place. I can feel the way it fills you. There's something to it, some aspect to that power you're drawing upon."

Jason could feel the energy coming up from within him, but he didn't know what she could feel. He couldn't deny that he was pulling upon power. He knew he was, much like he knew there had to be something he could do to hold onto that power, but he didn't fully know what that something was. He held onto the energy within him, trying again to better understand the power and the magic flowing within him. As he did, he could feel the shifting from somewhere deep inside him.

Once again, the power of the northern mountains began to flow, heading out into the distance and whipping around, filling him with its energy.

"My home was different than yours," she said. "Lorren raised me out here, beyond the mountains." She pointed into the distance, indicating the far south.

When she did, Jason stared, following the direction she pointed. He could feel the changing landscape, and as he started holding onto that energy, he recognized there was something else within it that he could feel, some aspect that seemed to flow within him.

"What was your experience out here?"

She looked into the distance, a bit of sorrow in her eyes. "Loneliness." She took a deep and steadying breath. "We didn't have much out here. He feared the people of Lorach, and he feared them coming for us, and he worried about what would happen if they were to acquire the dragons he'd been raising."

"Did you spend any time with Therin?"

She shook her head. "I didn't have the opportunity. He was before me." It wasn't surprising that Therin would have been before her. Jason didn't remember all that Lorren had said to him about training Therin, but he remembered Lorren's irritation about how Therin had abused what he'd learned from Lorren. How he had twisted it and used it.

"Therin is the reason that I came out of my village."

Jason looked down, the mountains and snow swirling around far below. They were nearly to the edge of the mountains, and as they continued to fly, Jason could feel the changing landscape drifting past them. Eventually, they would move beyond that, and then they would head toward a distant land, another place.

Beyond.

"Do you hate him?"

Jason stared off into the distance. "My feelings toward Therin are complicated," he said. And they were. He couldn't deny he'd been given an opportunity he wouldn't have had otherwise, but at the same time, he'd also been responsible for what had happened to the people of Dragon Haven, the dangers they had sustained, and because of Therin, there had been an attack on those lands and dragons.

Had he not come to the mountains, Jason might never have known about his connection to the dragons. He might never have been able to save the dragon misfits, and he might never have known the connection he now did about how to bind himself to the dragons, understanding that connection and feeling the power that came from them, joining with him.

All of that was because of what Therin had done.

In the distance, Jason saw something that worried him.

A dragon.

Strangely, he could feel the energy out there, and he could feel something that was taking place, but couldn't tell what it was or why he should be so attuned to it. He looked over at Janeya and found her staring out into the distance, her gaze sweeping across the mountains.

"Do you see that?" Jason asked, nodding toward what he had observed.

"I see nothing," Janeya said.

He frowned and borrowed quickly from the ice dragon's eyesight, looking through the dragon's eyes, but couldn't see anything more. Just a bit of movement.

His own dragon sight had allowed him to see that movement, and he hadn't needed to use the ice dragon's eyesight in order to be able to make out much else, though with that help, he could see a flicker. A glowing brightness was the energy that he detected and the energy that he recognized.

It was that energy which he needed to get to.

He motioned to the ice dragon and they started moving more quickly.

The ground streaked below them.

"What did you see?" Janeya asked.

"A dragon, I think."

"Why is that important to you?"

"Out here?" Jason looked around, but even as he did, he couldn't see anything more. "Out in these lands, dragons are unusual. It's either a dragon that I've helped, or…" The other possibility was that it was Lorach, and if it was Lorach, then it was reason to be extra cautious.

"Do you fear the dragons?"

He stared through the ice dragon's eyesight, using that to help him understand whether there was anything out there, but he didn't see anything clearly.

"I fear why Jessica has sent the dragons out here," he said. He swiveled so that he could look at Janeya, seeing her dark hair and silver eyes, her pale skin, and the hint of a smile that had been plastered to her face ever since they had taken to the air. She enjoyed flying with the dragons. He understood that feeling, having known it ever since learning of his connection to the ice dragon. Each dragon that he rode had a different style of flying, and each dragon gave him a different feeling as they traveled. It was as if he were meant to feel something distinct from the dragons.

"What makes you think this is her?"

"A feeling," he said.

The ice dragon streaked forward. If they were farther to the north, he could have powered through the energy of the ice, of the cold, but they headed up over large, grassy mountains, each of them carrying a different sort of energy and power that existed here. A warm wind gusted around him, mitigated somewhat by the cool of the ice dragon, but not so much that it offset it completely.

Then he saw the dragon.

It wasn't alone.

There were two dragons, and he knew why the call for help would have come.

Janeya's breath caught.

The dragons battled.

Jason focused through the ice dragon, trying to borrow his vision, but he couldn't see anything that way. There was the roar of the dragons, flames streaking from their massive jaws, and they ripped at each other, claws tearing at dragon flesh.

Jason needed to get there.

He needed to stop this.

He needed to know whether one of these dragons was from Dragon Haven.

The ice dragon streaked forward, and Jason recognized one of the dragons. A dark blue, massive creature, blood pouring down from his belly, a wound ripped through it.

He cried out.

"You cannot help him now," the ice dragon said.

"I have to stop this," Jason said.

The other dragon was all black, with three Dragon Souls on its back, and the power exploding from them washed over the blue dragon—David's dragon—as they attempted to try to tame him. To control him.

David would not have wanted that for his dragon.

Jason jumped, pouring power out of him so that he could streak upward, and he shot toward the Dragon Souls.

He did it without thinking, without even considering the implications or what might happen to him, knowing only that he needed to get there. Power carried him forward, and it was the power and energy of the north, power and energy of the ice, of the cold, and the power and energy of his home.

All of that launched Jason forward, and he streaked upon the wind, carrying him toward the blue dragon.

He roared.

Power filled him.

Jason didn't even know how much of the power came from the dragons, or how much of it came from him. At this point, he didn't have the time to stop and investigate.

He reached the blue dragon and grabbed for him, wrapping his arms around the dragon's neck, and then stood upright, anchoring himself with power in order to hold onto the dragon, worried that he wasn't going to be strong enough.

"Let me help," he said to the dragon.

The dragon roared, power exploding from him, and he continued to rip at the black dragon, but Jason could feel the weakness within the dragon, the energy that was within him already starting to fade. He tried to tear at the dragon, using all of his remaining power, pushing heat and energy into the attack, and sending more through it.

It was only then that Jason realized the black dragon had something clenched in his talons.

A bone.

Why would the dragon have a bone in his talons?

A burst of power struck him and he nearly tumbled free of the blue dragon.

He roared again, anger filling him.

David had died in order to protect this dragon, to

protect his people, and to provide understanding for the dragons, and now the dragon would be hurt?

He called upon ice and fire, mixing them together in a burst of power, and he struck it at the first of the Dragon Souls, the man sitting at the front of the black dragon and holding onto the dragon's spikes, leaning forward as if to control the dragon.

Jason would not permit it. He would not allow the Dragon Soul to get away with anything.

Other than dying.

Another burst of power exploded from him.

He struck the next Dragon Soul.

The woman was ready for it.

She used some barrier to protect herself, deflecting the blow, and Jason tried again, calling down ice lightning. It slammed into her, dislodging her from the dragon and sending her tumbling to the ground. He had no sympathy for her.

It left only one Dragon Soul remaining.

He turned his attention to the man. He was larger than Jason, with dark hair and black eyes so different than Jason's mismatched dragon sight eye, rage seeming to bubble within those eyes.

Jason felt the same rage.

Anger filled him.

He called on the powers that he could access, but something happened.

The blue dragon started to fall.

Jason tried to shift his grip, trying to hold onto it, but could not.

Even as he attempted to do so, he could feel something there, some aspect of it holding onto him.

He tried to help the dragon, but he didn't know if he could.

He called upon the ice and iron dragons, wanting to mix their two powers together, but even as he did, he couldn't help but feel as if there was nothing that he could do. He needed to find some way to help. This blue dragon needed his assistance.

But the other dragon…

"Stop him," the blue dragon called.

"Why?"

"He must not take the bone," the dragon said.

"I can help you."

"Stop him," the blue dragon said again.

Jason looked up. The black dragon was already starting away. If he didn't do anything, it would be too late.

He summoned the power within him and jumped.

The cold power of the north carried him, bursting him upward, and he soared above the ground, the energy carrying him, and power that Jason recognized filled him.

He held onto that energy, that power, and he continued to let himself be filled with it. As he did, he tried to grasp for something more, some other energy, but he didn't have enough. He needed more power.

He needed the iron dragon.

That energy carried him, and as Jason let that power lift him, he streaked higher and higher, drawing upon all of the powers that he could, and he raced toward the black dragon and the bone.

Somehow that was important.

Henry had told him that it was not the first time Lorach had gone after a dragon bone. There was power in the bones of dragons, though Jason had no idea why this bone, or why at this time, but he felt as if he needed to do what the blue dragon asked of him.

He couldn't look back to see whether the blue dragon needed his help, but there was a part of Jason that suspected he did. He feared what might happen to the dragon, and feared what would be happen if he didn't help him, but at the same time, he also didn't know whether he could stop what was taking place.

Power carried them forward.

It was an incredible burst of energy, and it helped him catch up to the black dragon.

Jason grabbed for the bone in the dragon's talons. It was a massive thigh bone, and heat radiated off it. He used the dragon bone to help slow him, and he clutched it, feeling the warmth within it, almost something that was familiar to him.

He scrambled along the length of the bone, using everything that he could in order to get to the top of the dragon, and from there, he needed to go farther.

He needed to keep moving.

He climbed up the dragon, and he could feel the

energy of the dragon, but he could feel something else, as well.

The influence of the Dragon Soul.

Jason needed to help this dragon.

He could do that from here. He was next to the dragon's flank, hidden from view, and as far as he could tell, the Dragon Soul had no idea that he was there, no idea that Jason attempted to scale the dragon's side.

He needed to take advantage of that.

He focused on ice and iron, the healing washing of power that he knew could work through the dragon, and as he did, he sent that energy through the dragon. He had healed countless dragons. Each time he did, there was the same reaction, that feeling of freedom from the dragon as he released it from the hold the Dragon Soul had over it. This time, there was a different bit of resistance.

He could feel it.

Jason struggled against that power.

The Dragon Soul was more potent than he would've expected.

Jason needed to borrow as much power as he could, sending it coursing through this dragon, but even as he did, he wasn't sure that he had enough strength.

He pushed outward again.

The dragon roared.

Pressure built from inside the dragon, coming from the Dragon Soul, pressing toward Jason, and the dragon started to shake, the power trembling within the creature, threatening to toss Jason.

"Just release the bone," Jason whispered.

He had no idea if the dragon would even listen, and no idea whether the dragon could listen, only that he believed that the dragon needed to listen.

"I can help you," he said.

He hoped that he could, but he didn't know if such a thing would even be possible. He hoped that the dragon could accept his help, but as he struggled, straining, Jason could feel the pressure building against him, pressure that came from some external source, someplace that he couldn't quite fathom. Not the Dragon Soul, but somebody who was far more powerful than Jason would've expected.

He had to get onto the dragon's back.

"Tip to the side," Jason said, sending the message with another wave of ice and iron power, pushing it through the dragon in a healing connection.

The trembling washed over the dragon and suddenly, the dragon tilted.

It was the break Jason needed.

He jumped at the same time as the dragon tilted, and he came to land on the dragon's back, near his tail.

The dragon thrashed and the Dragon Soul turned to him.

He had something in hand. It was oblong in shape.

Power emanated from inside it.

Dragon pearls.

The Dragon Soul used dragon pearls to command the dragon.

Anger surged inside Jason. They would use dragons against dragons?

Of course they would.

It was even more reason to overthrow Jessica. How could he not? How could he feel as if he could do anything other than overthrow her, especially given everything that she had done and all that she was willing to do?

He glared at the Dragon Soul, holding onto the dragon tightly, but as the creature continued to thrash, he almost wasn't going to be able to hold on.

The Dragon Soul crawled toward him.

Summoning the power of the fist full of dragon pearls, Jason wasn't sure if he would have enough energy.

He needed to use each of his dragon connections.

The dragon thrashed again.

And then a burst of power streaked down.

The Dragon Soul looked up, but almost too late.

Ice lightning shot toward him, but he raised his hands.

The lightning began to part around him, but more and more power poured out, and it pressed through him.

Jason scrambled forward and he grabbed the Dragon Soul's hand, prying free the dragon pearls. He jerked them away from the Dragon Soul, tossing them over the side of the dragon, where they scattered on the ground far below.

And then another burst of ice lightning struck, knocking the Dragon Soul off. He screamed while he fell.

Jason pushed a healing wave through the dragon, fixing the connection that the Dragon Soul had attempted, and he leaned forward.

“No time to rest,” the ice dragon said to him.

“Why?”

“He needs you.”

An image flashed in Jason’s mind, and he knew exactly who needed him.

The blue dragon.

13

Jason clutched the black dragon, holding onto him tightly, and they circled back around. The landscape below them was undulating grassland, a flowing hillside that would have been lovely under other circumstances. Not under the current one, though. He saw small copses of trees, clusters of flowers, and grasses that looked to be as tall as he was. The air carried with it the fragrance of the flowers, the warmth of the sun, and just a hint of humidity.

He turned his attention back to the dragon. He could see through the ice dragon's eyes that the blue dragon needed him.

"Why do you have the bone?" Jason asked the black dragon.

"They did not say," the dragon said.

It was part of some plan Lorach had, but Jason didn't know what it was, and he didn't know what it would take to overthrow what Jessica intended. All he knew was that they had some plan.

He let out a frustrated sigh.

He came to land next to the blue dragon, and he looked down. The blue dragon rested on a mountainside, trees rising up near him and heat radiating off him.

His belly bled.

"You can go," Jason said, looking over at the black dragon. "There are other free dragons. Find them. Stay away from Lorach."

"I can help," the dragon said.

"You have helped."

He hurried over to the blue dragon, resting his hands on the dragon's side, immediately calling upon ice and iron, trying to pour the two of them together, wanting to find some way to connect to the dragon in order to heal him, to help him, but even as he did, Jason doubted that he had enough strength to do so. He doubted there would be anything within him that would help.

As he pushed power outward, sending it flowing into the blue dragon, he could feel it flowing into an abyss. An emptiness. A void.

"Stop," the dragon said.

"I can help you," Jason said.

The ice dragon landed and Janeya climbed down, crouching down next to Jason, looking at the blue dragon.

"Stop," the dragon said again.

"But I can help."

"You have helped enough," the dragon said.

"I can help." Jason tried again.

The dragon twisted his head, looking at Jason. "You are everything he hoped you might be."

"I can do more for you," Jason said.

Why did this dragon's sufferings hurt him more than others?

Maybe because the dragon had always been free. Maybe because this was the last connection he had to David. Or maybe because Jason felt as if he should have been able to help.

"Find the rest," the blue dragon said.

"The rest of what? Dragons? I'm trying to find them. I'm trying to understand what I need to do."

"The rest of the ancestors," the blue dragon said.

He stared at Jason and in a flash, a vision appeared in Jason's mind. It was that of power, and yet, within it was a smoky appearance, something of a haze, and beyond that was a soft glowing, as if there were energy within it.

"What is it?"

"The ancestors," the blue dragon said.

"Let me help you," Jason said. "Then I can find the ancestors."

"No. You must find the ancestors, and then you can help me. You will understand. He has shown me."

"He?" Jason shook his head, looking over at the ice dragon and then back at the blue dragon. "David?"

"David," the dragon whispered. "No. The night." With that, the dragon closed his eyes, took a heaving breath, and then was no more.

Jason tried to pull upon heat and ice, mingling them together, but even as he did, he knew it wasn't going to be enough.

An emptiness filled the dragon.

And he tried, but there could be nothing done.

He crouched down, sitting for a moment, his hands resting on the dragon. "I should have been able to help him," he whispered.

"He knew it was his time," the ice dragon said.

Jason looked over at him. "He was young. At least, for a dragon he was young. There should have been something I could have done."

"It was his time," the ice dragon said. "Come. He wanted you to find the ancestors."

"You know where it is?"

"I did not. I do now."

Jason remained next to the dragon for a long time, holding his hands above his body, wishing that there was more that he could do and feeling regret that he could not.

"Come," the ice dragon nudged again.

Finally, Jason got up. Janeya watched him, saying nothing through it all.

He climbed onto the ice dragon's back and then waited for Janeya to join him. When she did, he shook his head. "I'm sorry. I tried to do everything I could for him."

"I know, but why?"

"Because he's a dragon," Jason said. "And he was a friend. He helped when others did not. When others could not."

The ice dragon took to the air and the landscape started to shift, taking on the appearance that the blue dragon had shown him. A hint of smoke and haze began to appear, and then they started to descend, dropping to the ground, following what Jason could see of the shifting and shimmering landscape until they came to the ground.

"This dragon was connected to an auran, someone who could have been a Dragon Soul but chose not to be. And because of that, the dragon was allowed to live free. I feel I owe it to this dragon to understand. I feel like I owe it him to do more."

She watched him before turning and nodding off into the distance. Jason looked, following the direction of her gaze, and noticed a slight haze hanging over the ground. Something like a fog, but he didn't think that was the case.

Mist?

Not the same as the mist dragon, though.

He headed toward it.

The ice dragon followed him, but the rumbling under the ground suggested that the earth dragons were coming as well. As he went, he focused on the haze and the energy there. He thought it was from the mist dragons, or even from the smoke dragons, but as he neared, he realized that wasn't the case at all.

While there was an energy here, it didn't seem to come from dragons.

At least, not living dragons.

He stared, looking around at everything, and realized there were bones around him. Some of the bones were small, little larger than a finger, and some looked to be claws, while others were enormous, bones that were longer than he was tall. All of them gleamed somehow, and not from sunlight, as a faint haze swirled around it. It seemed as if they gleamed from some internal power, as if they emanated the energy themselves.

There were dozens upon dozens of bones here. Hundreds of them.

A dragon boneyard.

Jason touched one of them.

It was a leg bone, at least as far as he could tell. When he held onto the bone, touching it, a surge of energy came up from within it. He looked over at the ice dragon, but the dragon didn't seem to feel that same surge of energy.

Why should Jason?

"What is this place?"

Janeya swept her gaze around, her eyes going wide. She clutched her arms around herself, and a shiver worked through her. Jason could practically feel the shiver, as if the ground itself, the earth dragon, or some other connection between them, helped him feel what she was feeling. He didn't know if that was real or not.

"It is a place of death," she said.

"Is it a place of death, or is it a place of celebration?" He stared, trying to pierce the haze all around him, and as he did, he could feel the energy and power here.

The ancestors.

That was what the blue dragon had said.

He headed to the next massive bone, this one a section

of a jaw. He could practically stand inside it. Power built off the bones, filling him again. He looked over at Janeya, but she wasn't looking in his direction. It was almost as if she didn't know what he detected.

Could she not feel it?

They were connected by the earth dragon, bonded through that.

Jason ran his hand along the smooth surface of the bone, recognizing the texture, but also recognizing warmth within it.

It was strange that there was still a warmth within the bone, but as he ran his hand along it, he could feel some aspect of the dragon still living within it.

"Tell me more about what Lorren thought about the dragons," he said. Lorren had collected bones. That had to be significant, though why would he have done that?

"I've told you his view on the dragons. You don't care for it."

"I don't, but I recognize he had a different view than I do. And with everything he had done, I have to wonder if perhaps there might be something I need to better understand."

"Such as what?"

"Such as why he was so willing to sacrifice dragons." He swept his gaze around, looking at these bones, feeling the energy coming off them and recognizing the nature of their power.

"Lorren believed dragons would come back, though I don't know if he ever thought there was a specific place or time when they would return." She looked around the dragon boneyard, her gaze settling on one particularly large bone. She walked over to it, holding her hand above it and closing her eyes. She leaned from side to side, leaving Jason wondering what she could detect. Perhaps nothing. Perhaps the heat. Perhaps something even greater than he could detect. "We didn't talk that much about it. He believed that dragons were part of a cycle, a part of the world, and that they couldn't ever be fully removed. He believed dragons were too critical to what existed within the world."

Jason wondered if that were the case or not, but even as he looked around, he couldn't help but feel as if there was some aspect here that he was missing. He headed deeper into the dragon boneyard and stopped at another long bone. It looked to be the spine, with ribs coming off it. Standing beneath it, he felt as if he were in some sort of shelter, as if he were standing within the dragon itself.

Jason pulled upon the power within him and began to focus it. He held onto that energy and mixed power together. As he did, he recognized something different. Some of that power began to flow into the dragon bones, but it flowed into him as well.

It was a strange tingling sensation, a warmth that worked through him, and a drawing sensation that reminded him of what he had done what he had dealt with the dragon egg. As he continued to push power out, holding onto something similar to the illusion, Jason recognized that something different was taking place.

By holding onto that power, by creating that aspect of the illusion, Jason could use it, but he also could feel that illusion starting to shift. He didn't have control over it.

"What are you doing?" Janeya asked.

"I'm not trying to do anything," he said. "Something is taking place here, but..."

He felt the way the power was continuing to flow out from him.

It was a mistake.

He tried to withdraw, trying to pull back that energy, but there wasn't anything that he could do.

He shifted what he was doing.

He couldn't push as much power out from the other dragons, not without risking weakening them, but what if he drew upon the power of the northern mountains?

In the back of his mind, he could feel the ice dragon roaring, though Jason didn't know why he was. He snapped his eyes open and looked around and found the ice dragon watching him.

"Go on," the ice dragon said.

"What am I doing?"

"I don't know," the ice dragon said, and yet, there was power flowing within him, power that suggested to Jason that he needed to keep pushing, that he needed to keep using his energy, that he needed to keep it flowing out from him.

In doing so, Jason could feel the energy coming off the ice dragon, the cold and familiar sense of the north, and used everything in his power to send that energy outward.

Surprisingly, it seemed almost as if the dragon bones stored that power, creating something of a reservoir. The power Jason was drawing started to fill the bones.

"What are you doing?" Janeya asked.

Energy continued to build, rising up within him. The bones pulled on power from him. That power flowed out through him, as if the bones themselves summoned it, trying to siphon it away from him. Even as he attempted to resist, he could do nothing to withstand it. There was simply too much power being drawn off him. It was power that flowed through him, calling upon the energy that filled him, and yet it was nothing he could control.

Unlike with the dragon egg, he was certain the energy came from him. It was flowing down from high overhead, a power he channeled. Jason was giving it as much strength as he could and he tried to prevent the bones from drawing on him, but there wasn't anything he could do. Surprisingly, he could feel something within him, a sense of energy that started to cry out, a screaming of power.

As he focused on it, he realized what it was.

The ice dragon cried out to Jason, calling out to him, demanding he continue to summon energy. He didn't dare test the connection between them to determine why, not trusting whether he'd be able to withstand the overwhelming draw power on him. If that energy continued to flow out from him, he wasn't sure he'd be able to withstand it, and he feared what it might do to him.

Jason held onto it as it flowed out around him, holding

it tightly within him. There was something within it. A reflection of power. A reflection of familiarity. It headed into the dragon bones, and it filled them with a strange surge of energy, of power that rose up from within, and it exploded.

An idea came to him.

He continued to push power out, letting it roll out and into the dragon bones. Then he shifted it.

By shifting the nature of that power, Jason could feel the energy changing, and he could feel something about himself changing. He used everything within him to shift it, drawing not only on the forest dragon from so far away, but drawing upon the power of the illusion from within *him*. Jason could feel that power over illusion within him, and he recognized some other aspect to it that he needed to contain, some other aspect that he needed to better understand.

And then he could do no more.

The illusion held.

The connection to the north, to the cold, to the energy of the mountains, began to take on a life of its own. As he held onto that power, Jason recognized that sense and knew there was nothing more he could do. The only thing he was in control of was the way he held that power. Only, now he wasn't even holding onto that power. The power was drawing from the north on its own, not even requiring his connection.

There was nothing to do. Nothing he *could* do.

It was an ongoing draw of power, but it connected to

something greater, some other aspect Jason no longer understood. Finally, he turned.

"What just happened?" Janeya asked.

"I'm not exactly sure."

"Look," she said, pointing behind him.

Jason turned.

There was a part of him that suspected that he would find a dragon, and given the way that he had fed power out to it, using the energy of the north, part of him suspected he might find an ice dragon, but instead of a dragon, there was a gleaming white egg.

A dragon egg.

More than that, the bones were gone.

"How?" she asked.

Jason could only shake his head. "I… I think Lorren was right."

14

Jason maintained his connection to the north, feeling that energy bubbling through him. He held onto that power and turned it to the egg. The energy of the north was familiar to him. Even without standing atop a mountainside, he knew the gusting icy wind, the pain of sharp needles of snow falling, the occasional rumble of the threat of an avalanche. All of that poured through him. Even as he did, he didn't feel anything from within the egg that seemed to summon power, not the way that the night dragon egg had called upon power. Jason continued to push, letting as much energy flow out from him as he could, and then he started to draw upon the power of the other dragons. Even as he did, he could tell there wasn't anything more within the other dragons that he needed to add to.

Jason trapped that power within the egg, trying to hold it there.

The egg had already fed, drawing upon the power he had provided it. Jason leaned down, holding his hand above the egg, feeling the power within it.

"What is it?" Janeya asked.

"I feel something within it," he said. "I'm not exactly sure what it is, only that there is a distinct sense of power within it."

He continued to hold his hand above the surface of the egg, and as he did, he could feel something more, some aspect of it that left him questioning whether or not it was tied to the other dragons, or whether this power was simply connected to the north, the same way the ice dragon had been.

Jason leaned down next to her, holding his hand up against the egg, feeling the power flowing out from it. "Why would this egg have formed?" he asked aloud.

"You're asking me?"

"You knew Lorren," Jason said.

"I knew him, but he didn't tell me what he had been doing with the bones."

"What *did* he tell you?"

It seemed to Jason that was the key. For them to better understand just what they were dealing with, and the reason behind everything he'd encountered so far, he thought he needed to understand more about what Lorren had been after.

He knew Lorren had been the one who had taught Therin about dragon eggs and how they could change, how the eggs were tied to the land. As he focused on that sense of power around him, he couldn't help but wonder if perhaps Lorren had been after this place in particular.

"Did Lorren send you looking for this?"

"He thought the dragons had a place of significance," she said softly, "but he didn't know what it was. Or where."

Power. It came from this place, and it came from everything all around him.

Was this what Lorach had come after?

He got to his feet, leaving the egg alone. He turned to Janeya. "When I first came for you, I felt a summons from the dragons, and I felt as if I *needed* to come to you. The earth dragon had shown me other places. He had shown me places of Therin." Jason reached into his pocket, pulling out the fragments of bone that he had carried with him. "He had shown me what Therin was after, but I didn't understand." He looked over to Janeya. "I think the earth dragon knew that I needed to."

Maybe it was more than just the earth dragon that had needed him to find this.

There had been an urging that had come from someplace deep within himself when the earth dragon had appeared.

Had it been him, or had it come from the dragons directing him in some way?

And then there was his friend.

The blue dragon had wanted him to come here.

He had died in a sacrifice so that Jason could know about it.

He turned to the other bones. The one that had drawn upon the power of the mountains, the energy of the north, had been a nearly complete spine.

He stopped near a skull. This skull was massive, and Jason could only imagine what kind of dragon it came from. There weren't any dragons alive that he had seen that would rival this creature in size.

As he stared at it, he wondered whether or not it would pull upon power the same way as the other bones had. He felt that power flowing, the way that it continued to sweep out from him, and he recognized power radiating away.

Something within him began to draw outward.

Strangely enough, Jason was aware of what was coming from him.

It was the power of the iron dragon. That heat and energy, and not only did it come from some place within Jason, but it came from the distant connection he shared with the iron dragon.

Jason had to be careful with it, not wanting the iron dragon to be weakened, fearing what might happen were this bone to hold onto that power, trapping it. There had to be something that he could do to ensure that the dragon bones didn't draw off too much power.

Jason held onto that energy, feeling it flowing from within him. He continued to call that power to him, trying to summon it himself rather than letting the iron dragon be the source of it. The more power he pushed through himself, connecting to these bones, the easier it was to ensure that nothing different took place.

He tried to separate from the drawing of power.

He couldn't do so. As he attempted to separate from that power, he felt a change, something within him, some aspect of it that made it so he couldn't pull away. He continued to let that power flow through him, trying not to fight it.

Fighting wasn't going to do anything, at least not the way he needed. Jason focused on it. He wasn't going to be able to pull away, but could he do something different? He was aware of the energy that flowed out of him, a mixture of each of the dragons, and he tried to withdraw so that he didn't take too much power from them, but his attempts failed. He could not withdraw nearly as much as he needed to.

"Can I help with anything?" Janeya asked, looking over at him.

Jason locked eyes with her. "I might need your help. The bones are drawing upon me."

"The bones?"

He nodded. "Somehow, these bones are drawing on me, just like the last set did. I need to try to separate from it, but I don't know if I can." Even as he felt for the power that was flowing around him, Jason tried to use something to separate, but he couldn't. There was too much power here, too much energy building.

He tried to restrict the bones from calling upon his

connection, but the control over the iron dragon power was different than what he had over that of the ice dragon. Even with the ice dragon, Jason didn't necessarily have any real control. He had strength, and he had a connection to the north, but anything else…

Janeya touched his hand and he felt the trembling within the earth, that same connection that had bound them together. By holding onto that sense of energy coming from her, Jason felt a changing, the energy around him pressing in upon him.

The earth continued rumbling.

"Why would these bones call on your power?" Janeya asked.

Jason shook his head. "I don't know. I can feel power rolling away from me. I can feel the way they're trying to draw energy from me. And I can feel the considerable power here."

Holding onto the connection he now shared with Janeya, he felt that power building, some aspect of it different than what he had felt before. He recognized something within the way that Janeya called power. It was a familiarity. It was almost as if he had known her before.

Jason tried not to think about it.

She looked at him, watching him. "What is it?" she asked.

"I don't know. All I can tell you is that—"

Jason didn't have an opportunity to finish. As the power continued to draw from him, it was too much. He strained, struggling to resist that power, and failed.

He lost control.

Energy exploded, called out of him, and he tried to hold on to what he could to counter the effect, but he couldn't.

There was far too much power coming out of him.

He tried a different approach.

Rather than attempting to fight it, Jason pushed power into it.

As he focused on it, he let it flow out from him, and pushed more and more power out. Jason gave the bones as much power as he could, squeezing it out, letting the energy of the iron dragon flow from him. When it did, it headed into the bones, and he could feel that power beginning to build much like it had the last time.

Would it create another egg?

Jason had to continue to push. As he did, he recognized something changing.

"It's too much," Janeya said.

Jason held onto the power, drawing it up from someplace deep within him. This power was different than that of the ice dragon. That was the power of the cold. The north. The power of his home. It was the power of familiarity.

This was that of the iron dragon. Anger and rage and the sense that he had of what could have been. It was different than what he had used before, and as he held this new energy, letting it flow to him, filling him, Jason tried to maintain his hold over it, but wasn't able to control it.

Perhaps he didn't need to.

Why should he fight?

He embraced the anger, the rage, the heat of the iron dragon. For the first time, he thought he understood where it came from. It bubbled from someplace deep beneath the ground, but it also flowed through him.

Jason had known that anger had flowed through him, and he could feel it, and he had known that to use this power, all it took was for him to find it, but this was something different. This was a matter of pulling power from deep within him.

Anger from his time in the mountains, a time where he had been teased and bullied, flared within him. It was part of the reason that Jason had found an understanding of the iron dragon, part of the reason that the two of them had bonded so quickly. It was not so different than how he had bonded to the forest dragon, understanding the desire to hide and conceal himself, the way that Jason had once hidden in the snowy landscape, hunting, but also hiding from those within the village.

Power filled the bones and created another egg.

This one looked different than the ice dragon egg. The egg was enormous, almost as tall as he was, and oblong, and a little lopsided. It was nearly perfectly white, though streaks of green and red worked into the white, and when he turned his head from side to side, it seemed to glimmer with other colors. They were faint, though, as if they were barely within the surface of the egg.

The egg glowed softly, and as he brought his hand

toward it, he recognized the heat radiating off it. It was the heat of the iron dragon, the heat of the earth, the heat of someplace buried deep underground. It was impressive, enormous, and it was something unlike anything he'd ever experienced before.

Jason held onto that power, and he tried to push more into it, but the egg was satisfied. He turned and looked over at Janeya.

"I don't even know what to make of this," he whispered.

"Lorren wanted to find something like this place, but I never understood why."

"How is this even possible?" Jason asked.

"I don't know," she said. "I also don't know how it's possible for you to call upon the power you have been."

"I'm drawing upon that of the dragons," he said.

"Only you are not. You're calling upon the dragons, but you're calling upon something else. Some other aspect of power."

Jason frowned to himself. She was right. He might be calling upon that of the dragons, but it came from *him*.

Strangely, as he focused on that power, he recognized that whatever he detected, whatever energy he was borrowing, it truly did represent some aspect of him, some way for him to connect to the powers that existed within the world in a way that he had never done before.

It seemed impossible that he had that kind of a connection to the powers of the world, the misfit powers, such as they were. Still, the dragons themselves were unique, so why shouldn't he be unique? The dragons had bonded to their environment, connecting to aspects of it, and Jason had bonded to those dragons, coming to know them. For him to understand the power of the world they connected to, he had needed to understand the dragons. Doing so may have connected him to the world in a way that others had not.

Maybe all he had to do was add power to these bones, turning this place into something more, using the energy that flowed within him, the connection that existed within him, and changing it in a way that created more power and, then, something different.

How many of these bones could be restored? How many of these could take energy and turn that energy into something more?

Better yet, how was any of this going to make a difference?

Somehow, they still had to stop Jessica and Lorach.

Jessica had to be after this for a reason. Could she have learned about the boneyard?

It seemed impossible to fathom, but her Dragon Souls had been out here. They had claimed bones.

It suggested that she had known.

Which meant she had known they could be used similarly.

He had to stop her.

And there was only one way he could think of to do so.

They had to get to the dragons. They had to get to those eggs.

Before Jessica accomplished whatever she intended.

Janeya watched. "What do you intend to do?"

"I think that I need to see if there are more of these bones that we might be able to use," Jason said.

She looked around and then nodded.

15

The boneyard looked drastically different than it had before.

It had only been a few hours, but in that time, Jason had transformed the boneyard into an egg yard. All around him were eggs. A dozen, each of them enormous, and each of them nearly as tall as him, so large that he had to walk a dozen paces in order to circle them. Most were the same pale white, and each was streaked with color, though there were two that had more color than the rest. Energy radiated from the eggs, and the strange haze lingered over the egg yard where it hadn't before.

Strangely, he had to wonder how many of these eggs would actually hatch.

Given all of the energy that Jason had fed into them, he hoped they would somehow hatch. He had seen the night dragon drawing upon energy, and had seen how the egg and the dragon within the egg had consumed the power. Would they be able to hatch?

There was energy around him. Within that energy was a sense of familiarity. Jason held onto that familiarity as he wandered through the egg yard.

A dozen eggs. Each of the bones that had once been here had summoned power from him, guiding him as to which of the dragon misfits' energy he needed to call upon. As he did, he had begun to feel that there was something more, some aspect of power he might be able to use that was different than what he drew through the dragons.

As he'd drawn through the dragons, he'd found he wasn't weakening them the way he thought he had.

What about *his* weakness, though?

The dragons may not have suffered, not feeling the effect of him summoning power, but he couldn't help feeling as if it was more than just the dragons he needed to be concerned about. It was more than just their energy he needed to focus on.

Jason focused on the power within him, and he tried to see if he was weakened. *Maybe a little.* Even as he felt that power, he could feel some aspect of a continuing flow into him.

It was almost as if the energy was starting to drift back to him, coming from someplace different, floating off the energy that he summoned, drawn off the power that he had a more direct connection to than he'd ever known. Finally, he let out a heavy breath.

He turned to Janeya. “Despite doing all of this, we still haven’t figured out what we need to do in order to stop the people of Lorach. We haven’t figured out how to stop the Dragon Souls or Jessica or…”

Coming here had been essential to understanding the misfits, though. He had felt urged to come here, drawn to the boneyard, and felt as if it were important to have done so, but perhaps doing it now had been a mistake.

Only… Could this have been how Therin had created his misfit eggs?

Perhaps this was what Jessica was after now. Something similar to Therin.

Jason had stopped Therin once, and he had stopped Jessica when she’d intended to hatch a dragon egg, but what if there was more to it?

She understood things that had been hidden from Jason, things that he had been forced to learn independently. She had the opportunity to study with the Dragon Souls, and she had knowledge that had accumulated over years of that study.

Jason needed to stop Lorach.

He was connected to other dragons. It seemed to Jason that Therin might have known how to summon power and feed them into the bones. That might be why Lorren had not shared the secret with anyone other than Therin.

With Therin, though, it had been about more than just bringing bones back together. It had been about finding eggs.

This had been about creating eggs.

Which suggested to Jason that Therin had not known. He may have suspected, but had he not known, he would not have been able to do anything.

Even another dozen eggs, if they were to hatch, wouldn't be strong enough to overpower the several hundred dragons still in Lorach. Maybe this new connection to other powers that he had uncovered would be enough.

Janeya watched him, and he couldn't tell whether or not she was concerned about the way he was calling upon power or whether there was something else to her scrutiny. There was considerable power coming from places around him.

"It might not be enough," he whispered.

"What are you trying to do?" she asked him.

"I'm trying to see if there's anything I can do with the power I'm holding."

"Let me help. I feel like I owe the dragons. After what Lorren did, the way he used the dragons, I need to do something more than what I've done. I need to take ownership of it."

"Even the two of us might not be enough," Jason said.

"We can try, though," she said.

He sighed. "We can try." He held onto the power within him, and he used the sense of the ice dragon, calling down to him. "It's time for us to return."

The ice dragon breathed out with an icy sigh. "What about them?"

Jason shook his head. "I don't really know what do

about the eggs. They could stay here, but I don't know that they are going to mature enough in time to help us." Even if they did, Jason wasn't sure that he would want to risk young dragons.

That was assuming that the eggs would even hatch.

"Are you sure that's wise?" Janeya asked.

Jason shook his head. "I don't know that anything is wise when it comes to the dragons. I've done everything I can to protect the dragons, and then I come here, find that there is a different place, and..."

Janeya took his hand and patted it, and he felt a strange and soothing comfort from her. Somehow, he would have to try to find a way to help the dragons of Lorach *and* the misfits. Coming here wasn't the way. They had found this place, found what Lorren had sought, but now...

Within him came a sense of the dragons. It echoed with the energy that came from him. There was something more, though. That something more seemed to come from what he detected of the eggs.

That can't be a coincidence.

The eggs were there, lining the ground, and within those eggs was a certain power.

It was the sense of the dragon, the sense of the power he had given them. But it wasn't only power that he gave them. As he studied them, he realized there was something more to it.

There was a different energy here, some other aspect that flowed from them.

Whereas he thought that the eggs were distinct, drawn on a single type of power that he had been holding, as he was here, focusing on that power, recognizing its energy, he realized there was a mixture of senses.

Not all of them were completely mixed, and there was a predominance of power to each of them, but the basic element of each of the misfits was there within them. Each of these eggs had that aspect.

The only dragon that wasn't represented by these eggs was the night dragon.

If he could use him, if he were able to draw upon his energy, Jason might be able to add something more to the eggs. They might be safer. More powerful. He might be able to call upon the power of the night dragon.

The night dragon was a distant sense to him.

It came to him as a distant and weak awareness buried deep in his mind, so different than the connection that he shared with the other dragons. Jason thought that he might be able to gain a better understanding of the night dragon if he were to have more time with it, especially as he had continued to change.

Jason reached for that power.

When he did, he felt the energy of the night dragon flow into him. It filled him. The energy of the night dragon was there, exploding within him. As he held onto that power, something changed. Darkness began to swirl around him.

"What is *that*?" Janeya asked.

Jason didn't get the opportunity to explain.

The darkness continued to build, flowing, and Jason suddenly recognized just what it was. It wasn't only the *power* of the night dragon.

The night dragon was coming to him.

That awareness deep inside his mind had not shifted at all, unlike when the other dragons approached. He was amorphous, a smear of darkness, but within that dark cloud of energy was the power of the night dragon and the truth of his existence.

The night dragon appeared before him.

He was darkness, he was the inky black of night, but he was also power.

Small—no larger than he had ever been—he was still incredibly powerful.

"How are you here?" Jason asked.

"Because you called me here," the night dragon said.

"Did you feel what happened?"

"Did I feel you using the energies of the world in order to create life?"

Jason looked over at the eggs. "Was that what I did?"

The night dragon laughed, a strange and dark sound. "In a way. Dragons leave behind something of themselves when they depart the world, and what you did was imbue that something with an aspect of life, an aspect of energy, and you added the power that you were able to grant and changed something for them."

The night dragon swirled around the eggs and tendrils of darkness began to shimmer, floating around the eggs, floating around the night dragon, and Jason felt the power the night dragon used on them.

It was a strange and subtle sort of energy, but the longer that he continued to push that power out, the more Jason was able to detect just what the night dragon was doing. He was cycling, circling around the eggs, but he was also influencing them. The power of the night dragon began to flow into them.

"What are you doing?"

"I am simply speeding along the natural progression of things," the night dragon said.

"Why?"

"Because it must be done," the night dragon said.

Power again filled the eggs, but this time it was different than the kind of power Jason had been giving them, a different sort of energy .

It reminded Jason of how he and the other dragons had fed the night dragon. It was connected to power, but it was connected to the power of the night dragon, not to anything else.

The power of the night dragon flowed into each of the eggs.

And then it began to build.

Jason questioned whether or not there might be something more that he might be able to add to it. As he attempted do, he felt the night dragon resist him. Darkness swirled toward him and the night dragon's face turned toward him, his eyes looking like black pools of night. The night dragon pressed that energy into Jason.

"No. You must save yourself."

Jason held onto the energy within him and focused, trying to see if there might be something more he would be able to add to what the night dragon did, but even as he did, he didn't know if it even mattered. The eggs started to tremble.

Jason backed away, looking over at Janeya.

The trembling took on the energy of the earth, the energy of the storm dragon, and it took on the energy of each of the dragons that made up these eggs. Gradually, Jason recognized that trembling, he recognized how that trembling continued to flow, building within those eggs, building outward, filling them with a source of power.

The night dragon continued to swirl around them, and as he did, the eggs trembled and power exploded in them.

There came a flash of darkness, followed by a strange light.

Then power bloomed.

Jason had never experienced anything quite like it before. The sudden blooming of power erupted all around him, giving him a sense of dragons, but also giving him a sense of the *power* of those dragons, the way they filled him with their energy. It came from all of the dragon eggs.

Not just dragon eggs. Not anymore.

Now they were dragons.

The dragons were drawing upon energy. It was different than the energy that had come off Jason, different than the power that he had exuded, and this energy was not just the power of him, or the other misfits, or even the powers of the world.

This was a power that connected them to each other.

He realized what they were doing. They were feeding.

Only, the way that they were feeding was different than what he had seen other dragons do. These were feeding through the connection he had added.

He tried to push more power into them, focusing on that energy, but even as he did, he wasn't able to add much more to it. He didn't need to.

The dragons were drawing upon the power on their own. They were growing larger. As they did, he realized something else. The dragons were taking on the size and scale of the bones he'd used in order to create the eggs. The dragons transformed on their own, using the power that he held onto, and they turned that power, becoming something else.

They were powerful. Massive.

And not surprisingly, the most massive of them was a dragon connected to the cold.

Jason turned to that dragon, looking over at the ice dragon hiding behind him, and realized something.

A female.

Females were rare, so having another female was incredibly rare.

That wasn't all.

All of them were female.

"Do you see what I'm seeing?" he asked Janeya.

"This shouldn't be." She shook her head again. "None

of this should be. We shouldn't have any of these dragons. And more than that, to have all of them be female?"

Female dragons, especially like this, misfit female dragons, would change everything. How many other dragons would there be like the night dragon?

How many other dragons would there be like the other dragons he had known?

He looked over at the night dragon. "Did you know that they would all be female?"

"You were needed," the night dragon said.

"I don't understand."

"Don't you?"

Jason had felt something that had urged him to come out here, though he hadn't known what it was. At the time, he had thought it was tied to understanding the misfits and that he would find that understanding of the misfits out here, and he had, but not the way that he had expected.

"You knew." There was the trembling he'd detected. The connection to earth and the earth dragon. The night dragon *had* told him that Jason needed to go. Here he'd assumed it was to go find what Lorach intended with the dragon bones, but what if it was about more than that? "Were you responsible for sending me to him?"

"You were needed."

This was a powerful dragon, and the dragon had to have had some reason, some purpose, in doing what he had done. That something was beyond just a dragon misfit.

He could feel that sense coming from the night dragon.

"What else are we supposed to do for them?"

"You will do what you must, Jason Dreshen."

"And these dragons?" If Jessica learned of these female dragons, all of them misfits, he could easily imagine what she might do with them. The way that she might try to use them. If she were to do that, Jason didn't know if there would be anything that he would be able to do to help them withstand it.

He would try. He would fight. He would resist.

Given what he'd already experienced, the power that he had detected in the way Jessica was using the other dragons, Jason didn't know if it would be enough. Everything that he might do would be not successful. Jason would fail.

The dragons would fall.

And Lorach would gain a dozen female dragons.

When they did, these dragons would suffer.

The world would suffer.

"What do you think that she will be able to do compared to their power?" the night dragon asked.

"I don't understand."

"Don't you?"

There came an urging from the night dragon, and Jason recognized what the night dragon wanted him to do, the way he wanted Jason to turn his attention to the other dragons, to focus on their power.

When he did, he recognized something else within them, some aspect of power.

Not only were they connected to the other dragons, but they were somehow bound together. Because they were bound together, they called upon the energy of the other dragons, and they called upon the energy of the world.

That was what would protect them.

The dragons weren't in any danger.

Not the way he had thought.

The dragons were safe.

He turned his attention back to the night dragon. "That's what you were after. Did you know they would be bonded in such a way?"

"You gave them power, Jason Dreshen. Much like you gave me power."

"I didn't give you power. The others did."

"You permitted the others to do so. And in doing so, you have changed dragons. It's time for you to return. You're needed."

"Why am I needed?"

"You must see it." There was an urgency to his words, and Jason studied the night dragon, wondering what it was. "Power."

It seemed to Jason that the night dragon struggled to put into words what he wanted to say.

"Where do we need to go?"

"Where I hatched. Follow."

The night dragon stretched out, spreading wings of shadows and darkness, and with that, he took flight. He hovered high overhead, a dark shadow in the sky.

From where Jason stood, it seemed almost as if the dragon were larger than he appeared on the ground, though Jason knew that was nothing more than the shadows. Nothing more than an illusion.

He stared at the dragon, staring at the power he detected coming off him, and he stared at the energy that he detected. Within that dragon was a familiar sense. Much like within these other dragons was a familiar sense.

The dragons pushed outward with power, and it was that power which flooded into Jason, the same powers that he could connect to. It came from his understanding of the dragon misfits, an understanding that had bound and bridged their magic together. It came from his understanding of their connection to the world, and the way that he had called upon that power.

He focused on the connection he had to the other dragons and felt a connection to these dragons too. It filled him, that understanding. It radiated up from someplace deep within him. Jason could use that.

He sent forth a request.

Not a requirement. Not a demand. Not even a command.

A request.

These dragons were young, but he had a sense that there was something about them that was different from the other dragons. The night dragon had sped along their development, using his own unique power, that of the darkness and the shadows, and now they were there in front of him, fully formed dragons, and Jason had to ask whether they would help stop Lorach. That was what Jason needed to do now. The only thing that he could think of doing. With dragons like these, Lorach wouldn't be able to slow them.

But would they help?

The night dragon had changed them. He could feel that change. And that power.

They were *more* than they should be.

Which was the advantage they needed against Lorach.

When the dragons answered, they did so without hesitation.

16

They veered toward Dragon Haven, staying high over the ground. The landscape shifted beneath them and Jason stared down at the ground, holding onto the power of the ice dragon, letting that energy fill him, searching for what was down there.

"I can sense something is wrong," Janeya said to him.

The farther they traveled, the more he felt it as well. It bothered him.

An absence.

The night dragon had warned him. Something was going on. Something the night dragon wasn't able to explain. Whatever it was reflected power.

Lorach.

That had to be what it was.

But what had Lorach done now?

The night dragon had come to the boneyard, but then disappeared again.

You're needed.

At the time, he hadn't given it enough thought, but he should have.

Now…

"I don't know what it is," Jason said. "The dragons are missing." Not the misfits; he could feel them within himself, though the sense of those dragons had faded somewhat. This was about the Dragon Haven dragons.

He focused on Janeya for a moment, a sudden concern filling him that perhaps she was responsible for it, though he didn't think that was the case. If she were responsible, he would have felt that influence before now.

Whatever else it was, it wasn't her.

As he continued to focus, straining and feeling for the power that was out there, he realized he detected the absence. It was that absence which troubled him the most. Within that absence there was something more, the lack of the dragon power, connections, people. All of it should be there. Something about it was off, though.

Janeya turned so that she could face him.

"Is there anything I can help with?"

"Maybe. I don't know," Jason said. "I don't really know what's going on. I don't really know what has happened, and I don't really know whether there's anything that we can do differently."

"Tell me what you're looking for."

"Dragon Haven."

"This is the rebellion?"

Jason nodded. "The rebellion. Other dragons. I placed

an illusion around it to shield it, but there's something off."

"There has been an illusion around all of Dragon Haven since I placed it, but now the illusion is different." It was almost more robust, as if it were fortified. Still, some part of the illusion felt off to him, something Jason couldn't quite place and didn't know how to explain. Power, but not the kind of power he had expected to be here.

What about this had the night dragon wanted him to see?

"Is the city missing?"

"Not missing," he said. Through the illusion, he *thought* he could still feel that, though wasn't entirely sure. "But something is wrong."

As he glanced over to her, it felt almost as if they had a shared connection, though he put that thought out of mind. It was strange that he would have some sort of connection to her, but Jason was certain that was what he felt. A connection.

She was lovely. Dark hair, silver eyes, and power that emanated from her. There was something quite potent and intriguing about her.

He had to push those thoughts away. It was dangerous, not only because he didn't know her at all, other than her connection to the dragons, but it was dangerous because of what he thought had been a growing affection between him and Sarah.

Perhaps there hadn't been, though.

With everything Sarah had been doing while searching for her parents and trying to protect Dragon Haven, Jason had been an outsider. Not because she had made him one. It was more because he had no other choice. He had wanted to continue searching for the dragons, wanting to protect them, and had been less concerned about the people of Dragon Haven. It had started to drive a wedge between him and Sarah, which had only worsened with her need to lead in Dragon Haven now that her parents had gone missing.

Now as he looked at Janeya, he didn't even know how to answer.

He tapped on the ice dragon's back. "We have to go see what happened." Turning to Janeya, he said, "I don't know what took place, and I don't know if you are going to be in any danger here, so I can't promise I will be able to protect you."

She ran her hand along the surface of the dragon, and he could feel something through that connection, though Jason wasn't at all sure what it was or why he should feel something from her, only that there came a connection, something distinct and formidable from her. She nodded, as if making up her mind.

"I accept the risk," she said.

Jason held her gaze for a moment, then he tapped on the ice dragon's back again.

They descended.

They streaked toward the ground.

The dragon seemed to know exactly where he needed

to go. The power within the ice dragon filled him, and then the treetops loomed into view. That was all Jason could see. Trees. There was nothing else.

Is this illusion?

The illusion was far more extensive than what Jason had placed. Incredibly powerful, vast, and far more believable than the illusion that he had placed.

The dragon turned, heading farther inland.

Jason called upon the power of the ice dragon, but he shifted that, changing to grab for that of the iron dragon. The iron dragon was somewhere nearby. Jason could feel the sense of him, though he couldn't see him.

He focused on the dragons connected to him, but only those that had been connected to him the longest. The ice and iron and forest, and even the storm dragon. By holding onto those dragons, Jason could track through that connection, and he could feel something greater, some other aspect to it, and he felt beyond that connection.

It was there in the back of his mind. He detected it faintly, but definitely there.

He reached across that distance and added a hint more power.

Something shifted at the edge of his vision.

It was faint, but even as he probed, he recognized the power there.

There.

The shimmering came again.

When it did, Jason hung onto that sense of power,

latching onto that connection. He detected something buried within the connection, and he felt a faint and faded sort of sense. This time, Jason recognized that the power was within him even though he could feel that energy out there.

"The night dragon is causing this."

The illusion stretched all over the land. Not just over Dragon Haven, but over much more than the city. It seemed as if the illusion was used to conceal the city, the forest, and everything.

Had the night dragon feared Lorach finding them?

Why would he have done it otherwise?

The question Jason had was *why*?

You're needed.

What had happened here?

The shimmering changed around him. Jason used everything in his power to overwhelm what happened near him. The illusion the night dragon had created shattered.

Jason felt a flash of the other dragons mixed with the energy of Dragon Haven. The ice dragon must have felt it as well. They hurried toward that sense, focusing on it, and he recognized the power within it. He still felt no sense of the Dragon Haven dragons.

They streaked toward Dragon Haven.

There came an increased sense of power building from him. The earth dragon granted him a connection. Only, it wasn't that of the earth dragon.

He jerked his head around.

Janeya added to him. Because they shared a connection to the earth dragon, they were somehow connected.

"What are you doing?"

"I could feel the way you're pushing on power," she said.

"You can feel it? How?"

"I don't exactly know, only that I can detect what you're doing and I feel as if there's something I might be able to offer to help."

Jason tried to maintain his hold over that power and he held onto it tightly, gripping it, and could feel some aspect of the way she was pushing out with her own power, giving him more than he would have been able to handle on his own.

Jason turned in place, holding onto the ice dragon and letting the dragon's power fill him. As he did, he recognized there was some aspect of the magic of the ice dragon he hadn't tapped into yet. It was a connection to the cold overhead, a distinct and direct connection to the ice and the mountains and the wind and the snow.

As he stared down below him, he could see the forest, and that was it. That was all he saw, though now that he was aware of the illusion, he knew to look for it, and he knew to look through it. There was enough here that he could see, and though he tried to penetrate the illusion, Jason couldn't do so easily.

What had the night dragon done?

The ice dragon dove.

Jason held tightly and Janeya shifted, spinning around

in place so she could grab onto the dragon's back. She cried out, and for a moment Jason thought that she was scared, but that wasn't the sound he heard from her.

This was excitement.

She enjoyed flying with the dragons.

More than that, she seemed to enjoy the ice dragon, and she seemed to enjoy the power of the dragon beneath her. It was a strange thing to feel through another person, through a connection that they shared, bound by the earth dragon.

He pushed away that thought. That thought brought him into dangerous territory.

The dragon dove down toward the ground, heading toward Dragon Haven, and then landed in the clearing near it. Jason hopped off the ice dragon's back, and so did Janeya. The dragon yard stood empty.

His heart started to hammer as he turned to the ice dragon.

"I need you to keep watch. Do you think you can find us again?" Jason asked the ice dragon.

"You are here, so I can find you."

With that, the ice dragon took to the sky. He leapt to the air, his wings shaking icicles and letting a hint of cold water come raining down.

When the ice dragon was gone, he started toward the city, casting one more glance toward the empty dragon yard.

"Dragons are missing," Jason said when she found him staring. "There should be several over there." More than that around the city. All of them were missing. *You are needed.* "There's something off here, and I don't know what it is," Jason said.

The night dragon had wanted them here.

He would have known, so why not tell Jason?

Maybe he couldn't.

Despite how he came across, there were things about the night dragon that still felt foreign to Jason. He couldn't communicate everything on his mind as well as some of the dragons, so maybe he couldn't have expressed *why* Jason had needed to come here.

And why had his illusion covered so *much* of the forest?

As he hurried toward the city, he glanced over, wondering if perhaps he was making a mistake by bringing Janeya with him. He didn't think so. In the time he'd been around her, he hadn't the sense from her that she was dangerous, and even more so now that he was somehow connected to her through the shared bonds of the earth dragon.

By holding onto that sense of energy, that connection, Jason recognized that there was something within her that reminded him of a familiar sensation. It was his same desire to protect the dragons. He could feel that from within her. Somehow, the earth dragon had bound them together, giving them that bridge of connection.

"I can feel something," she said softly as they ran.

Jason looked over, holding onto her silver gaze as he started to slow. "The other dragons?" If they were outside of the city, then he should go there first. Maybe Sarah had moved them.

"Not dragons. Something else. It's strange. I've always had that connection to the earth dragon, but there is something within it." She looked at him briefly. "As long as I can remember, the earth dragon has allowed me to connect to him, and I've been able to use that power and draw upon it. This is something else."

He nodded again, starting back toward the city. Not the other dragons, then. "I think what you're detecting is me. I think it's the shared connection we have to the earth dragon, and somehow that allows us to share some sort of familiarity."

Her brow furrowed and something about her expression darkened.

"I didn't ask him for this," he said quickly.

"That's not it. It's just…" She looked around for a moment before turning her attention back to him. "Lorren taught me to be alone. That I had to be prepared for it. That I should learn to work with the dragons and…" She swallowed, shaking her head and leaving Jason wondering what else Lorren had wanted her to learn. "I haven't needed to connect to anybody else. Having to have this connection to you, and having some sort of connection like this is difficult." She said the last softly.

Jason chuckled. "I haven't had this sort of a connection before, either."

He spoke carefully, feeling a hint of guilt in it. He didn't want the misfit dragons to know; he didn't want

Sarah to know. It felt almost as if he were betraying her by having this connection to Janeya, especially now that he was back in Dragon Haven.

Dragon Haven, but where are the dragons?

Where are the people?

Through the earth dragon, he sensed uncertainty from her. He felt it as well.

Jason held his hand out, and she took it.

17

The inside of Dragon Haven was quiet. He had never seen anything quite like it before. There had never been crowds; the city was home to only a few thousand people at most, all of them part of the rebellion, but the sudden absence of everything here was striking. Jason could feel that absence.

Where was everybody?

You're needed.

There had been an illusion around everything, enough power that had covered the city, the forest, everything.

Could it be an illusion now?

It wasn't just that the Dragon Guard was missing. Dragons were missing. Those who had a connection to the dragons were missing. He stared at the empty streets. The city was never the busiest of places, but now it was totally empty, devoid of people and strangely quiet.

He closed his eyes, using each of the dragons that he

connected to and trying to understand whether there was anyone here, but without a dragon connection to the people, Jason wouldn't be able to find them. If anyone was still here, he wouldn't even know.

"I thought this was a home to a great number of people," Janeya said.

"It was. It is."

Is this part of the night dragon's illusion?

Therin had performed a powerful illusion on him once before, and had made it so that he hadn't been able to even find Dragon Haven. Jessica had similar abilities. What if this was her now?

Still, there was something about this which felt real.

Then there was the issue of the night dragon's illusion around the entire forest.

Protection.

But from what?

He focused on the misfits. They were still there.

Which meant the illusion would have to be selective.

If that was what it was.

He felt increasingly worried it was something else, though.

Not illusion.

Jason nodded to Janeya. "I need to see if I can find anything."

Dragons *or* people.

He guided her through the city, through the empty streets, nothing moving around him. There were the sculptures of dragons lining the streets. They were lifeless, almost as if they were trying to taunt him, a memory of the people and their pride that had been here before.

The city was empty. No people. No dragons.

Completely empty.

His sister and mother. William. Henry. Sarah.

Countless others he'd come to know and had said he would protect.

And he'd been gone.

That hit him harder than he would have expected. Jason had been away, working with the dragons, when this attack had come. He could have been here for them. He *should* have been here for them.

Lorach. It has to be.

But... how?

Jason had been focused on the dragons, finding the misfits, understanding the bones, that he'd forgotten what he had promised to Sarah—and in effect, Dragon Haven. He had been asked to find what Lorach intended.

Now he was too late.

This felt different than anything they had faced from Lorach before. Those had been targeted upon the dragons, ultimately to try to find a way to capture and control the Dragon Haven dragons and ultimately to destroy the entire city, but for whatever reason, this felt personal. This felt as if he had been attacked, that Jessica had targeting the city, emptying it of power, as a way of coming after him.

Jason focused, and he sent out a request to the dragons, using the strength of his connections to them. Now was not the time for subtlety.

Something had happened to Dragon Haven. It was time he respond.

Power flowed from him to the dragon misfits.

All of the dragon misfits, including the night dragon, wherever he ended up.

The night dragon knew something and Jason needed to understand what was going on. He had been the one who had wanted Jason to come here.

Suddenly, a glistening white dragon dropped from the sky. The ice dragon shot toward them. The iron dragon started to slither out of the forest.

Jason could feel a trembling beneath him. The earth dragons. More than that, the mist dragons and the smoke dragons somehow found their way toward them too.

As they did, Jason stood in the clearing of Dragon Haven.

An empty Dragon Haven.

He thought about the first time he'd ever come here. He'd been the outsider then.

Now Janeya was the outsider, but she still seemed comfortable—far more comfortable than he had been when he had first come here.

The iron dragon rumbled, radiating heat along his side. Janeya stared at him.

"How is this dragon even possible?" she whispered.

"I've asked that about all of the dragons before," Jason said.

"He's… amazing," she said.

Worry overwhelmed him but he needed to be calm. For her, for the dragons, and for himself.

He forced a smile. "Don't spoil them too much. I'm sure he would love to hear the compliments, but I don't know if it's good for them." Heat radiated down the sides of the iron dragon. Jason held his hand out, turning toward him. "I'm going to need your help. Was it Lorach?"

"I don't know."

Jason wasn't about to ask how the iron dragon didn't know. He'd been watching the night dragon as Jason had asked.

"If it is, you know what I'll have to do."

"I know."

"You don't have to do this if you don't want to, but…"

The dragon snorted. "I will do whatever we must to protect the others."

Others.

That meant other dragons.

He tried again to reach for the night dragon, but that connection was faint and fickle. There was a wisp of it in the back of his mind, but barely more than that. He believed he could reach it, but he grasped for power he did not have.

As he felt power coming off the iron dragon, the energy coming through the iron dragon glove once again, he breathed in the energy and heat, recognizing that power within him. He glanced over at the ice dragon. Power radiated off him too, only his power was of the cold and the mountains and the north wind channeling through him.

What he felt was something more than just channeled power. Jason had to understand that, only he hadn't taken the time to do so. He turned to the ice dragon. They didn't really have that much time right now for him to question, but he had to know.

"Am I somehow drawing upon that power myself?"

"It's possible that you are," the ice dragon said. "Perhaps you were changed by your time in the mountains. You could have been changed the same way that I was. Could not the people who have power of the dragons be influenced the same way that the dragons are?"

Jason hadn't considered it and didn't think that was the case, knowing he had only a connection to the dragons, not necessarily the power of the dragons.

Only, that wasn't entirely true. The one thing he had learned about his connection and the power he possessed was that it was different than others. The only other person he had ever met who had a similar power to him was David.

The auran had a way that he was able to draw upon power, a way to summon it without even using the dragon pearl, reminding Jason of his own ability. If only Jason had an opportunity to better understand that.

Jason focused on the connection to the dragons.

A shimmering came from high overhead.

He looked up.

He pushed through the illusion and the forest dragon

came swooping down on a breath of wind, landing next to the other dragons. She got a greater reaction from Janeya than the other dragons had.

"She's your connection to illusion."

"She is, but it's different than the way you use mist."

"I suspect the same outcome can be achieved in many different ways," Janeya said. "At least, that was what Lorren had always taught me. You could do the same sort of magic by connecting in different ways."

There were things he could do that the Dragon Souls could do, even though Jason didn't use the power of traditional dragons. He used misfits, but the kind of misfit power that he had access to was so different than that of the other dragons.

"What else are we waiting for?" Janeya asked.

"I'm waiting for the other dragons." Lorach *had* done something here. He was sure of it. He might not know what it was, but Jason understood what he would have to do to end it.

He needed his dragons.

All of his dragons.

Jason, and the misfits, would find a way to end Lorach.

He could feel they were, the energy coming from within them, that power that continued to flow from someplace distant. There came the rumbling of earth, that ongoing trembling sensation, which Jason continued to feel building.

The newly hatched dragons were coming. Jason could feel them. The connection might be different, their power more unusual and perhaps more like the night dragon, but they came at his request.

He focused into the distance.

A burst of thunder rumbled, lightning crackled. The storm dragon came.

Janeya looked up. She wasn't concerned.

She must've known it was a dragon, and through their connection to earth, she might even know about the storm dragon.

"Lorren warned me there was a dragon like that out here," she said. "He was concerned about him because he didn't know what kind of power he had."

"The power of the storms," Jason said.

"That must be an impressive ability," she said.

"I haven't had that much time to work with him."

He could feel that power coming off him, the energy that came from the storm dragon, and he tried to reach for it, but there wasn't anything to that connection that he felt strongly. It was there, distant and faint within him.

It was a trembling energy, the electric source of power he could summon, and within it came the thunder, that distant rumble that echoed within him every time the earth dragon shook. It was almost as if the storm dragon and the earth dragons had connected in some way. Perhaps they did.

Finally, lightning crackled high overhead.

He looked over at the forest dragon. "Can you ask him to land?"

"He's not going to like that," she said.

"He needs to. Until we understand what's going on, the other misfits need to gather."

That was how he would gather his forces.

Misfits.

All of them would take the fight to Lorach.

The forest dragon let out a shriek. It was an undulating sound, almost like a cry, but it was not at all like that at the same time. A summons.

Thunder rumbled, lightning crackled, and a massive dragon appeared before them.

Janeya regarded the dragon with an appraising eye, sweeping from his head to his tail. The storm dragon was all smoke and clouds and indistinct lines. Energy crackled along the surface of his body, and he kept his wings curled around him, though Jason didn't have the sense that the dragon needed to use his wings in order to fly. From what he understood of this dragon, he could probably take off from a standing position, shooting into the sky using the power of the storms.

"The earth dragons are almost here," she said.

The rumbling he felt distantly began to build, coming steadily, rising with an intensity. As it did, Jason watched and felt for that power, wondering how long it would take for that energy to come, concerned about when it would appear.

He didn't know whether the other dragons would even react. They didn't seem to be doing anything. They were standing there, waiting.

They knew.

The dragons could feel that energy coming. They must have been aware of the power coming up from beneath the ground, and he wondered if they were as aware of the other misfits as he was.

Perhaps they were.

With his connection, the bond that had formed between them, it was possible the dragons did know everything that he knew, the same way that it seemed Janeya knew what he knew.

Why would I have this connection with a stranger?

Power built from them, from her, and he felt the rumbling. Then the stone near the edge of the clearing began to shift. Three dragons appeared. They were enormous.

The dragons emerged from the ground, almost as if hewn from the rock themselves, made of gray and brown stone, dirt clinging to their sides, with massive bodies but small wings. These were not dragons that would be able to fly. These were dragons designed to move underground, to navigate easily in the vast darkness beneath them.

And these were dragons who shared a very different connection to the world than any others that he had ever met.

Jason still didn't know where the night dragon had gone.

He was the reason Jason had returned when he had. *You're needed.* Otherwise, Jason might have searched for more dragon bones, wondering if he might be able to save more dragons. Instead, he felt a different urgency—one that filled him with a desire to destroy Lorach for good.

He had felt that before, but now… now it burned in him.

The iron dragon roared his approval.

The earth dragons lifted from the ground, rising up quickly.

One of the earth dragons rumbled toward him, taking lumbering steps, carrying power within him. He stopped in front of Jason, lowering his head. This was the earth dragon Jason had bonded to.

Jason watched the dragon, feeling the power coming from the ground. In the distance, he recognized something else, the power coming toward them. It came from someplace distant. It was the energy of other misfit dragons, the energy of that of the mist dragons, that of the smoke dragons.

"The two of you have found a shared bond," the earth dragon said.

"You formed that shared bond," Jason said.

"By necessity," the dragon said. "You were needed."

You are needed.

It was the same thing the night dragon had said.

The earth dragon and the night dragon had been communicating.

Within that shared bond, Jason was able to feel something more, some power, and he recognized the energy within it. He looked over at Janeya, and then he pushed outward. They *were* connected.

He wanted to ask the earth dragon if he knew what Lorren—or had it been the night dragon?—had planned, but power still built around him.

More dragons were coming.

There were more than he had expected.

But then, between he and Janeya, they had connections to many misfits.

Maybe even enough to stop Lorach as he planned.

A fog began to swirl around them, layering on the distant trees, and within it, Jason noticed some shimmering shapes. The mist dragons. Not only that, but there came wisps of smoke drifting around: energy from the smoke dragons. They were near enough now. Now that he was here, feeling the power of the smoke dragons, he couldn't help but wonder if perhaps he could use the bond he shared with her in order to reach to those dragons.

One of the smoke dragons turned toward him and appeared out of the smoke. It lingered for a moment, then it disappeared again. There was something playful about it. The mist did the same thing when he turned toward it.

"What are you doing?" Janeya asked.

"We're going to have to work together. But it's more than just having to work together. We're going to have to fight, but I'd like us to save the dragons. I don't want to fight the other dragons. I don't want to hurt them."

"I've never wanted to hurt the dragons," she said softly. "Lorren told me we might have to sacrifice some in order to save them. Lorren believed the fire cycled." She reached her hand out. Smoke swirled around it.

The dragon appeared and she rested her hand on his long nose. The dragons's smoke spiraled around her before settling. "It does make sense if you begin to understand the nature of the dragons the way Lorren believed in them. He believed the fire cycled. There were only so many dragons, and that by freeing certain dragons from the control of Lorach and others like that, we were allowed to find them anew. We could bring them back, and we could save them in a different way."

Before the boneyard, he hadn't given much thought to what happened if the dragons died. There had been dead dragons that he'd experienced over the time that he'd been fighting with Lorach. Unfortunately, there had been more than he had cared for.

Now that he had been to the boneyard, Jason wondered if death really was an endpoint. If the dragons cycled the way it seemed, then perhaps losing one dragon wasn't really a loss.

Jason focused on the power within him and pushed outward, focusing on the smoke dragons, the mist dragons, even the earth dragons. They were there, powerfully connected to him.

"We are the bridge between them," he said.

Janeya looked troubled, but didn't say anything about that bridge. "What are we waiting for?"

"I'm waiting for the rest of the dragons to arrive. Including the night dragon."

Gradually, he saw the night dragon.

He was a swirl of darkness, a massive cloud that constricted as he descended.

As the darkness abated, Jason looked over to the night dragon. "All of this was you?"

"Something happened," the night dragon said. Jason sense to struggle within the night dragon, and he realized where it came from. The night dragon tried to explain what happened but could not. "I did what I could. There is nothing more that could be done."

"You placed this illusion."

"There is something more. I had to protect the others."

"What others?"

"Others."

An image formed in Jason's mind, and he saw the dragons that had been in Dragon Haven flicker through his mind; he thought that perhaps they were still here, but then the image faded. The dragons were gone.

"It's not your fault," Jason said.

"I did what I could," the night dragon said.

Jason should have been here. Had he been, he could have offered protection, and Lorach wouldn't have been able to claim the dragons or the people of Dragon Haven.

"We will take the fight to them."

The night dragon roared and darkness swirled around him, and suddenly Jason felt it fill him. It was enormous. The power of the night dragon raged within him, something more than he had ever experienced before.

It called from all of the other dragons he had connected to.

Only, there were some he had not yet added.

Jason could *feel* them.

There were other misfits. Jason had suspected they were out there but had never known with any certainty.

Now he could feel them.

It seemed as if the night dragon summoned them.

He pushed that aspect into the connection with the night dragon. Water and sun and grass and wind and a few of the others he could feel coming toward him. They were drifting slowly, almost as if they fought the desire to join them, but at the same time, they seemed to know the need to.

Suddenly the night dragon swelled with even more power and darkness became absolute around him. It was a pocket of darkness, but that was it.

The night dragon roared.

The other dragons roared in response.

It was more than just reaching them, though. Jason understood that, but he suspected the night dragon did as well. Jason had been bringing the dragons together. But once they were together, he had a vision of what they could be. How they could fly freely.

To do that, he would have to fight Lorach.

Strangely, he wasn't afraid of something happening to the dragons the way that he had before. Knowing the dragons would cycle, they could be reborn, leaving him feeling something more for them.

Hope.

Streamers of shadows swirled toward him, and he had

a feeling of the night dragon that fluttered in the back of his mind.

The night dragon had wanted him to know this.

The night dragon came toward him. Darkness swirled around, the energy of the night filling Jason, giving him a strange and powerful sensation, something he had never detected before. The dragon roared. His roar was far deeper than Jason would've expected for a dragon as small as he was. It filled the night around him.

Only, it wasn't night around him.

It had been daylight before they had started all of this, and yet, it seemed as if the night dragon had changed everything.

The other dragons waited for Jason.

They watched Jason, and at first, he didn't know why. He looked over to the night dragon, waiting for some understanding, but none came to him.

He could feel these dragons, though.

All of them.

They were misfits. Like him.

As Jason glanced over to Janeya, he wondered if she were a misfit like him.

She certainly had a connection to the misfits in the same way that he did.

The dragons waited on him.

"We will stop Lorach. And the dragons will fly freely once again."

18

Jason rode atop the ice dragon, feeling the familiar cold radiating beneath him, the energy that wafted off him, and he stared down at the ground. He borrowed from the power of the iron dragon, mixing his eyesight with that of the ice dragon, mingling them together for their search in the lands surrounding Dragon Haven.

Dragons spread on either side of him, a small fleet of them. Seeing them spread out in this way, it was not nearly the numbers he knew he needed to rival Lorach, but they were all he had. His misfits.

Somehow, it felt like there were so many—and not enough.

The misfits helped him search, looking for what happened to Dragon Haven.

In the distance, Jason thought that he could feel something, though it was vague. He had no idea what it was, but it was all they had. They followed the strange sensation, following Jason's direction.

They followed and allowed him to lead.

Perhaps that was what he needed to do.

Janeya sat on the ice dragon front of him.

It was strange that she needed his help to fly, but the other dragons she had connected to didn't give her the gift of flight. The earth dragons tunneled under the ground and the mist dragons didn't have the ability to carry her. They were almost too insubstantial, too wispy and light to carry anyone. The smoke dragons were something else altogether, and Jason had a growing understanding as to why Janeya hadn't crossed the mountains herself.

Somehow, Lorren had managed to do so, though he had used a different technique. By leaving her behind, he had trapped her. Had he known that?

Jason suspected he had. Knowing Lorren as he did, which wasn't all that well, he suspected Lorren hadn't done anything without knowing all of the consequences.

Jason looked down, searching for any sign of the others.

"How are you looking?" she asked.

"By connecting to the dragons, I can look out through their eyesight. It's a strange thing to be able to do, but with the ice dragon and the iron dragon, I'm able to mingle the two ways they're able to see, though…"

He hadn't even tried adding the other dragons to it. Jason thought perhaps he should. The more that he focused on the energy down there, the more he thought that he could use the other dragons to add something more.

The mist dragons flew along with them as well. Jason reached through Janeya and borrowed their power. They saw things in a crystalline fashion, almost as if they saw things within the mist. Of course they did. Still, in doing so, there was a heat to the way that they looked at the world.

He mixed what they saw with that of the other dragons.

It mingled, creating something greater than it had been.

Could he borrow from the smoke dragons?

As he added the vision of the smoke dragons, Jason couldn't make anything else out. There was power, but in looking outward, he didn't see anything more than what he'd already seen. He removed the smoke dragons, trying not to use their power.

The earth dragons would have exquisite eyesight in the dark, or perhaps some other way of navigating. Jason didn't really know. He would have to wait till they came up.

He turned his attention back to Janeya. "Do you see anything?"

She turned and looked out into the distance. "What are you doing to see through the dragons?"

"I am borrowing from the dragons. I don't really know how to describe it any other differently than that."

"How do you borrow from them?"

Jason focused, thinking about what he did, the specific way he connected to the dragons for this purpose. The dragons themselves seemed to give him an ability to look into the distance. He thought about how he had connected to the dragon. Strangely, he was able to detect something about that power.

"I borrow from them the same way I borrow their power," he said.

"If that's the case, then you should be able to borrow every aspect of what they can do."

He'd already seen that he could reach for the power of the dragons in a different way, that he could connect to them more directly so that he could call upon their power. Even if he could reach just a little bit of what the ice dragon or the iron dragon or the forest dragon possessed, it would grant him a more direct connection than needing to reach through the dragons. It would remove the possibility that he would overwhelm them as he called on their magic.

By focusing on their energy, he realized what he detected was tied not only to them, but it was tied to the power that flowed within him. They were bound together, wrapped up in the connection that was a stirring deep within him. It was that connection which allowed Jason to understand that power, to know it.

It bonded to him, connecting with him, the energy of the dragon that shifted, flowing through him. And gradually, Jason began to understand there was something more to it that he might be able to understand.

He was connected to those dragons, but he had something more as well.

It started with what he was able to detect from the ice dragon. By holding onto that power, Jason recognized that he was bound to energy high above him. Ever since he had started working with the night dragon, some aspect of his understanding of the dragons—and in particular, the ice dragon—had begun to shift.

In this case, and in the case of the other dragons, Jason could feel that power, and he recognized the way it was flowing and just how powerful it was. He recognized that he was truly connected to the energy of the north.

Could he feel something similar with the iron dragon?

He knew the dragon, and he knew where the dragon's power came from. This time, it wasn't even borrowing. It was drawing from the same source. By calling on that power and energy, Jason could use the same energy as the dragon. He called from the anger that stirred within him. It was in a deep place.

It was connected to the anger from everything he had experienced his entire life, the time spent on the mountaintop, time spent isolated, hunting, searching, struggling to live. Now that he was able to connect that power, he could feel the way that the dragon connected to his power, and he could draw upon it as well.

What about the forest dragon? Hers was different. Jason remembered the first time he had connected to the power of the forest dragon, the way that he had felt the wind rustling below, the energy of the wind as it guided him.

Jason could feel that now and he breathed it in, letting the energy fill him. There was a vibrant sense of it flowing within him. He recognized the way she was connected to the forest, the wind, to other aspects of life. He might be able to do the same thing.

He attempted to call upon that power. When he did, he felt something stirring within him. Slowly, he again connected directly to that power.

Finally, he opened his eyes and looked over.

Janeya watched him, and he tried to figure out how much time had passed, but realized all of that had happened in no more than a blink of an eye. A few heartbeats at most.

"What are you doing?" she asked.

"Connecting to the power of the dragons."

She watched him for a moment but said nothing more.

Jason wasn't necessarily drawing from the dragons, either. All he was doing was calling on their power, but he was connecting to it the same way they did. They were misfits. *He* was a misfit. Together, they had a different connection, and they were able to use more power, more than he had ever had before, and he was able to finally begin to understand the nature of what a misfit meant.

The dragon banked off to the side.

He noticed something.

He stared in the distance, borrowing from all the

connections to do so, but he didn't see anything. This time, he *felt* it.

That was what he had to continue to focus on.

Power stirred someplace deep within him. Jason let it out.

It washed away from him, sweeping across the landscape.

He felt life, movement, energy. Jason was aware of all of those things. It was different than it had been before.

There.

He pushed that connection through to the ice dragon, guiding the dragon toward what he detected. The dragon gave him a stirring within their bond, and he surged into the distance.

The dragon flew quickly toward what Jason detected.

"I can feel something out there. I've *been* feeling something out there. I just..." He wanted to know what it was, but he couldn't tell. Power, perhaps, but from where?

And what did it have to do with what had happened to the people—and the dragons—of Dragon Haven?

"What is it?" She studied him, a curious tilt to her jaw.

By focusing on the power within him, focusing on what he could detect of the earth dragon, he sent his connection over to her.

She gasped. "How was it that you were able to detect that?"

"I don't entirely know," Jason said. "It's tied to the energy of the dragons."

"This is different than drawing upon the energy of the dragons," she said.

As he called upon that power, he could feel how different it was, but he didn't have any idea why it would be that way. He could feel the dragons, he could feel the energy, and he could feel how the power continued to explode away from him.

It was something familiar, but it *was* different as well. He couldn't figure out what else there might be down there. Janeya did. He could feel it within her.

He turned to her, realizing she had some connection to what was down there, some energy within her, an awareness of the way his power built from him. "What do you detect?"

"I'm not exactly sure," she said. "I'm using what you are calling, and as I do, I can feel…" She sat up, looking outward. "I can feel it *calling*. Don't you feel it?"

Jason didn't, and he wondered if that was because he was wrapped so thoroughly in the power he held onto—or was it that because of what he had done, the way he had started to call power of the dragon, he could not.

He couldn't tell whether or not the dragons were tied to that same calling and whether there would be anything within them that would be drawn by it, but as he looked around, he pushed through the energy he had shared with Janeya, and he felt the calling through her.

He pushed through the dragons, starting with the ice dragon. By doing so, he recognized the calling within him.

It was distinct. That was what he'd been detecting since leaving Dragon Haven.

Ever since leaving the protective illusion the night dragon had placed around it.

And that sense was close.

The dragon settled to the ground. Jason hopped off his back, racing forward. Janeya followed. Jason could feel that power coming off her, and he recognized the energy she was holding onto, and he wondered if perhaps there was something else within it that he might be able to understand.

He focused on what he could feel out in the distance. There was definitely the sense of something out there, some energy that he could detect. It was almost as if it *were* trying to summon him.

He raced forward, using the energy he detected within him.

Where were the missing Dragon Haven dragons? The people?

He held out his hand and Janeya slowed.

"What is it?" she whispered.

"I'm not exactly sure. I can feel something..."

He still didn't *see* anything.

Illusion.

Of course.

Knowing what he did about Jessica and the way she would use power, he wouldn't be surprised at all that she would use illusion so convincingly.

Drawing on the power of the forest dragon came

slowly, but he recognized there was something more to it as well. Some aspect of it flowed deep within him. That was what Jason called upon, no longer drawing upon the energy of the forest dragon herself.

Now he called upon the power he detected around him, that energy that existed throughout him. It was like the breath within his lungs, like the energy he held.

He had to use that power.

Jason continued to call on that magic, letting it fill him.

Finally, he felt something more within it. It was the power of the illusion.

Jason exploded that out from him, slamming it into what he detected.

Strangely, when he did that, there came a shifting and a shimmering, almost as if the power he pushed against bulged against him but then resisted.

Why should it resist?

Better yet, *how* did it resist?

The energy managed to oppose him.

He had to try another tactic.

Jason scrambled, sending more power out from him, searching for some way to use that energy and to see if there might be something more within it. Power bubbled up from within him. That power came slowly, building gradually, and the more he felt it, the more certain he was that he wasn't reaching for what he needed.

Jason borrowed as much power as he could from the forest dragon, calling upon as much energy as he could from his own connection with the dragon and the forest and the energy all around him. Finally, as he pushed, he could feel the surge of energy as it exploded away from him.

He used that and drove it outward.

There was power around him.

It was the power of dragons. The power of someone else using illusion.

That he was able to feel that other power suggested to Jason that it was Jessica. She was holding onto enough power that she was able to draw upon the energy of the dragons, and he had to fight off what she was doing.

He used all of the power of the other dragons, letting it join together. In doing so, Jason could feel something else within it.

Janeya ran alongside him. She held onto her connection to the dragons as she ran. By default, she reached for the energy of the dragons she had bonded to, much like he reached for the dragon energy he was most bonded to. Each of them had a different connection, one that was stronger than he expected.

Jason continued to use that of his familiar misfits, not borrowing from the energy otherwise.

"She's out there," he said. "Jessica. She has power. It's different than the kind of power that most Dragon Souls have. Hers gives her the ability to override what I have done."

Janeya motioned for him to slow. When he did, she turned to him. "There are some who have this ability that you described."

"Not all of the Dragon Souls have the same power."

"No. The power these Dragon Souls possess is different. At least from what Lorren always told me. He warned me there was a kind of power out there, some different magic that existed, where the people who had the ability to connect to the dragons could do so more directly than others. I was one of them, but so was he."

Jason nodded. "It's the same thing I possess. I can connect to the dragon the way that others cannot."

"But it's something more than that," she said, looking over at him. "Lorren never had the opportunity to tell me. He warned me that when I found out, it would change everything that I knew." She shrugged. "Lorren had a way of talking like that. He liked to make everything seem as if it were grander."

"Did he say anything about the rulers of Lorach?"

"Only that I needed to avoid them," she said. "He feared them. He feared the control they had over the dragons. Which is why I think he used his influence on the dragons the way he did."

"There has to be something more to it," he said.

"I don't know what else might be. All I know is that he—"

Janeya didn't have the opportunity to finish. A burst of power built around them.

Jason looked around, but he didn't see anything. It troubled him that there was still nothing other than that sense of illusion. He pushed out again, drawing upon his own power. When he did, he felt the crashing of the illusion.

It faded, flickering. When it did, he realized something.

They weren't alone.

He looked over at Janeya. "Did you see that?" She nodded slowly. "I think it's Dragon Souls," he said.

He had seen the Dragon Souls multiple times recently; they had been going after bones each time. How many Dragon Souls were there going to be now?

The last time he had encountered them, there had been multiple Dragon Souls per dragon. If they had the same again, would they be strong enough to withstand an attack?

Jason pulled upon the power within him, focusing on it, letting energy build within him. When it did, he turned and looked around. He squeezed, surging power away. Once again, there came a shimmering, a flickering as the illusion started to fade.

Jason added his own connection, his touch to the illusion, and he changed reality.

Janeya added to it.

He recognized the way she augmented him, the assistance she gave him.

Jason pulled upon that power, using it to help. As he did, he pushed again.

Suddenly, the shimmering around him solidified. Jason could make out people around him, a dozen Dragon Souls. They were dressed in dragonskin, and each of them had a glowing object clutched in hand. Dragon pearls.

Power emanated from them, and he feared that the moment they were able to see him, they would target him, attacking him in unison. A dozen Dragon Souls should not be more than he could withstand, but it was not only him he feared for. It was the others with him and his concern to keep those dragons safe.

Distantly, he felt something more.

The north wind. The cold from high overhead. The energy of the ice dragon—only not necessarily from the ice dragon. He used that.

Flinging his arms out to either side, ice shot from him, streaking toward the Dragon Souls. He twisted, feeling the resistance around him starting to fade, shifting a little bit. Jason continued to push, adding more power, using everything in his ability to override that energy, and threw icicles again.

How am I doing this?

It was something to consider another time.

As he held onto that power, he continued to fling the energy of the north.

The longer he did this, the more he began to feel something changing.

He pushed again. Cold whipped around him.

When he had used cold before, he had done so with an illusion.

He had shifted reality, using that energy in order to be able to summon that cold, to create it around him, but in this case, what he drew upon was not necessarily the illusion, and he didn't have to even shift anything. This was him calling upon the cold, creating a swirling wind mixed with snow and sleet and the energy of the north.

It raged around him.

Jason stood in the midst of it, feeling that energy, feeling something familiar about it, a sense of power that roared within him.

He had known that power and that cold his entire life. He had known that energy, and he had known throughout his entire life that there was some way to use it. As he focused on that power, Jason let it rage within him, roaring up through him. He filled with that power. He didn't fight it.

There was no reason to fight it. Jason could feel that energy; he could feel the way it flowed and the way that power needed to be unleashed. Cold came through him.

Jason called it down.

A burst of ice lightning streaked from the sky.

When he had felt it before, it had come through the ice dragon, and this time, it had come because Jason had summoned it.

And then everything was quiet.

He looked over at Janeya and found her watching him.

"That isn't the power of the dragons," she whispered.

"I don't know what it is," he said.

"I don't either, but I fear we need to find out."

There might not be time.

Now that the Dragon Souls were down, the resistance shifted and there was no more pressure building around him. Jason pushed against it, drawing on the power of the forest dragon. When he did, everything shifted around him again.

People appeared.

For a moment, Jason thought they were Dragon Souls, but that wasn't it at all.

They were the people of Dragon Haven.

And they were all in front of him.

19

There were hundreds lining the road, all those who had an affinity for the dragons, far more than he ever would've imagined that Dragon Haven contained, but all of them seemed sensitive to the power of the summons. Some of the people were dressed in jacket and pants while others were dressed in their small clothes, as if they had been called out of bed.

Were Sarah and Henry down there?

What of his mother and sister?

Others that he knew. The Dragon Guard. Even William.

He couldn't tell. It was difficult to see through the illusion, and other than that they formed a line, he could not make out much about them.

"How are there so many?" Janeya asked.

They marched, heading in a line along the ground. Somehow, whatever power that Jessica used on them called them forward. Somehow, she must've found some way to summon these people, using power she didn't have before.

Jason stared at the people of Dragon Haven, horror filling him. It looked as if they were in some sort of trance. These were people that he knew. People he cared about. All of them were drawn.

But not *all* of the people of Dragon Haven, though.

As Jason looked along the line of people, he couldn't help but wonder where the others were.

There were hundreds here, but not the thousands that occupied Dragon Haven.

The ones here consisted of those he knew to be in the Dragon Guard. Henry. Sarah would have to be here. Maybe William?

People who were dragon sensitive.

"I don't really know," Jason said.

"What are they doing?"

"It seems that they're responding to a summons, though they shouldn't. I thought that by shattering Jessica's illusion, they would be able to get rid of the effect, but..."

Even as he focused on it, the illusion started to form again, taking hold. Jason tried to stand amidst it, feeling the effect of it, but the illusion formed around him, yet excluded him. It was almost as if he were separated from it. What about Janeya?

"Do you see the illusion Jessica is forming?"

It had to be her, didn't it?

Jason tried to look beyond but could not see what he needed. He couldn't tell the source of the illusion, either, only that there *was* illusion.

She shook her head. "I don't see anything. When the pressure starts to build"—she frowned, wrinkling her eyes as she did—"they disappear. At least, they start to disappear. Then you do something and they reappear."

"I push against the illusion, but I have to actively maintain that connection in order to know just what they're doing."

"There's still the calling," she said, looking over to him. "I'm fighting it but it's almost too much."

Jason felt the pulling as well. It *was* almost too much. The dragons offered some protection, but not enough.

"Is there any way for you to separate the summons?" she asked.

"I'm not sure. I can't even tell what they're doing, or the way she's doing it."

That was the hardest part. Jason could feel the effect of the summons, but he couldn't feel just what Jessica was doing or why she was doing it. He didn't know how she could call the people of Dragon Haven.

She shouldn't be able to.

All these people were connected to the dragons, and all of them marched forward. Jason wasn't able to intervene. The people of Dragon Haven continued to march, heading forward.

Jason tried to override the illusion and the summons—they *had* to be linked somehow—hurrying through the crowd of people. Where was Henry? Sarah? William? His sister and mother?

It was almost as if the energy Jason detected, that of the summons, was hidden from him. The people continued to move past him.

Jason pushed against it, surging outward, trying to shatter the illusion, but it didn't seem to matter. They were focused on their march. They headed directly toward Lorach. *It would end the battle with the rebellion.*

He focused on his connection to the night dragon. It was faint, wispy, but he thought of all of the dragons, he would be the one to help Jason look for what happened to the others. The night dragon could sneak away, and given his small but fast size, Jason couldn't help but think that the night dragon would be able to look.

"Find the others," he said, sending it through the faint streamer of a connection he shared with the night dragon. "Please find them."

"I will do this."

In summoning the others, Jessica intended to end the rebellion without any fighting.

There was a part of him that wondered if perhaps that was not necessarily a bad outcome. The rebellion had lasted a long time, and the people who had been a part of the rebellion had battled for more time than most even knew. If they were somehow able to stop that fighting, able to end the rebellion, end the war, the people of Lorach and the people from Dragon Haven could come back together, and…

And the dragons would still be held captive.

Even if they were able to come back together, that didn't mean the dragons would be freed. That was what Jason ultimately wanted, the reason for the rebellion.

More than that, it was what the people of Dragon Haven wanted. They had wanted the dragons to be safe, freed, not under the danger of any summons, and not under the training of the Dragon Souls. If he did nothing, the dragons would be in perpetual danger.

Jason focused on the energy within him, feeling for the power that grew within him, and he continued to call to it, letting it flow. He recognized something more within it.

The power pulsated.

"Do you feel that?" he asked Janeya. "There is something about the summons. I feel it pulsing."

"Where is it calling them?"

Jason frowned, focusing on that power. The people marching in front of him were all dirty. Filthy. Some of them were half-clothed. They all looked weak. Some were barefoot. All of them compelled.

"Lorach. It has to be." Though there *was* something about the direction they were heading that didn't feel right.

But Jason had only been there a few times, and knowing the power of Lorach, knowing what was there, he recognized that there was a certain distinct energy to it. It came from the dragons, but it came from something else as well.

Maybe it wasn't coming from Lorach, at least not directly.

He needed to see from above. In the distance, he felt the ice dragon flying high overhead. Did he even need the power of the ice dragon in order to travel? Jason didn't even know any longer.

He held onto power, letting it fill him. Then he summoned the ice dragon.

The ice dragon streaked out of the sky, hovering overhead. Jason grabbed for Janeya, and he used a burst of cold energy to shoot them upward. When he landed on the ice dragon's back, he tapped on the dragon's side and they began to move.

They flew, traveling quickly. He could feel that power flowing within them and continued to recognize the beacon in the distance.

"Are you aware of that?" he asked the dragon. The ice dragon roared. "What is it?"

"Something that should not be here," the dragon said.

The dragon pushed an image across their connection to him. It was unexpected. It was a shimmering oblong shape with colors streaking through it and energy radiating from it.

An egg?

Jason's breath caught. "Why would that be here? And why wouldn't Lorach have it better guarded?"

In the image the dragon revealed to him, there was nothing but the egg. Nothing more that suggested they feared losing the egg.

But if Dragon Haven had been defeated, there would be no reason to fear.

"What is it?" Janeya asked.

"An egg," he whispered.

It had to be another attempt to create a dragon misfit. Considering how Jason had seen Lorach chasing dragon bones several times, it had to be the same reason.

Jessica wanted her own dragon misfits.

Jessica wanted that power. She understood the energy of the dragon misfits. She had seen the evidence of what happened when dragon misfits were hatched. Not only through what Jason had experienced, but through what Lorren had done.

Those dragons were powerful, and he could imagine her wanting to use that power to control the rest of the dragons.

They raced toward it, but even as they did, Jason felt something else. Dragons.

The sky was filled with darkened forms of dragons. A hundred of them, possibly more, all of them blackening the sky. Seeing the dragons flying like this was something Jason had longed for. He had wanted to see the dragons circling and flying freely.

But not like this.

These dragons were not freed.

For a moment, Jason thought that this was nothing more than another illusion.

He had seen illusions like this before. It would be similar to the kind of illusion Therin had once used on him, but when they neared, Jason could feel the power of the dragons, and they were familiar to him. This wasn't any kind of illusion that he had ever detected before. If it was, then it was a powerful one.

Jason tapped on the dragon's side.

Some of the dragons he saw in front of him looked familiar. There were several that Jason recognized, dragons he had once freed, and now were captured once again. Somehow, Jessica had found a way to overpower what he had done.

Anger flowed up from someplace deep within him.

He would have to find a way to overpower the energy they were using to control the dragons. He might be able to borrow from the power from each of the dragons, but what he needed was a greater connection. He closed his eyes, trying to borrow that energy from the dragons, and then started to push it out.

"There are too many," Janeya said.

He hated that she was right. "There are too many," he agreed.

"What do you propose?"

"I don't really know. The people of Dragon Haven are marching here, and I don't really know what she intends to do with them." He turned to the ice dragon, focusing on the power within him. "Are you certain that there's an egg here?"

"I am."

The ice dragon sent that awareness to him, connecting Jason to the power of the egg, allowing him to feel the energy flowing from it. The people of Dragon Haven were still a ways behind them. Why bring them *here*?

He tapped on the ice dragon's side and they streaked upward.

The ice dragon moved with incredible speed, flying high and quickly. Jason held onto the ice dragon by the spikes, and he tried to look down, using the ice dragon's eyesight in order to see the Dragon Soul dragons, but there were still so many that it made it difficult to focus on them.

He looked down from the ice dragon, watching as those dragons circled. Sadness filled him.

"Why do I feel… sadness… from you?" Janeya asked.

"There was a time when I feared the dragons," Jason said softly. "And then there was a time when I began to understand the dragons were different than anything that I had ever known before. I began to realize that they were misunderstood, and that the belief I had of the dragons was different than the truth about them. I vowed to do everything I could in order to protect them."

He squeezed his eyes shut, but even with his eyes closed, he could still see. He borrowed from the energy of the ice dragon and was able to see far down below, even without his eyes open. "And now I find that I want to protect them, but I don't know if I can. It seems everything I have tried to do, every way I've attempted to intervene on behalf of the dragons, has led me here, but here is a place where I can do nothing."

"There are things that you can still do," she said.

"I'm not entirely convinced there are," Jason said. "Had I not intervened, had the dragon misfits not been freed and bound to me, I couldn't help but wonder if Lorach would have stopped attempting to come after them."

In the time he'd been working with the others from Dragon Haven, he had come to know that the rebellion wasn't really all that effective. There were aspects of it that had continued fighting. The Dragon Guard had continued to battle, trying to put some distance between Lorach and Dragon Haven, using their attacks to disrupt Lorach from learning where to even find Dragon Haven. Still, everything he had done didn't matter the way he once believed it did.

"There was a time when I would've wanted to see hundreds of dragons flying the way they are, flying apparently freely, no Dragon Souls riding atop them." He closed his eyes briefly. There was that vision again, the one he *wanted* almost as much as the dragons. And it was here… only it was not quite what he'd dreamed. "There's something wrong to it, as well."

The energy of the dragons was all off. As he stared, focusing in the distance, looking down into the darkness of the swirling dragons, Jason could feel just how wrong it was, and he was aware of the power that was down there, power that seemed to influence those dragons, power that seemed to affect them in a way that it should not.

As much as he wanted to overwhelm it, he couldn't.

He stared, feeling the energy, feeling the power, and distantly, he was still aware of that pulsation and that summons that continued to draw the dragons, but also the people of Dragon Haven, toward this location.

The egg. That was what this was tied to, though Jason didn't have any idea why she would be calling them here toward an egg.

He had to help the people of Dragon Haven. And the dragons.

That had been his purpose since being freed from his village.

Protecting the dragons was obvious, but there remained a debt he owed to Dragon Haven. He owed them his safety, a debt that had permitted him to find something he hadn't known before.

Purpose.

When he had been in his village, Jason hadn't known any purpose. He had known nothing other than the cold and the torment and the sadness that life in the village offered. It had taught him about the cold, about being taunted and bullied, and it had taught him about camouflage. It had taught him lessons he had needed to first connect to the dragons. They were lessons he had not known he needed, but without them, Jason would never have been able to connect to the misfits the way that he had.

Coming to Dragon Haven had changed that for him. It had given him something else, something he had not known, something he had not even known he had wanted.

It had given him a bond and a connection he still didn't fully understand. It had given him a way of reaching the dragons, and it had given him people who were like him, people who wanted for something more than just themselves.

Perhaps that was the greatest part of it all.

Because he had come to Dragon Haven, he began to know the power of the dragons.

He closed his eyes, feeling the dragons there, the sense that flowed out around him. In time, he had freed a considerable number of dragons. He still wanted to free the remaining dragons, and he still wanted to do everything in his power in order to protect them all. The difference now was that he didn't know if he would be able to do so.

He took a deep breath, letting it out.

"After we deal with this egg, we have to go to Lorach," he said to the ice dragon. "It's time to end this for good."

"Yes," the ice dragon said.

"I don't know if we can do it," Jason said. Or should. Heading to Lorach might be exactly what Jessica wanted him to do. He turned to Janeya. "We have to disrupt what Lorach has done to the people of Dragon Haven, along with the dragons I had once freed."

He looked over at Janeya and could feel her within the connection to the earth dragon. That connection seemed to be building the longer that he shared it with her, and she shared with him an understanding of her desire.

He looked over to Janeya. She had been willing to help so far, but what he asked from her now would be something more.

He would be asking her to fight.

"You don't have to do this. The fight with Lorach is not yours. It's mine. I can return you to wherever you want to go."

And he didn't even need to return her. The dragon could do so. Any of the dragons would do so. All Jason had to do was ask.

"You're doing it for them?" She swept her gaze around, looking up at the other dragons.

Jason nodded.

"If you're doing it for the dragons, it must be a good fight."

"It is."

She looked at the others around her before turning back to him. "Then I will help."

20

The misfit dragons circled overhead. The newly hatched dragons were massive and immense, and they moved swiftly, powered in ways that the dragons of Lorach were not. It was not just anger within them, but other powers of the world. The swarm of dragons showed him the way the skies should look if dragons were permitted to fly freely.

The ice dragon streaked toward the rest of the misfits, and Jason looked through the ice dragon's eyesight, searching for signs of Lorach. They had to be here somewhere. They wouldn't have left the egg unguarded.

All he saw were dragons. Hundreds of dragons.

And the misfits.

They stayed together, and somehow the misfits remained shielded from the drawing off of the egg. Jason would have to consider that later.

"There was a time when I would've given anything to have seen these dragons flying like this," she whispered. "I can't help wondering what they sacrificed to travel like this. I can feel the conflicted energy within them."

Jason connected to her, and as he did, he realized there was something more within the dragons. He wouldn't necessarily call it a conflicted energy, though he did recognize there was some aspect of their power that troubled them.

"It's getting stronger," Janeya said. She clenched her jaw, and strangely, through the connection that he shared with her. "Do you think this will be enough?"

Jason didn't know. Even with all of these dragons, it still didn't feel to him like they had enough power to overwhelm the dragons he'd seen swirling around the egg. If all of those dragons were under the influence of the Dragon Souls, controlled in the way their power could be used against them, then Jason didn't know if they would be enough.

He couldn't help but wonder if the drawing was an attempt to call power like the eggs in the boneyard had called power. It had to be similar. That energy had drawn rapidly, as the eggs in the boneyard had developed.

This seemed so similar to him.

Strangely, it was also stronger.

Jason had no intention of harming the people of Dragon Haven. He had come hoping to rescue them, but because of the danger from the influence of Jessica and the others of Lorach, he didn't know if he could.

He stared into the distance, sitting astride the ice dragon, feeling the power of the dragon underneath him, that energy that continued to flow, building with each moment the dragon spread his wings, beating at the air with the frosty north wind gusting beneath him.

It felt to him that all of this had been building up to a battle he was ill prepared to handle. It was a battle Jessica had waged her entire life. It was a battle she had trained for, which meant that it was a battle she was far more equipped to win.

Jason shifted so that he could look down and see the people of Dragon Haven more effectively. He stared, trying to get a better glimpse of them, but from his vantage, even borrowing the ice dragon's eyesight, he could not see anything more.

Only the long lines stretching across the ground.

He had to turn away.

They weren't here for the people of Dragon Haven yet. They would have to be a part of what he and the misfit dragons did, but first he had to ensure that whatever Jessica attempted to do with the freed dragons—and the dragon egg—was stopped.

Far below them, dragons swirled, blackening the sky.

Somehow, they had to stop these dragons from attacking. "I'll take any suggestions you might have," Jason said.

"The dragons seem to have an idea," Janeya said.

Jason looked over at the dragons, realizing she was right. As he watched, he realized the dragons had begun a circle, but it was more than just the way they circled. They formed a pattern, and within that pattern, he felt a growing power. It was the power of the ice and the northern wind. It was the power of heat and the anger of lava and metal. It was the power of the earth rumbling distantly. It was the power of the wind and that of illusion. It was even the power of the wild storms raging in the distance. All of that built from within the dragons as they circled. It crackled between them, radiating all around.

"What are they doing?" he asked the ice dragon.

The ice dragon roared, and through the connection, Jason realized he needed to look at not only what the ice dragon and the other dragons were doing, but what the night dragon did.

The forest dragon sent darkness swirling among the other dragons. Within that darkness came a sense of energy, and it seemed as if it subdued what the other misfit dragons created.

Not to squelch that power, but to mask it.

The forest dragon created an illusion.

It was a kind of illusion that was different than what Jason had learned to create. This wasn't an illusion to alter the image of reality. This was simply hiding the power, blackening it out, changing day to night.

Thunder rumbled and lightning crackled within a storm cloud, coming from not only the storm dragon but from these other dragons, all of them having some distant connection to the night dragon and the storm dragon. As they held onto that power, and as it continued to crackle around them, Jason searched for something within it that he might better understand.

Only, as he focused, he felt nothing other than that growing buildup of power.

Suddenly, the dragons below began to call. The sound echoed, piercing the masking that the night dragon created, the shriek of a hundred dragons coming to him.

The Dragon Soul dragons knew something was taking place.

Even with the dragons knowing what was taking place, Jason didn't know if there was anything they were able to do to stop it. Given the power of a dozen female dragons and all the other misfits, there might not be anything they could do against it.

Jason stayed on the ice dragon's back, feeling that energy building around him. It was their attack. Only, what kind of an attack?

The pulsation around him persisted, that strange drawing sense.

There was something about all of this that struck him as the way Jessica wanted to pull power. If it was about misfits, then did she intend to destroy them or was this only her way of trying to control them?

Jason had been to the boneyard and recognized a sensation similar to this, but it wasn't quite the same.

Maybe it could not be the same.

"I have to be down there," he said. "That's the only way I can deal with this summons." He had to help the egg.

Wasn't helping dragons what he'd always done, anyway?

It might do what Jessica wanted, but Jason thought he could save the egg—and the dragon—and use *his* connections to ensure she didn't get to use them.

"How do you expect to get down there? There are too many dragons."

Jason met Janeya's eyes and held her gaze for a moment.

This was somebody he had not known very long, but somebody that he now felt a strange and strong connection to, somebody he wanted to ensure remained protected, avoiding danger. There was one way that he could watch over her.

"Protect her," he said to the ice dragon.

With that, Jason jumped.

The fall jarred something within him.

Wind whistled around him, cold and biting, the sound overwhelming. Despite that, there was a strange calmness everywhere around him, something that left him feeling as if he were dropping, but dropping alone.

Perhaps he should have been more careful. Perhaps he should have taken the ice dragon with him, descending together, rather than jumping and plunging, risking himself in this manner, only Jason wasn't sure that going with the dragon would have permitted him to penetrate the dragons swirling around. This was something he needed to do by himself. This was something he could do by himself.

The wind seemed to intensify. This speed with which he dropped increased.

Panic set in.

For a moment, Jason questioned what he had done and the reason he had done it.

This was foolish. This was death. Almost certain death.

Only, Jason knew it wasn't. He had used his power in a way he knew he could control. That was what he had to do. He needed to reach the egg and keep it from feeding—and off the dragons, along with the people of Dragon Haven.

He reached the energy swirling off the misfit dragons. It crackled around him, the energy of lightning and thunder and ice and fire and everything.

Then he was through it.

Jason barely had a chance to react.

Once through that cloud of power, he realized what these other dragons were doing. They created a shell of power.

That shell held back danger. That shell held back the darkness.

It was power.

Jason fell through the heart of it.

Somewhere distantly, dragons shrieked. It came from overhead, and then other dragons shrieked, calling after him.

Jason ignored that. He focused instead on the power within him, the power of his fall, and trying to control it all.

That was what he had to do now. He had to control it.

Somehow, Jason had to find that energy within him, a way to hold onto that power and to maintain his control over it. He began to focus on the energy of the north, the cold wind.

As he did, he could feel it flowing within him.

Darkness swirled past him.

Jason was dropping so fast that he barely gathered that it was a dragon before he was past.

A streak of flames shot toward him, but Jason, wrapped in the cold, ignored it.

He wondered if it would even bother him anyway. He was tied into the cold of the north, but he was also tied into the heat and fire of the iron dragon.

By holding onto that connection, Jason wondered if he might be able to use that power in a way that would grant him a greater connection, something more than what he already possessed. Jason held onto that energy, letting it fill him.

He had to focus on the power within him in order to not crash into the ground. It involved using the energies that he connected to. Not just the northern wind that he had somehow bonded to, but that of the iron dragon, perhaps the earth dragon, and even that of the forest dragon.

He used that power, pushing outward, attempting to slow himself.

Finally, as he started to slow, Jason turned.

Dragons were everywhere around him.

He dropped through them.

Suddenly, dragons turned toward him.

Jason used a hint of wind and then reacted again, twisting.

It took his connection to the wind to cycle him down.

That was what he needed to do. Jason held onto that energy, feeling the way that he was cycling, and began to focus on it, feeling the way that it needed to spin, using that same connection to the power within him.

It was that same wind he had known his entire life.

Jason swirled.

By holding onto that connection, feeling the wind as it swirled around him, he understood there was something more, some other aspect of it that he could hold onto. He swirled the way ice had always swirled around him when he was younger. It was a familiar feeling.

Dragons swirled around him, but much like the wind, his swirling avoided the obstacles. He avoided the danger. He avoided everything as he dropped toward the ground.

He lost himself in the swirling of the power, the energy that continued to cycle around him, and Jason let that energy continue to build as it circled around him. He wanted nothing more than to hold onto it, to see if there might be something within the swirling that he could use, but even as it continued circling around him, there was just the energy.

He let that power work around him.

By holding onto it, Jason recognized the way the north wind held onto him, circling around him, giving him the power that he needed. Jason embraced that energy and power, and by holding onto it, he continued swirling, circling, moving.

He felt one with it.

And then he slammed into something.

He lost control. He gusted off to the side, pain shooting through him.

He borrowed the energy of the ice and the iron dragon, sending it through him. A healing wave washed over him.

Then he slammed into something else.

Again, hot fire raced through him, and again he had to respond, pushing the healing energy through him.

What is it?

Dragons.

As he slammed into the dragons, he realized he had fallen too far. Too fast. He no longer had control.

Now he was nearing the ground. Now he felt the energy as it continued to work around him, swirling, and he couldn't tell if there was going to be anything that he would be able to do to stop the nearest dragon from—

Another dragon slammed into him.

Jason cried out.

He embraced the cold. He embraced the fire within him.

Everything exploded.

A bubble of energy worked around him, forming a barrier.

It was the raging winds of the north. It was the angry fires of lava deep beneath the ground. It was the heat and the cold. It was everything. Jason used that energy, and he let it fill him, holding onto it, and power coursed through him.

Now the barrier surrounded him entirely. He continued to drop, now holding onto the barrier, determined to ensure that when he did land, he would not be too far off course. The distant sense of the egg pulsing below him guided him, and Jason knew he needed to find his way toward it, to focus on that power and energy, to feel where the egg was guiding him. As he flowed with the north wind, that power streaking him toward the ground, Jason could feel some other aspect to it. He had to welcome it. He had to know it would guide him down.

He created more of a barrier. And then he caught a flash of darkness.

The ground.

Energy came up from the ground.

He focused on that energy.

It was the egg pulsing.

As he raced toward the egg, Jason focused on the power within it, and used it to guide him. Something about the egg felt off. It was a painful sort of sensation. As he neared it, Jason realized it was calling to the others, feeding the way the eggs in the boneyard had fed, but something about it felt wrong. There was more power building than the egg should have.

It was the last thought he had before he reversed the power of the north mountains through him, and he slowed his descent. When he landed, he came crashing next to the egg.

Seven Dragon Souls surrounded the egg.

21

The Dragon Souls stood near a pile of pale white dragon bones. They were of different sizes. Some looked like legs, some looked like ribs, and he saw part of the skull. Jason didn't have much time to process it. Whatever Lorach intended with the bones was tied to the egg, but he didn't have any idea as to what—or why.

The Dragon Souls started toward him, turning their power toward him.

They were all connected to dragon pearls.

And they were powerful.

But Jason was *more* powerful.

Connected as he was to the dragon misfits, he reacted.

He found himself reaching for heat and ice, iron and ice mixing, creating steam that surrounded him, a fog that enveloped the Dragon Souls.

From there, he used the energy of the forest dragon.

He created an illusion, an empty void all around him, and solidified it.

The Dragon Souls screamed.

A thought came to him.

Maybe it was his own, or maybe it came from the dragons, but whichever it was, Jason didn't care.

These Dragon Souls had intended to harm him. The dragons.

They had intended to do something that would destroy others.

He solidified the mist around him. Freezing it.

And then he borrowed from the earth dragon, and he collapsed it down.

The Dragon Souls disappeared.

Jason shifted the illusion and looked over to the egg, ignoring what he had done.

It was enormous. Larger than any other egg he'd seen.

He turned toward it, holding his hand out to it. This one was strange.

It was drawing upon power. It was feeding. He turned, looking at the freed dragons, then looking at the people of Dragon Haven, and he could feel the energy coming off them all.

The power continued to drain. Up close, he could tell it was drawing off him, drawing off the dragons, and drawing off the people of Dragon Haven.

Somehow, he was going to have to find a way to stop that egg from drawing the power of the others.

The egg pulsated with that power. It was simply too strong.

He could feel that the new dragons, the misfits flying overhead, had used their power. That energy continued to build, swirling around, and as Jason became aware of it, he felt something more within it. He tried to focus on that power.

He was connected to the misfits, but if he were to borrow that power, then he would be taking from them. Weakening them when they needed strength.

Jason had another possibility—holding onto the power that came through him.

It started with the north.

The energy Jason had to call upon came from the mountains. He borrowed that, letting it flow through him, and rather than pushing it into the egg, creating a ring that encircled the egg. From there, Jason added the heat and fire of the iron dragon. That energy was there within him, building, and it was that energy which he thought he could maintain, holding tightly to it.

Next, he went to the storm dragon. It crackled softly within him, a distant sense of the storms, of the weather changing. Jason had never been fully connected to that before, but as he tried to focus on it now, he could feel the energy building, the power of the dragon, the power that existed high overhead, the power of the clouds and the wind and the rain. It crackled within him and started to streak down, drifting toward him. Finally, Jason added that of the forest dragon. As he did, a rumbling echoed toward him.

He frowned.

It was a rumbling that came from the earth dragons, but why should he feel the earth dragons now? There shouldn't be a reason to be so aware of them.

Though he had a connection to one of them, Jason didn't have a connection to earth in that same way. Not yet.

Perhaps in time, Jason would develop that connection, and he would be able to understand how that power flowed within him, but for now, he didn't have it.

Only, that sense of earth continued to rumble, building up within him, feeding him its power and energy. And feeding him the power and energy of Janeya.

That sense was there within him.

He looked around. She was near.

Had the ice dragon brought her down here?

As he looked around, he searched for any sign of her, but he didn't see anything.

No sign of the ice dragon, but the sense of Janeya continued to flow through the earth connection.

It was above him.

Jason looked up and saw the shimmering of something moving high overhead.

As he did, he frowned, focusing on what he detected.

And then he understood just what it was.

Janeya had dropped from the ice dragon.

He had been separated from the ice dragon and hadn't

paid any attention, but now that he was focusing on that energy and that connection, he realized what she had done, and he felt her descending.

As he thought he needed to add something to what she did to slow herself, he realized that wasn't even necessary. She had the power of the earth, and she brought it up in a way that allowed her to slow. Three Dragon Souls tried to attack, but Janeya used blasts of earth mixed with smoke, and they tumbled to the ground, crashing near him. Before Jason had the chance to do anything, the earth rumbled, separating enough for it to swallow the Dragon Souls.

She came to land on the ground next to him.

"I wasn't about to let you have the only fun."

"I'm not so sure this is fun," Jason said. "Can you feel the power coming off it? I think the egg is drawing on the power of the other dragons, along with trying to draw on the power of the people of Dragon Haven. Maybe even us."

"The same reason the eggs in the boneyard did. It needs to feed."

He had to stop this summoning, somehow, though he had no idea what was going to take for him to stop it as he focused on it. He could feel the energy of it and feel how the egg attempted to feed, but what did attempt to feed upon?

Could it be the people of Dragon Haven? Was it their dragons? Or was it all of it?

Whatever it was, Jason had to stop it.

"I sensed you doing something," she said. "I'm not exactly sure what it is that you're doing, only that I can feel it."

"I'm trying to separate the egg from us."

As he held onto that power, he could feel the energy of the egg flowing through him, though. Jason reasserted his control over the cold and ice, adding the heat and fire, finally adding the storms. To that sense around him, he detected Janeya adding energy of the earth.

She shrugged at him. "I can feel it was needed."

Finally, Jason focused on the power he had been connected to through the forest dragon. That power connected him, binding him in a way that allowed him to use it. But it also allowed him to use that power on everything around him.

The egg was different than those in the boneyard. Larger. Stronger.

He had no idea what Jessica did to make this egg, but he worried about what it meant.

There had to be some way for him to shield the egg and the power it was sending off of it.

Illusion.

That was what he could do.

With a strong enough illusion, Jason thought he could prevent the egg from drawing off everyone around it. At least for now.

He created a barrier around him and then solidified it. It created a shielding, nothing more, and he didn't try to twist the reality around him too much. That would potentially toss him out of the illusion and toss the egg out of an illusion. All he needed was to hold it.

"What did you do?" Janeya asked.

"I used the forest dragon, making it real," he said.

"It wasn't real otherwise?"

"It is, but this is something more."

He squeezed power and pushed it around the egg.

The sense of pressure coming from the egg began to ease. Jason held onto the power and could feel Janeya using her connections to do the same thing.

"How long can we hold this?" she asked.

"I don't know. I don't know how long we have to hold it," he said.

"Long enough for the dragons to escape?"

Jason looked up, but he didn't know if he could feel anything from the dragons high overhead. He could feel their energy, and he suspected there was something to that energy that he might be able to better understand, but it would take time. Unfortunately, time was something he didn't have right now.

He needed time to get the people of Dragon Haven away from here.

Jason looked high overhead, continuing to focus on the power, and he felt for something within him. Janeya took his hand.

Holding onto her, he could feel her connection, and he could feel the energy of earth through her, and he could feel something more. Confidence. She didn't fear this egg, and she didn't fear for the people of Dragon Haven. She didn't fear for the dragons.

These weren't her people.

Which gave her the ability to act in a way that Jason couldn't.

Turning toward the egg, Jason held onto the energy within him. The egg continued to pulse. Jason strained against it. Even as he did, he wasn't sure if the way he used power was enough. He couldn't tell if he were drawing upon enough energy or whether he was pushing out too much.

Janeya held onto his hand, squeezing tightly. Power came from her, the energy of the earth, a soothing sensation that rolled through him. He had to seal off the egg.

"The egg is resisting me." The more that Jason focused on the sense of the egg, the more certain he was that was exactly what he detected.

It was fighting him.

More and more energy from the egg seemed to seep out, convincing Jason of that. If the egg was fighting him, then somehow he was going to have to find a way to overpower that fight, to keep it from overwhelming him.

Sealing it off like this didn't seem to be as effective. Jason tried to trap it but could feel the egg pushing. It was connected to something else. The more he held onto that power, the more certain Jason was that whatever he detected was tied to some distant and deep power.

Distantly, Jason felt the connection.

It came from Lorach.

There was some strange connection here, and it seemed to be drawing away.

Connecting to the egg, but connecting beyond it as well.

Somehow, the egg had a stream of power coming off of it that came from Lorach.

What was Jessica doing?

Somehow, this egg was tied to Lorach, and it was tied to whatever else he detected there. He had known it was bound to Lorach, but feeling the way it was connected startled him. It came from someplace distant.

Jason studied the egg.

There was heat within it, though it felt different than the eggs in the boneyard. Those had been warm, pulsating with the power of each of the great energies within the world. This one seemed to try to draw upon him, and was almost oily and unpleasant when he rested his hand upon it. He wanted to immediately withdraw away from it, only he wasn't sure that he could or should just yet.

There was only one way to stop this. He had to feed the egg the same way he had fed those in the boneyard. When he did, he had to think that he could overpower Lorach.

Jason held onto the power within him, feeling the energy flowing from each of the different dragons. He tried to call upon that and then started to push it outward. As he did, the dragon within the egg started to pull on him.

It happened gradually, but then began to pull even

more, the energy starting to siphon Jason, drawing even more power off until he could feel nothing but the energy coming off the egg, funneling through him. There was a considerable amount of power that flowed. It was that of the northern mountains. It was that of the flame from the iron dragon. It was that of illusion. It was even that of the night dragon, cascading energy around all of it.

That power filled Jason, and it poured into the egg.

He started to step away but hesitated.

He had to guide the egg. He had to ensure that the egg would not harm anyone else.

Suddenly, the egg cracked, and there was a small dragonling inside it.

It was tiny, not nearly as large as the other dragons had been.

It might be small, but as Jason probed for the power in the dragon, he couldn't help but feel as if it were incredible. Strangely, there still seemed to be that streamer of a connection to Lorach.

Jason had to sever that, somehow.

With another powerful misfit, he couldn't help but wonder what else was going to change. As this one got as large as the other misfits, how would the world change?

They had grown larger because of how the night dragon had fed them.

Jason pushed a bit of power out, connecting to this small dragon, and then sent a bit of soothing energy through, creating an illusion around the dragon and then solidifying it.

The dragon fell asleep.

Hopefully it would hold.

He turned to Janeya. "We're going to have to step outside of this illusion."

He took Janeya's hand, and drawing upon the north energy, that power deep within him, Jason pushed off. It blasted them up and beyond the illusion. As soon as he was through the darkness that swirled around them, he saw the dragons high overhead. They seemed to fly without the same purpose and intensity that they had before.

Jason circled with them, staring off into the distance, straining for the people of Dragon Haven. They continued to march this way.

"Do you still feel it?" He looked over at Janeya. "I can't tell if hatching the egg has separated the summons or not."

There was still a strange and powerful draw from Lorach. Jason had no idea what it was, only that it stretched away from the dragon.

But not from anything else around him the way it had when the egg had been feeding.

"I don't know," she said, closing her eyes. "I can feel *something*, but I can't tell if it's what you did or if it's something else."

Jason looked up at the dragons.

He focused on the ice dragon, and the ice dragon dove toward him. A surge of ice lightning streaked with it, clearing a path through the other dragons. They darted off to the side, giving the ice dragon the freedom to descend.

Jason chuckled softly. "I should've thought of doing that when I dove."

"You can do that?"

"Not as well as the dragon, but something similar."

The ice dragon hovered over him.

"Do you detect anything?" Jason asked the dragon.

The dragon circled overhead. He was powerful, and he radiated the energy of the cold and the north, and his wings battered at the air, holding himself above Jason.

"I can't tell if what we have done has been effective."

There was only one way to tell. He had to talk with the people of Dragon Haven. He had to know whether or not the influence was still there.

He looked at the ice dragon. "Take me to them."

22

Jason held onto the ice dragon, and they flew overhead. By looking down through the ice dragon's eyes, he could see the landscape shifting below him. It was a line of people, making it difficult to pick out one person from another. There were hundreds of people, and they were filthy, but not all of them. Some he recognized as Dragon Guard, dressed in their dragonskin, though others were and tattered clothing that had worn out. He had no idea if they were still influenced.

Overhead, the misfits still circled. The other dragons had disappeared, leaving them isolated, as if by hatching the egg, those dragons had been pulled somewhere else.

The misfits had not followed. Jason wondered if it was even necessary. They could track what he could feel of the dragons without needing to chase them.

"We're going to have to get closer," Jason said to the ice dragon.

Janeya shifted in front of him, holding tightly to the ice dragon. She seemed comfortable on the ice dragon from the beginning, so different than anyone—even those in Dragon Haven—had been with the misfits. Janeya had a connection to them, different than even Sarah had.

I have to stop thinking like that.

He stared into the distance. A steady sense started to build within him, a calling sensation. He grabbed for Janeya. "Are you ready?"

When she nodded, Jason jumped.

Jumping this time was less concerning than the last time. He understood what he needed to do, and as his fall carried him down, he used the power from the cold northern wind to guide himself down.

At the last moment, Jason blasted the energy through him, using the cold to swirl him gently down to the ground. Wind whistled around him, and when he landed, he did so surrounded by Dragon Haven people. He had seen the people of Dragon Haven on the ground, marching.

He couldn't help but wonder where the others that were not dragon sensitive had gone. He closed his eyes briefly, focusing on the night dragon, and though he searched, he did not see anything.

What had Jessica done with them?

There were hundreds of them, all marching forward, ignoring him, as if whatever had happened to them had left them unmindful of everything else in the world around them. He still didn't know how Jessica had done it.

Not the egg.

Had it been the egg, they would have improved by now. He looked over at Janeya. "It's not better. There's still something here."

"I feel it, but I don't know what it is."

He could feel her holding onto power through her connection to the dragons, and he could feel the rumbling of energy through her that came from the earth dragons, but it also came from the mist dragons and the smoke dragons.

Now that he was on the ground, he looked at all of the people of Dragon Haven. As Jason stared around him, he could see them in a line. A blankness washed over them, and Jason needed to find a way past it.

He found a woman he recognized, a dark-haired woman named Mandy who had worked with Sarah's parents. "Where's Sarah?" he asked, touching her on the shoulder. The woman looked at him, a dazed expression in her eyes. "Mandy. Where is Sarah?"

Mandy stared at him with a lost expression in her eyes.

Jason moved on.

How many others were going to be like Mandy?

That worried him. It meant that maybe there was something else going on. Maybe Lorach had some other plan at play.

Maybe they all would suffer, all of them struggling with the nature of this attack.

Jason began to work his way through the line of people. He continued to search for anyone who might be able to help him. By looking through the crowd, he strained, wanting to find someone. Anyone.

Where was Sarah?

He had felt her, Henry, and William from above.

Even his sister and mother.

All he had to do was see if he could follow the energy they put off.

Jason was aware of that energy. He could feel it and the way his sense of them built within him. He recognized something about it, a familiarity. It was different than detecting their dragons. This was detecting them, and their connection.

Why should I be suddenly aware of it?

He darted through the Dragon Haven people, moving from one to the next, focusing on the power he had detected before. That energy was there, that sense of familiarity existed, and all it took was for him to reach it.

There.

Jason approached, moving through the line of people. Janeya held onto his hand.

He found Henry first.

The old Dragon Soul was dressed in his dragonskin, and he had a sense of power to him. He was a burly man, with a thick beard, and even without the heavy furs he'd worn when Jason had first met him, something was intimidating about him. His dark eyes stared blankly, and his hands were empty, hanging loosely at his sides. He shuffled forward, his lumbering gate making him look as if he were injured. Maybe that was nothing more than just the effect of the summons and the trance that had been placed upon them.

"Henry," Jason said, touching Henry on the arm. Nothing changed. He stared blankly. "It's Jason Dreshen," Jason said.

Still, there was no reaction from Henry. Jason touched him again, trying to tap on him to get his attention, but there was nothing.

Only the confusion in his eyes.

He continued looking at Henry, watching to make sure that he wasn't building any power. He added energy to his tapping, using a hint of water and heat, mixing them together, sending it washing over Henry. Henry blinked, and for a moment that confusion cleared, but then it returned.

"Something's not quite right yet," Jason said, looking back toward the hatched dragonling. There was a vague sense of it, but also the illusion he'd formed around it in order to shield the dragon from Lorach. "I thought hatching the egg would make a difference but it hasn't."

He pushed power out, focusing on it, letting it wash over Henry, trying to heal him. That still didn't work.

"What if there's another egg?" Janeya asked.

"We'll have to find it." He focused on the dragons overhead. They would have to help, as well.

He would deal with that after he separated the people of Dragon Haven from what Jessica and the egg did to them. First, he would do that, then he could figure out if there were other eggs like this to be concerned by.

Could I use illusion?

If he were to do that, he thought that he might be able to bring Henry back, but it would involve twisting the illusion in such a way that would carry him out of the mind trap that he was in.

Jason had used something like this before.

He studied the man in front of him, feeling the power coming off him.

He was fighting.

That was why Jason had been able to detect something. Henry struggled with whatever was happening to him. What must he be experiencing? It was within his mind, the same sort of power and illusion that Jason had once experienced when he had gone to Lorach.

"Maybe there *is* another egg still feeding and calling them forward," he said.

How could he separate them from what Lorach had done?

Healing hadn't been enough.

A strong enough illusion *might* work, but it would have to be powerful.

Jason focused on the energy of the forest dragon, borrowing from her power, letting that sense of energy fill him. There was something within it that he needed.

The illusion formed, pushing out from him, and he drew upon as much as he could to separate his illusion. He focused on the ice dragon and the iron dragon, then he added that of the forest dragon, and by pushing all of them together, he squeezed in a way that created a surge of power.

Finally, it washed over the others.

He could feel a shifting. Jason maintained that connection, holding onto the power that was shifting, and he let that energy wash out from him. When he did, he could definitely feel something change.

Henry looked over, then he blinked. "Jason?"

Jason sighed.

It worked.

He could feel it holding. More than that, he could feel what he needed to do to maintain it. He pushed a hint more, maintaining his connection to the illusion, mastering everything that he could as he held onto that power, letting it flow into him.

"Henry. It's good to see you back."

"Back? What happened?"

Jason looked around, focusing on the power he still held. There were too many people here for him to be able to use this illusion the way he needed.

"All I can say is that somehow you were targeted by Lorach," Jason said.

"Targeted? I don't understand."

He shared with him what happened, the egg, and the way the people of Dragon Haven had been used. As he did, Henry looked at Jason with a strange expression in his eyes that burned with uncertainty. It was the expression of a man who had suffered, and strangely, Jason understood it. He had gone through something similar, and he knew just how hard it would be to explain. At the same time, Jason needed to get to Henry quickly, and he needed to convince him to be of assistance.

He hadn't shared with him the boneyard. Yet. He would have to know about those dragons soon. Jason looked around, motioning to the plains. "Do you know where we are?"

"This is the Flor Plain. It's the outer edge of Lorach. All these people are here as well for the same reason?"

Jason motioned toward the egg. "The egg summoned you." He still felt that energy within him. "I don't really know how to explain otherwise, only that there is some sort of power calling to you." He looked up at the dragons, a mixture of Dragon Haven dragons and those that he'd freed. "It's also calling to the dragons. Feeding on them too."

"Where are the others?" Henry asked.

Jason shook his head. "I don't know what happened to the others. I have one of the dragons looking, but I can't feel anything from them." Henry arched a brow at him, and Jason ignored it. He couldn't feel anything, which was all that mattered. Until they found the others of Dragon Haven, he wasn't sure it mattered anymore.

Even if they did, unless Lorach actively attacked them, there was nothing that Jason needed to do for them. Right now, he had to protect the dragons.

"How did this happen?" Jason asked.

"We'd seen movement from Lorach. The Dragon Guard had identified it. You were gone. Sarah decided to take matters into her own hands and went searching." His voice caught. "I wish she would not have."

"What happened?"

Henry shook his head. "She found them. Both of them. At least, their bodies. They were outside of the city a couple of days by foot, lying near the mouth of a cave. She saw a pair of dragon pearls she suspected implicated Lorach, so she went after them."

"*She* went after Lorach?"

"She was hurting. Angry. And when she attacked, they were powerful. They chased her, us, and then… this."

Cherise and Olaf were gone.

Jason had known they probably were, but hearing it this way was hard.

It had to have been devastating for Sarah.

And he hadn't been there for her.

She'd found them on her own.

How angry must she have been?

Angry enough to go after Lorach.

Henry went on, oblivious to what Jason had been thinking. "I remember… a pounding. I'm not sure what that means, only that there was a sense of a pounding, and I remember how it was coming toward us, the power pulsating within that pounding." Henry looked over at him, frowning. "What does that mean?"

Jason shook his head. "I don't know, only that whatever caused that is likely tied to the egg feeding energy that called you here."

Henry looked around him, shaking his head a moment

before turning his attention back to Jason. "Can you help these others?" Henry asked.

"It is taking a considerable pull on all of the energy for me to be able to free you. I worry that if I were to let it go, you'll be drawn in again."

"Is there any way to solidify it?"

"There might be," Janeya said, looking at Henry. "I've done something similar before, though not quite on this scale."

"Who is this?" Henry asked.

"This is Janeya. She trained with Lorren."

Henry glowered at her, and Jason had to hurry to head that reaction off. He needed them to work together, not against each other. It wouldn't do for Henry to look at her in that way.

"She's with me, now," Jason said. He needed to head off any issues before anything happened. "She wants to help. She wants to stop Lorach. She wants to save the dragons."

"I can feel something within him," Janeya said. "I think that if I use the power of the earth dragons, mixing with the mist dragons, it should be enough to change things, and we should be able to hold it around him."

"Try it," Jason said.

She turned to Henry. "You will have to hold steady."

Power flowed from Janeya. Jason recognized way that she was using it, swirling the mist dragon energy around, and she anchored it with the earth dragon.

The combination was strange, and the way she held onto it was impressive. By holding it that way, by anchoring it downward, Jason recognized it would hold steadily.

Then she tamped it down. "This is as much as I can do," she said.

Jason focused on what she was doing. He thought he might be able to recreate it.

It would be challenging, especially as he didn't have the same connection to the mist dragons as she did, though he could reach through the connection he shared with her, and together he thought they would be able to draw that power out, and he could feel how she had used it in order to seal the illusion.

And she wasn't just holding it; she was adding to it.

He looked at Henry. "What do you feel?"

"Nothing different. Should I feel anything?"

"She anchored it. Hopefully it will hold."

"Hopefully?"

"I don't know what will happen if it doesn't. If it fails, then I worry you'll feel the summons again and you'll end up right back here. I managed to hatch the egg, but..." He closed his eyes. He could still feel the energy coming, as if another egg were summoning power. Jason looked around. "Where's Sarah?"

"Seeing as how I don't remember anything from before this all happened, I'm not sure I can help you find anyone."

Jason focused on the power within him, and he weaved his way through the people, Henry following. By the time he found Sarah, he knew exactly what he needed to do. He mixed the combination of the ice and iron dragon, then added the power of the forest dragon to it. In doing so, he washed it over Sarah and could feel the pressure there.

There was resistance, but then he pushed past that resistance. He overpowered it, and Janeya hurriedly added her own connection to the mist dragons along with the earth dragons.

"Sarah? Are you there?"

She stared blankly for a moment before blinking. Clarity returned to her eyes and she looked over at Jason, hurriedly noticing Janeya, along with the way that Janeya held onto Jason's hand. A frown crossed her face.

"Jason?"

"Do you know where you are?" he asked. He wanted to ask about her parents, but guilt kept him from doing so.

"I…" Sarah closed her eyes for a moment, then opened them again. That clarity blinked for a moment, almost as if it were going to disappear, but then it returned. She swept her gaze around before settling on Jason and then on Janeya. "I guess I don't."

"Lorach has been summoning you." He told her about the egg and how it fed, her eyes widening. "All of it is similar to how Lorren tried to use the dragons. Now you're well outside of Dragon Haven. Lorach called you here."

Sarah looked at Jason, irritation in her eyes, though it was irritation that he understood, irritation that he recognized, irritation that he thought he deserved.

"Where have you been?"

"I'm sorry," he said. "I shouldn't have left."

She shook her head. "No. You should not have. I found my parents."

"I heard from Henry. I'm so sorry—"

"Where did you go?" she demanded. "You'd said you were going to be there for me. To find them. And you didn't."

He swallowed while looking to the sky at the other dragons. "I was summoned. Directed, possibly." Jason didn't even know which it was. If he thought too much about it, he believed the night dragon had been a part of *why* he'd gone after Janeya. "You know that I would do everything that I can to protect the people of Dragon Haven. I wanted to be there for you."

"I don't really know that," she said. "All I know is that you disappeared."

"To figure out what was going on with the dragons."

"But you didn't tell us what you were doing. You didn't tell us where you were going. You didn't..." Sarah shook her head, and she looked over at Janeya. "My name is Sarah L'aral. Who are you? And why are you with Jason?"

The ground rumbled beneath Janeya as she summoned power. It was dangerous having these two together, especially as he could *feel* irritation coming off Janeya. "My name is Janeya Arnson."

Jason's breath caught. "What did you say?"

"I'm Janeya Arnson."

Jason shared a look with Sarah for a moment, his heart hammering.

Arnson.

He knew the name.

David Arnson. Jessica Arnson.

She'd told him of Lorren, and how he'd rescued her.

Or stolen her.

She was related to them.

Her control over the dragons, so different than most, made more sense.

Jason thought of the conversations he'd shared with David, discussions about the purpose of the dragons, discussions about how the people of Lorach would not have recognized the power of the dragons and would have feared it. Discussions that even now, Jason thought, shaped some of his opinions about the dragons.

"How is that possible?" Sarah asked.

Janeya frowned. "How is what possible?"

"Your last name," Jason said.

"What about it?"

Jason reached for her, ignoring Sarah's hard glare. "It's the same as the king and queen in Lorach."

23

He sat off to the side of the road where they had tried to help as many of the people of Dragon Haven as possible, looking over at Janeya where she sat beneath a tree. She chewed on her lip, and every so often, she would look up at the sky, as if she might find answers there. Jason knew there would be no answers there, just as he knew there were no answers about what had happened here. The only thing he knew with any certainty was that he needed to help Janeya.

"How could I be related to them?" She looked up at Jason, her eyes tinged with red.

"I don't know. Without knowing what Lorren knew, I don't know that any of us can have that answer. The only thing we know at this point is that you share the name."

He could feel the steady pulling from Lorach, and he knew they didn't have too much time to linger, but he felt as if he needed to take whatever time he could now. Janeya needed it.

"He never talked about it. Not when I was younger. At least, not much when I was younger. He said he saved me." She looked up at Jason. "What you think that means?"

"I don't know that I have much of an answer for you. I had secrets kept from me when I was younger, as well. My family, my parents, were Dragon Souls. Those secrets were kept from me until I had uncovered the truth on my own. It's not quite the same, but… I guess what I'm saying is that I understand."

She swallowed. "What does that mean for me?"

This time, Jason quirked a smile. "I think it means whatever you want it to mean."

"You still intend to stop Lorach."

Jason nodded, looking up at the dragons. "I think we have to. To save the dragons, we have to stop Jessica."

"Who I'm somehow related to."

Jason nodded. "Apparently."

She sighed. "I think I need a few moments."

He got to his feet, and he found William watching, looking over at him. His hair standing tall, dirt staining his face, and the bewildered expression on his face leaving Jason wondering if he was still influenced by the summons.

"I won't even pretend to know what happened," William said, waving his hand. "But I am curious who she is. I saw the way you were looking at her."

Jason glanced over to Janeya. "And what way was that?"

"Like you just saw your first dragon." He laughed softly. "Just don't hurt Sarah."

Jason breathed out. "I don't think that Sarah and I were anything more than friends."

William pressed his lips together in a funny looking frown. "Maybe not. Maybe she's always been interested in me, anyway."

"If you think so." He clasped William on the shoulder.

"I understand we have to keep searching?"

"You don't *have* to do anything," Jason said.

"If it's to stop Lorach, I'm going to be there. I'm done with all of this."

Jason nodded at him. "If it's any consolation, you should be pleased to know that you obviously have a connection to the dragons. You wouldn't be here if not."

William glowered at him. "Of course, I have a connection to the dragons. I've been telling you that all along."

"You *had* been telling me that you were lucky."

"You don't think I'm lucky?"

"I think your kind of luck has its own quirks."

William stayed with him as Jason made his way through the line of people from Dragon Haven. When he came across Kayla and his mother, Jason stopped.

Kayla looked over to him. Her eyes were damp, tears had streamed down her face. His mother attempted to console her, an arm wrapped around her shoulder. It was odd to see, especially since there had been a time when Kayla had been the one providing the caregiving, and their mother being the one who was sick and injured.

When he approached, they watched him.

"What happened?" Kayla asked, her voice a whisper. She glanced from Jason to William, who stood a step behind Jason, looking over at her.

For all his talk about going after Sarah, Jason saw the affection in William's eyes for Kayla. It was almost enough to bring a smile to his face. Under other circumstances, maybe it would have.

"This is Lorach," Jason said. "They're making their final move."

His mother frowned. "This is not any final move."

"Against Dragon Haven," Jason added. He looked up, and he could feel the dragons' energy in the air, even if he couldn't see all of the misfits. He could still feel power pressing on him. It left him thinking that there had to be another egg, but where? "They found Dragon Haven, figured out a way to summon those who have the potential of dragons, and now…"

Now they had all suffered for it.

"I don't want this to happen again," Kayla said.

"I don't either," Jason said. "Which is why I'm going to end it."

His mother looked at him, and she frowned. There was a strange expression in her eyes, and Jason wondered if it was disappointment or not that burned there. She had once been a Dragon Soul, as had his father, but even though they had served Lorach, he didn't think that she still felt that same sympathy.

"What can you do?" Kayla asked.

"I don't know. I have to figure out what they're after, and then we will stop it." He looked over to his mother. "Help her get back to Dragon Haven. Kayla is going to be needed there."

"I will. And…" She looked to Kayla, a pained look on her face before it faded. "Perhaps I can start working with her myself." She turned to Jason. "That is, if you don't have any objection."

Jason sighed in relief. "That's *exactly* what we need. What others need. To learn a connection to the dragons. Maybe a different one. When this is over, you'll need to use your connection to forge something new."

"What something new?" Kayla asked.

Jason shrugged. "I don't know. And that's the beautiful thing about it. You get to decide."

"Are you sure?" Kayla asked.

Was he?

The only thing Jason knew was that if they stopped Jessica and Lorach, there would be a void of dragon connections. They would have to fill it—the right way.

"I'm as sure as I can be."

After hugging them, he started forward until he reached Henry, who talked to Sarah, and he motioned for them. Henry watched him, as did Sarah, and they frowned. "I need to show you what is pulling on you."

When the ice dragon descended, Janeya joined him,

climbing onto the ice dragon's back without saying a word.

They took off, and several other dragons followed. The energy that was pulling upon him was easy enough for him to track, but he wondered how far they would have to go.

He was not surprised that they didn't travel far when he could feel the energy coming off of another egg. The energy here was faint but it was growing stronger, and if he didn't do anything, it would be more potent than he wanted. It was likely to harm not only him, but the people of Dragon Haven.

He stopped in front of an egg and the others joined him, taking a moment to create an illusion around the egg, trying to seal it from influencing others. Jason didn't know if it worked the way he wanted, but he *thought* it did.

Sarah, Henry, William, and five Dragon Guards joined Jason and Janeya at the dragon egg. They stood in front of it, feeling the power, the illusion circling around them to hold it in place. The illusion of this egg pulled upon him, calling to him. There was something quite potent about it, though Jason couldn't quite place what it was. Perhaps it was just of the potency of the illusion, or perhaps it was more about the egg itself. Either way, the energy within it continued to call to him, and he could feel it radiating from the egg.

"This is what summoned us out here?" Sarah asked.

She hazarded a sideways glance, looking at Janeya as she spoke.

"One like this."

"Why?" Henry asked.

"To feed." Jason studied the egg. It was larger than the last, and the coloration on it was different.

"Probably to destroy all of the people of Dragon Haven," Sarah said.

Could that be it? He didn't know if feeding the egg would destroy anything. He didn't have that impression, but he could have been wrong. "It's a summoning, but it also seems to be feeding, drawing upon power. It's doing the same thing to the dragons."

Jason looked up, but the illusion he'd created made it difficult to see the dragons overhead. He knew they were there, and so far, they hadn't gone anywhere. They continued to circle high above him.

"Why does the egg need to feed?" William asked.

"To create..." He glanced up again, thinking of the *new* misfits and the eggs he had hatched. "Something more. A different kind of dragon."

"So they are trying to create some sort of super dragon," Sarah said. "Sort of like your night dragon."

"I don't know. I suppose it's possible," Jason said.

"Possible? If they are trying to use the power of a hundred or more dragons in some egg, then it's more than just possible," Sarah said.

William approached the egg and reached out toward it. Power burst from the egg and slammed into his chest, knocking him back. His hair stood on end, more wildly than usual, and he staggered in place for a moment.

"Maybe that was a mistake," William said.

Jason held his own hand out, feeling for the egg, recognizing that there was a power within it. By holding his hand toward the egg, Jason understood its surge of power. He maintained his connection, feeling for that power, reaching for a sense of something within it.

He looked over at Janeya. "This one is different," he said. "It's drawing differently than the others."

"I can feel it." Janeya glanced toward Sarah as she spoke.

Sarah frowned and looked at Jason, then Janeya, before shaking her head. She still looked angry, though Jason couldn't quite place the source of her anger. Maybe it was about Janeya, or that Jason had been spending time with her, or perhaps it had more to do with everything they were dealing with when it came to the attack on Lorach.

Jason worried that there was irritation between the two of them.

He breathed out heavily and strained toward the egg. There was definitely a connection there, something that flowed from the egg, a power that radiated from it.

Jason focused on the sense of the forest dragon. She had been the key to his illusion.

The egg needed to feed. That was how he would stop the pull on the dragons. Feed and then this could be over. The only problem was that he didn't know if his new connections would be enough or if he would have to draw upon the dragons.

He forced power out.

Surprisingly, so did Janeya.

Between the two of them, they pushed power out of them.

As Jason looked over, he realized something about her.

All this time, he had come to believe that he was a misfit, much like the dragons he worked with. Until meeting Janeya.

He had a similar sort of power as hers. He had a similar sort of power to that which Lorren had possessed. Even Therin and Jessica had demonstrated something similar to Jason.

He had to finish feeding the egg.

He pushed, sending more and more energy out from himself. As he did, he could feel the way it funneled away from him, drawing on the cold, the anger, the illusion powers that coursed through him. It drew upon the rumbling of the earth, the flash of smoke, and the mist Janeya had control over.

Then the egg hatched.

This one was even smaller than the others. Jason could feel the pull of Lorach coming from the egg, coming from the dragon, and could feel how it still tried to draw upon the dragon.

He created an illusion, swirling around, and solidified it. Janeya anchored it using earth. He looked up to see the others with him staring at what had been the dragon. He understood that feeling, but he needed something more from them now. He needed help.

"For this to be over, we're going to have to take the fight to Lorach," he said, looking at the faces around him.

"We've tried, and we have failed," Sarah said. "It was my fault Lorach found Dragon Haven. I knew better and I—"

"Did what I should have done," he said softly. Her parents had died trying to take the fight to Lorach. Could he really ask more from her? This was his fight now. "I will do this," he said. It was what he'd planned when he'd departed an empty Dragon Haven. It was what he still planned.

"Jason," Henry said, turning to him. "When we've attempted to defeat the Dragon Souls before, they overwhelmed us. They overwhelmed *you*. Think about what has happened when you have encountered dragons controlled by more than one Dragon Soul."

"They won't be able to do so this time," Jason said.

"What makes you think we could do this?" one of the Dragon Guard asked.

"I can feel energy within me that's different than what I had before." He looked at them. "I no longer need to call through the dragons for that power. It's almost as if the dragons themselves taught me how to connect to that energy in a way that grants me my own source of power."

"That shouldn't be possible," Sarah said.

"I know it shouldn't be, but I'm telling you it is. I can

use the power of the north, that of the iron dragon, even that of the storm dragon without drawing through them."

"You're bonded to all of them, though," Henry said. "How are you sure that you're not calling upon it from them?"

"I can feel the power more directly," Jason said. "I don't know how to explain it in any other way. I realize there's pow1er that's out there, and I can feel it filling me." Even now, Jason was aware of the energy of the north mountains, the power that slammed into him from high overhead, the power of his homeland. By holding onto that awareness, he could call that northern power and use it when necessary. He was connected as well to the power of the ground, to the lava flowing deep beneath him, and to the power of the rage of molten lava. It mingled with the energy of the storm clouds. All of that flowed within him, mixing within him. All of those powers were accessible.

Maybe that was why he was somehow tied to the misfits.

His power was a misfit, as well.

"You need to be careful with that power," Henry said. "Even though you can draw on that energy, are you sure that it's going to be enough to defeat the Dragon Souls?"

"We have something they would not be expecting."

"What is that?"

Jason realized he still hadn't revealed the presence of the dozen female dragons. It was time for Dragon Haven to know about them, to know about that power, and to be prepared for the world changing because of it.

He embraced the sense of power coming from those dragons, feeling the energy coming off them, and he wondered if there might be something more he could detect from them. He should have focused on that power before. Now Jason had to find a different way to use his own connection and to see if there might be something that he could draw from them.

He focused on what he could feel of those dragons. There came a faint, distant sense.

It was somehow tied to him.

The dragons were here because of him. He had given them strength and he had created them, using his connection to the various misfits and his direct connection to power, to channel something different, something greater.

He focused.

Then he motioned for the others to follow him. Jason looked up at the dragons. They continued to circle, swooping around, and though there were the dragons from Dragon Haven and dragons that he'd helped free, the females were also present.

Energy radiated from them. Jason realized just what it was that he felt. It was the power coming off those dragons. He could feel it forming in a shell, creating something around him and around the dragons. It continued to build, rising all around them, and it swirled, reminding Jason somewhat of the north wind swirling around him. He doubted was coincidental. More likely that had been intentional, and that was the same sort of power that the dragons intended to call to them.

"What's going on?" Sarah asked. She continued glancing toward him, then toward Janeya.

"There's something else that I haven't shared with the rest of you yet."

Henry looked over. "What else?"

"Janeya and I found something."

More than finding it. They had created it. Together.

Sarah watched him.

There was a distance there that hadn't been there before.

It came from losing her parents, but it came from the way she looked at him.

He *was* a misfit.

An outsider to Dragon Haven.

She had welcomed him, but at a distance.

I can still help the dragons.

That was the thought that stayed with him. That *had* to stay with him.

It was why he would fight.

Jason focused on the energy within him, and he let it flow outward. In doing so, he felt the power and the connection to those dozen female dragons. The power exploded toward them. It took a moment, but they continued to circle, making their way gradually toward him.

The dozen dragons descended. They were larger than the dragons of Dragon Haven, larger than the dragons of Lorach. When he'd traveled with them, he had seen them as the same size as the ice dragon. And they were. Only, the ice dragon was incredibly large, much larger than any of the other dragons, even larger than the other misfits.

Gasps came from all around.

The dragons were enormous, large enough that they would attract attention, but they would attract more than just attention. They attracted fear. It was an irrational sort of fear, but Jason had seen that sort of irrational fear before. He had known it himself.

"What are these?" William asked. Of the people from Dragon Haven, William was the only one who seemed interested enough to try to approach the dragons.

"These are dragons we resurrected," Jason said.

"Resurrected?" Sarah asked, looking back at him. "What do you mean you *resurrected* them?"

"I found a dragon boneyard. It's a long story, but with enough power and dragon bones, I formed an egg."

Sarah was shaking her head. "That's not how dragon eggs work, Jason."

Jason held her gaze. There was still darkness in her eyes. A hollowness. He doubted that anything he would be able to do or say would remove that from her.

She'd lost her parents. And he'd not been there for her.

Everything he did even now was for the dragons.

He really *was* a misfit.

"I know it's not how it is supposed to work, but given everything that we've seen with the other misfits, it makes sense." He glanced over at Janeya. "Lorren believed the dragons never really died. He believed they cycled and their power came back, resurrected somehow. It fits with that."

Sarah stared at the dragons. "They're all female."

"They are," Jason said. "I think this is how we are going to beat Lorach."

They were powerful—more so than dragons that Lorach had experienced before. They had a connection to different powers—much like the night dragon. As Henry had described them, they *were* something like super dragons.

More than that, they were willing to fight.

"What now?" Henry asked.

Jason stared at the dragons, then he looked overhead, feeling their energy. "After we deal with the other eggs, it's time for us to take the fight to Lorach. Now it's time for us to reclaim her throne." He looked at Janeya.

She looked back at him, uncertain.

24

Jason pulled Janeya aside. "I know you don't know whether you can believe it or not, but that has to be the reason Lorren wanted to work with you."

"Why wouldn't he have said anything to me?"

Jason shook his head. "I don't really know." Had Lorren shared with them what he had been after, the reason that he had done what he had, Jason had to believe that there would have been something they could have done. Maybe he wouldn't have been so aggressive and they could have worked together.

Only, that wasn't quite true.

He had seen the way Lorren had been willing to attack the other dragons. He had seen how Lorren gave little thought to the Dragon Souls, along with the dragons.

But now I know they can be resurrected.

It changed things for him. For the dragons.

All of the dragons.

"I don't know why Lorren had taken you. Maybe he thought to protect you. Maybe he thought to use you. Either way, now you get to choose. It's the same as anyone else."

Jason wouldn't have changed anything. He would've done the same as he had done, and he would have tried to ensure that anything Lorren did to the dragons would be stopped.

"What if you're wrong?" she asked.

"If I'm wrong, then I'm wrong," Jason said. "It doesn't change what needs to happen. All it changes is who you might be. Regardless of whether or not I am right or wrong, I could use your help with this."

"I'm willing to help. I'm willing to do what I can to help the dragons. I've told you I will, but I'm not what you think I am."

"If you are, all I ask is that you consider what you might be able to do."

"And what might I be able to do?"

"I don't know," Jason said, grinning at her. "I don't have those answers. We can find them together."

He looked at the dragons all around them. They had the dozen female dragons, they had the other misfits, all the dragons so far proving they could not be influenced with whatever Jessica attempted.

"I will do whatever I can to help," she said.

That was all he could ask.

He focused on the energy of the ice dragon, adding to that what he could of the iron dragon, mixing that of the storm dragon, and finally bringing in the forest dragon. Distantly, Jason felt the earth dragon, though he recognized how the earth dragons responded not only to him but also to Janeya.

With his connection to these other dragons, along with his connection to the power in the distance, he didn't know that he needed to borrow that of the earth dragon. Even if he did, he could borrow power through his connection to Janeya.

"I am taking the fight to Lorach," he said, looking at everyone all around him.

There were faces around him that he recognized, along with faces he did not. He could feel the way they were connected, which surprised him. Jason had never known that before. More than he had expected had some connection to the dragons.

Somehow, he was aware of it.

"I'm going to free the remaining dragons. I'm going to stop Jessica. And I'm going to bring the dragons back together." The people around him began to murmur. Jason had no idea whether they agreed or not. Maybe it was little more than discomfort at what he said. "The misfits will fly with me. The new dragons will fly with me. And as many of the dragons as I can free will fly with me."

He wondered if he would have the strength needed to be able to free those dragons. He would have to try. As he called upon that power within him, he realized something.

The female dragons began to exert their influence. As they were connected to each of the other dragon misfits, their power similar to his, they were able to use illusion—and alter reality—as well.

But stronger.

The dozen dragons, all of them connected to something more and something greater, held onto illusion in a way that Jason wouldn't have been able to do, not without weakening himself.

What about the influence of the mist dragons? He needn't have been concerned. These dragons had that in them, as well. They had that of the earth dragons. There was nothing more he needed to do.

Jason marveled at it.

The dragons began to circle with more force.

"Look at them," William whispered.

Jason looked over at his friend, and he realized that William indeed had a connection to the dragons. That was how he had been summoned, the reason that he had been influenced. Because of that, William was here, trapped along with the dragons and the people of Dragon Haven, drawn into something that Jason thought he should not be.

"The dragons feel it," William said.

"Are you sure you want to do this?" Henry watched Jason, and the look in his eyes suggested that whatever else they decided to do would leave him uncertain. The old Dragon Soul had been through so much in his time serving, and shouldn't he want to rest?

Shouldn't Jason want to help him rest?

"We have been dealing with Lorach and their attack

for long enough. It's time that we do something different. It's time we stopped them for good. It's time the dragons are truly free."

Henry looked at the sky, and a look came to his eyes that Jason recognized. "For that reason alone, I would fight with you. I imagine the others as well. If you have some way of finally ending this war, then all of us will fight with you."

Jason looked at Sarah.

"What about you?"

"I don't know if I can do this," she whispered. She looked at the people of Dragon Haven. "I have wanted to help the dragons. That's all I've ever wanted, but now..." She shook her head. "It's my fault Lorach found Dragon Haven, but I needed to know. And now that I know my parents are gone..."

"The people need a leader," Jason said.

She looked down.

"They have one," he said, knowing that it was true, but knowing as well that she needed to do what she intended. Much like he needed to do what he intended.

Jason took a step forward, reaching out for her, and he saw Sarah tense.

He understood. She didn't need him to comfort her.

He hadn't been there when she had wanted him to be, and even now, their goals were not aligned. She wanted nothing more than to help the people of Dragon Haven, whereas he wanted to protect the dragons. "The rest of your people are still out there," he said softly. "And I need to go find the rest of the dragons I can help."

She watched him for a long moment and then turned away as a dragon descended. Her dragon. At least he remained free. Jason had to find the others, too.

Sarah looked over at him. "Be careful, Jason."

Given everything they had gone through, he hated the idea that Sarah wouldn't be here with him. Except, recently, she hadn't been there with him, anyway. Jason didn't like the idea, but at the same time, he understood.

She'd never wanted to fight. She'd wanted to rescue dragons.

With what he intended, he would have to fight in order to rescue the dragons. She didn't need to be a part of it any longer. She could let him do it.

Sarah needed to lead.

With her parents gone, the people of Dragon Haven *did* need someone like her. They needed a leader. They needed somebody willing to stay with them, to work with them, and that someone was her.

Jason, on the other hand, was a fighter. He had become that in his time working with Dragon Haven, and had he not, so much more would've been lost, but because he had been willing to become that fighter and had been willing to do the hard and necessary work, others had been able to thrive.

If they could stop Lorach, they could finally find peace. They could finally thrive.

First, though, the people of Dragon Haven had to get to safety. Find the others.

Rebuild.

That would take time.

And a leader like Sarah.

She turned them, marching back toward Dragon Haven.

It would be a long walk, but better than to march into Lorach, toward the danger, and toward the possibility of their own suffering.

Climbing on the ice dragon, he waited for Janeya to join him. One by one, the rest of the Dragon Guard, along with Henry—and surprisingly William—began to climb onto the backs of dragons.

He looked around, and then they took to the air.

The dragons flew with a wild intensity. As they reached their peak altitude, Jason glanced behind him and found Janeya watching him. He forced a smile, but he could tell through their shared connection that she knew what he was thinking.

They flew, and he found the drawing energy of another egg calling him, pulling him forward, and he recognized that the source of it was nearby.

His dragon started to descend, moving quickly, and as he did, he realized that there was something there, some aspect of energy that was calling upon him, dragging him forward, and he felt it pulling him.

As it did, he realized there were other dragons. They were not alone here. But the dragons were on the ground.

"Another egg?" Janeya asked, motioning to the dragons on the ground.

"I'm not entirely sure," he said.

He followed the pull of the egg. As that power pulled upon him, the ice dragon started to circle, lowering to the ground until he came to rest near a circle of two dozen dragons surrounding an egg. Other dragons with them descended, though didn't get close to the dragons, as if they feared getting too close to them.

These dragons were dying.

He jumped from the dragon's back and tried to look around, worried about whether there might be anything that he could do to help the dragons, nothing seemed to be obvious.

He headed toward the oblong, pale shape in the center of the circle.

It was pulling on the dragons around it. It was feeding on them.

Destroying them.

That's what would have happened to the people of Dragon Haven.

To their dragons.

And Jessica doesn't care.

"They're gone," Janeya said.

"The egg pulled too much," he whispered.

Was that what would happen to him if the egg would pull too much from him?

"Can you help them?"

Jason turned to the egg. The only way he thought that

he could help would be by pushing power out and connecting to the egg and trying to add enough energy that it would hatch, but even as he did, he could feel that there was some resistance.

He tried, pushing on power, letting it flow out from him, but the egg continued to draw from the dragons.

And then it cracked.

A small dragon emerged. It was multicolored: red, orange, green, blue, and black. As Jason looked around him, he realized the dragon was the color of the dragons that had surrounded him.

He formed an illusion around the dragon, pushing power out and solidifying it.

The dragon fell asleep.

Jason hurried to the nearby dragons and rested his hand on the first one, but there was nothing that could be done. He moved from dragon to dragon, but they were all gone.

Cold.

They had been fed upon.

Power had been stripped from them, and now there was nothing remaining.

"How could she have done this?" Janeya whispered.

"I don't know. She's terrible. She sees the dragons and their power as tools to be used. Wield it against her people and those who she thinks oppose her."

Janeya stared at the fallen dragons. "I would never have thought that anybody would do anything like this."

She looked up at Jason, and he noticed a resolute look in her eyes.

Jessica had learned something, but then she had used it against the dragons. It was her way of destroying his free dragons. He swallowed and made his way over to the ice dragon, and they took to the air.

"We need to find the other eggs."

They found nearly a dozen other eggs. Almost one hundred dead dragons. The dragons with him had increased with each Dragon Soul they'd pushed off a dragon, freeing the dragons again, but it hadn't felt like enough. They were still too few.

The Dragon Guard, Henry, William, and others flew with them.

It wasn't enough.

Jason had been able to help none of the injured dragons.

His heart was heavy and anger filled him, but it was a useless sort of anger.

Through the earth connecting them, he could feel Janeya's anger as well.

He needed to find some way to get past it, but had no idea what it was going to take.

He wasn't sure if he was going to be able to recover from this, either.

Janeya rested her hand on his back, and he could feel

something through the connection that they shared, but it did not matter. How could it?

All he could think about was what had happened. All he could think about was what had been lost and how much Jessica had taken from the world and the way that she had destroyed the dragons.

And it was destruction.

Hopefully he'd managed to get to the dragons first, and with his connection to them, the illusion that he placed over them, along with an attempt to place a healing over them, he had to hope that he would be able to do enough to protect them.

"We have to stop her," she whispered.

"We will," Jason said.

Even by bringing the dozen female dragons back into the world, could there be enough? There were new dragons he had hatched, and he would do everything that he could to protect them, but would that be enough?

Did the dragons she'd formed make up for all she'd sacrificed?

They headed toward Lorach.

As he flew atop the dragon, he saw the misfits spread out on either side of him. Not only the misfits, though. The Dragon Guard willing to come had joined him. Henry was there, and even William sat atop his red dragon. They flanked him, surrounding him. Jason could feel those dragons but worried it wouldn't be enough. Jason had no idea what they would all be able to do, if anything.

Perhaps they wouldn't be able to do anything. That didn't mean he wouldn't try.

They were coming to Lorach to end this. To bring about the final chapter of the war.

And they would do that together.

And the anger continued to fill him, bubbling within him. That was what he had to hold onto. It was the only thing he could hold onto.

Jason stared outward. The energy of Lorach continued to draw him.

"That is Lorach." Jason sighed, holding onto the power within him. "It's different than it was the last time I was here," he said.

The city was enormous. It stretched for miles, built of towering spires, impossibly tall buildings, and gleaming white stone. All of it was filled with the power of dragons. At the heart of it was the palace, twisting spires and towers that stretched high into the sky, creating a burgeoning source of energy.

Through all of it, though, was an undercurrent of something else.

It was something Jason was distantly aware of, something that he could feel as he approached the city. Perhaps it was the fear of the people who lived here. Perhaps it was the terror they felt toward the dragons, something that gave them an edge.

Jason recognized it all too easily.

As they came close, he could feel the energy of Lorach,

though it was somehow different than what he had detected before.

"What do you propose?" Janeya asked him.

He motioned to the dragons around him. They followed his lead the same way the misfits had when he had wanted to come to Lorach.

"First, we need to head to the dragon pens," he said.

"How many dragons do you think will be there?"

Jason shook his head. "I don't know. I doubt all of the dragons we need to free will be there."

"How many Dragon Souls will still be there?"

They had destroyed so many, but there were always more. That had been his experience with Lorach. They could always throw more Dragon Souls at them.

"I don't know, but probably not all that we will need to stop." Jessica wouldn't have kept everybody there. She would've brought them somewhere else to make it more difficult to be ambushed.

He leaned forward, holding onto the energy within him, feeling the power of the ice dragon beneath him. He felt the energy of all of the misfit dragons there within him.

There was dragon power all around him, and in feeling it, Jason tried to hold onto it, knowing that he might need to use a bit more of the energy within him, but knowing as well that there might be limits to just how much of that power he could draw.

"I see something," Janeya said.

Jason looked into the distance. He didn't see anything, though he was certain there was power out there.

"I feel it, and I..." She shook her head. "I'm not exactly sure, to be honest. There is something to it that is out there, some connection to that power that feels as if I should be able to utilize it. There's a connection within me."

It was different for him, but at the same time, he recognized what she meant. Vaguely, he could feel pressure beginning to build. They still hadn't reached the edge of the city of Lorach, though he could feel pressure or dragon energy that suggested that the people in power were nearby.

Where were the Dragon Souls?

The other dragons, freed and those from Dragon Haven, near him circled, flying high and powerfully, making their way through the sky. They were ready.

Jason could feel the tension within those dragons, their readiness, and was aware of what they were prepared to do. In addition, he recognized the power of the dragon females.

They called upon a different sort of energy that flowed within them, drifting to him, giving him a feeling of the power that existed within them.

Those dragons were trying to fuel him with power, as if they knew that he needed something more than just his connection to the dragons, though Jason wasn't entirely sure what it was. Perhaps it was merely the power that came from the female dragons that he had helped in the boneyard. He held onto that power, trying to draw it through him, needing to access it.

The people of Lorach tried to exert their influence, trying to push upon him. Jason didn't know if it came from the energy of the Dragon Souls or if it came from whatever Jessica attempted to do. Power continued to build around him.

He looked at Janeya.

Everything outside Lorach looked odd. There were dragons filling the pens, and there was pressure upon them, but the pressure was strange.

"Why aren't the dragons going anywhere?" Janeya asked.

Jason shook his head. "I have no idea. I don't know what she's doing with them, only that I can feel something out there."

"It is pulling on me," she said.

It was the same power that he'd been feeling for quite some time, only he had no idea why he would still feel it, or why that power would draw on him, leaving him trembling. At first, he had believed that what he had felt came from the attempt to fill an egg, but now it was something different.

Now he was drawn toward Lorach, and he still felt as if he were pulled upon.

"She's doing something to these dragons." Not only his dragons. To her dragons.

And the Dragon Souls.

He looked down, saw the dragons, and recognized the

power that was down there, a power that could not be altered. He had no idea what he could do about that. He had no idea if there was anything that could be done about it. The ice dragon swept over the penned dragons. There was no sign of the Dragon Souls.

"This is wrong," he whispered.

"What is it?" Janeya frowned as she leaned over the side of the dragon. "I can feel this," she said.

"I don't know what it is, only that whatever we detect is calling all the dragons that don't have a natural resistance." Which meant it called *all* the dragons other than the misfit dragons.

With the pull, he realized something else.

There was a pull on him.

Which meant the misfits would feel it as well.

The ice dragon could feel the drawing. Through the connection they shared, Jason could feel that, much like he could feel it from the iron dragon. The misfits weren't immune.

Even as he attempted to resist, he could still feel the energy coming off him, some power that drew upon him, as if it was attempting to drain him. That energy was more than he could withstand and he struggled against it, trying to fight off what was happening, but he knew he had to find the source of it.

He turned away.

"Is it just the dragons?" Janeya asked.

"I..."

It couldn't be just the dragons, could it?

If it was just the dragons, he would've expected to have seen something else.

Jason circled, sweeping over the city, but with each pass, the ice dragon began to get weaker. He didn't know how long the dragon would be able to withstand this.

For that matter, Jason didn't know how long *he* would be able to withstand this.

It was calling on him, pulling upon him, and it was potent.

Almost *too* potent.

He tapped on the ice dragon, and he connected the ice dragon to the cold of the north, shooting it down toward him.

The ice dragon didn't need his help with that, though. The ice dragon had his own way of connecting to the north and pulling that power down. All Jason did was add a hint of a connection to it, acting as a bridge, but even in that, it was probably unnecessary.

He tapped on the ice dragon's side and they continued to circle.

In the distance, he saw movement on the outside of the city.

It was slow, a march toward the city itself.

There was a pull, and it reminded him of what he had seen of the people from Dragon Haven.

Dragon Souls.

They were moving slowly, lumbering, and he didn't even need to latch onto the ice dragon's eyesight in order to see what had happened to them. He could feel it, even if he wasn't able to look down and see it.

"She's calling her Dragon Souls," he whispered.

Janeya looked over. "Why?"

Jason had no idea.

There was power calling to them, drawing off him, and he could feel it pulling, but he had no idea why or where it was coming from. There was considerable energy out around him.

I need to get into the city.

"Can you stay with the dragons?"

He pushed outward through a connection he shared with the dragons. All of the dragons. He needed them to circle and defend. *Be prepared.* The Dragon Souls could still attack.

Only… he didn't know if they would. Or if they could. Not like this.

"Why?" Janeya asked.

"Because they are going to need your protection. And I have something else that I need to do."

"What do you think you need to do?"

In the distance, Jason could feel the energy coming from someplace within Lorach, but he didn't know what it was or where it came from. All he could tell was that there was power out there, and it was radiating toward him. It was incredibly powerful, drawing off him.

"I have to stop this before she drains all of the dragons."

25

Jason focused, and he could feel energy flowing around him.

His old friend was there, and his mood matched Jason's mood. Rage.

It had been about the dragons and the eggs, but Jason had felt that strange pulling when he had come across each of the eggs. It had drawn toward Lorach, and even after the egg hatched, that pulling sensation was there.

And it was there now.

It pulled toward the tower.

The tower.

It was a place of power.

He had felt it when he'd been captive here. Not only that, but he had *used* it when captive here. Jessica used that power now. Whatever Jessica intended, he needed to stop it.

He looked over at Janeya, holding her gaze for a minute, and then he jumped.

He found the iron dragon, swirling, glowing.

But draining.

Like all of the misfits.

He tapped his hand against the iron dragon's side and connected to him. When he did, there was a surge of power that connected them, joining them together, and he held his glove against the iron dragon's side.

"We need to find her," he said.

The iron dragon streaked off, moving with a flicker of molten hot flame.

From there, he had to find something else.

He pushed forward, but there was something around him.

Movement in the sky.

He looked up. For a moment, it looked like there were dragons. Hundreds upon hundreds of dragons. There were so many dragons that they seemed to blacken out the sky. It was an impossible number. All different colors, all different sizes. Thousands of them. All with Dragon Souls seated atop them. It made seeing anything else impossible.

No.

Jason could feel the illusion. He knew exactly what it was. It was close, and the fact that there was an illusion like that told him that she didn't want him to be here.

Jason blasted energy at the illusion.

It shattered.

The city loomed below him, and there was some place down there that called to him.

The palace. He understood why. That was where he had been before. That was where he had felt a strange energy before.

He jumped from the iron dragon's back.

Energy started to swirl around him, and suddenly, a dragon streaked toward him. It was an enormous dragon, possibly the largest he'd ever seen…

Which means it isn't real.

Illusion.

He forced power at it and shattered the illusion.

He tumbled toward the palace, using the energy within him and that of the dragons to guide him. He landed atop the tower, determined to find Jessica. He could feel energy all around him, and he could feel the power that existed, the way she called it to this tower.

He was not surprised to find her standing atop the tower.

Even as he approached, he could feel the power coming off of her.

Off of the tower.

That power was immense. Overwhelming.

And pulled on him.

Jessica wore her familial dragonskin, and she watched Jason, anger flickering through her silver eyes. Her black hair streamed behind her, and power seemed to surround her. She was about his height, and she reminded him of Janeya now that he was near.

Could they have be cousins?

If only David had lived, Jason might have had an opportunity to learn more about how they were family, but maybe it didn't matter.

They were family.

"You're trying to drain the power from the dragons," he said.

She turned to him and energy crackled at him, but filled by the power of the mountains all around them, Jason didn't struggle with it the same way he had before. He created a barrier around himself.

"It was you who gave me the idea. I would never know about this had it not been for you. I suppose I should be thankful. You gave me the means to stopping Dragon Haven once and for all." She waved her hands all around her. "When you came here. You drew upon the power of this tower. We knew there was something to it, but we weren't exactly sure what it was. When you started to draw upon it, we realized there was a way of accessing it and we could use that."

"You already knew you could use it at that point," Jason said.

"I suppose that wasn't the only reason that we knew there was something more," she said. "And now you'll all fail. You've brought everything here that I wanted. That you are here tells me it has worked."

"I came here by choice, not because you summoned me."

"What if that's what I wanted you to think?"

The power continued to build. Jason felt something within it. It was a summons. The message. It was power. It pushed upon him, which meant it was pushing upon all of the dragons—misfits, freed dragons, those of Dragon Haven, and even the Dragon Soul dragons—flying above him.

She grinned at him.

"I knew I was never going to be able get all the dragons drawn here. We have been trying to do so, but even that wasn't too subtle. I found a way to summon dragons, but it was slow. The bones are the key, you see. That surprised me. We've been collecting them, and now they have powered this as much as I need."

Like the bones had created an egg.

Was *that* what would happen with this tower?

It was powerful. Too powerful.

If it fed on the dragons, the Dragon Souls, the people of Dragon Haven, Jason knew what would happen to them. The same as what he'd seen from the dragons outside of Lorach.

"Why would you even want to do that? Won't it harm the Dragon Souls?"

"Do you think that I care about them?" she snapped. "The only thing I care about is the power they grant me. By drawing upon the energy within them, I can use it to draw this." She waved her hands at the tower. "My family will be strong enough to use it. I'm going to be strong enough to overwhelm it. And now I can finally end this foolish rebellion. I have uncovered the key to calling the power of the dragons. All of the power of the dragons. And it is here. It has always been here. My family has shown me the way."

"It's not going to work. The dragons will continue to fight you."

"No. They won't."

With a sudden surge, the power pushing against Jason began to build.

He could feel it pulsating around him, the energy building and building. It was more powerful than he had felt before. Within him, he recognized how the dragon misfits suffered.

They felt the same power. There was nothing they could do against it.

They tried, straining against it, and Jason added whatever he could in order to try to oppose what he detected, but even as he did, there wasn't anything within him that could override that power. It was far too much. It was far too powerful.

It was connected to the tower. Jason tried to tap into that same power. He had been here before and he'd been able to do it then, but he found it didn't react to him now.

She looked over at him. "You can do whatever you want when it comes to the dragons, but all you're going to do is draw them toward me." She grinned at him. "Don't you even notice it?"

"Notice what?"

"Notice the way that your power continues to drain." She sneered at him. "I must admit that it took me a while to fine-tune this, and after much exploration and testing, I finally feel as if I have the right combination."

As she said it, he realized what she was doing. She was feeding on him. Draining him.

It was the same thing he used to do when it came to using the power of the dragons. Only, she didn't know that he had power connecting him to something else. Jason had opened himself up to that. It wasn't just that he had opened himself up to the power of the north. He had opened himself up to all of the powers that were out there, everything that he could connect to.

More power continued to build, and he started to feel it flowing through him. He added to it, building it within him. When he did, he started to push, and there came an explosion of energy. The explosion was what he needed. He was going to have to use that explosion in order to be able to overpower what was happening to him.

It fed on him the way the eggs had attempted to feed.

Jason pushed against it.

If nothing else, he could use the energy that he was able to channel to try to protect the dragons. Even when he did, he could feel that energy pushing away from him, but then was drawn back.

Jessica had truly figured out a way to defeat him.

She had figured out a way to call the power he could access, and in doing so, she was going to stop him. He wasn't going to be able to do anything to prevent her from destroying the dragons.

They were going to be drained. And all of the power would be stored here.

Dragons. People with dragon connections. Maybe even the residual power of the bones. All would be drained.

There would be no return for the dragons. Not from this.

She laughed. "I can see from your face that you recognize how futile all of this is. You realize you won't be able to stop what I'm doing."

"Why would you do this?"

"Because it must be done," she said. "The dragon power can't be controlled. You've shown that. David never understood. He thought we could work with the, but he saw how people reacted to the dragons. With fear." She took a step toward him. "You should see that by now. My people deserve better. Your misfits won't keep attacking. Destroying." She shook her head. "Ruining lives. Now they will fear no longer. Not dragons. Not someone like yourself or Lorren, who prove that not only don't we have a control over it, but they will use it. This is the only way to ensure that the throne in Lorach is secured and the people of Lorach are safe."

It pained him that he understood. At least in part.

But not completely.

There were others ways. Better ways.

She had never wanted to understand the dragons, only control them.

Now—destroy them.

"By draining all of the dragons?"

"By storing their power."

He thought about saying something, considering that even if she were to draw their power away, it wouldn't destroy the dragons completely, but he wasn't sure he wanted to reveal that fact to her. He could imagine that she would use it in some way.

If she did, the power of the dragons would be lost.

Distantly, he was aware of the dragon misfits. He could feel Jessica's summons, the call to power she held onto, changing things for them. That summons continued to build, sending energy all around.

Jason had no way of fighting. No way of overpowering it.

Because it was calling through him.

He lunged toward her.

A burst of power exploded against him, sending him slamming back into the tower.

"I would like you to watch this. Given everything that you have done for these dragons, just how much you have offered them, I would like you to be witness to it as Lorach is strengthened and your rebellion is defeated."

He focused on all of the dragons, even the distant misfits, the new dragons, but as he felt for them, he recognized there was something within what she was doing that continued to overpower them.

"There is just so much power out there," she said.

"David would be disappointed in you," he said.

It was the only thing he could think of saying, but he

knew it would have no effect on her. They had never been close. He doubted she even mourned the loss of her brother.

"David never really understood the nature of this power. He always thought the dragons were intelligent creatures that needed our care and never understood how they were tools."

"You really *are* like Therin," he said.

She smiled at him. "I will take that as a compliment. He understood the need to serve the people. He understood Lorach could never be completely free when there remained the threat of dragons in the world."

Jason attempted to use an illusion, attempting to shift reality, but it failed. He tried another approach, trying to spin power, but even as he did, it failed again. The way she called on that power, using the tower to lock onto it, was too much.

He was at Jessica's mercy.

He tried to lunge after her again but she slammed into him, pushing power at him.

"You're going to weaken your people," Jason said.

"I will *strengthen* my people. I'll be able to protect them without fearing losing control of the dragons. My family and I will be able to direct this power. My family and I will be able to ensure the safety of Lorach. My family and I will be able to stretch the borders of our kingdom." Names that Janeya had mentioned drifted through his mind. Vistel, Hamthen, Loth, Jol. She would attack them. "We will do it all without fear of dragon attacks. My people will finally be safe. Because of what my family has done!"

Jason blinked.

She and her family.

He knew what he needed to do.

The connection was still there, but it was faint. He focused on the earth dragons and their rumbling, and he focused on the ice dragon. It was a danger calling the ice dragon here, especially not knowing what Jessica might do to him.

It had to be done.

Jason held onto that power, and he let that energy fill him, and he sent the summons out to the ice dragon, but he also pushed within it a connection that attempted to tell the ice dragon what he needed. Along with that, he pushed out toward Janeya. He got to his feet and staggered toward Jessica.

"You aren't going to be able to stop this."

"*I'm* not going to stop it," he said, his voice growing weaker by the moment. He wouldn't be able to withstand this for much longer, but he didn't think he had to.

Just long enough.

Jessica looked up. The dark-shadowed form of the ice dragon circled, heading toward them. She chuckled. It was a dark and angry sound. "Do you really think a dragon will harm me? In this place, with the power I have controlled all around us, there will not be anything one of your dragons would be able to do."

"Not one of the dragons, either," he said.

Power shot toward them. It wasn't the ice dragon. It was ice lightning.

Janeya streaked toward the ground.

She dropped with that ice lightning and he buffered her fall with the north wind. It swirled. Jason used everything within him, summoning power through him, and he created a swirling wind that guided her down toward the tower.

Then she landed. Her dark hair streamed around her, and the power of the dragons filled her. She really was beautiful.

Jessica looked at him. "Another woman?" She sneered at Jason. "What will our Sarah do? That is her name, isn't it? I remember when you were here before, how much she cared for you. How much she was willing to do on your behalf. And now, look at you. You have betrayed her."

Jason ignored her. "Use the tower," Jason said, ignoring her and focusing on Janeya.

Janeya frowned at him. "Use the *what*?"

"The tower. Can you feel that power?"

Janeya could scarcely look away from Jessica. He didn't blame her. There was so much power coming off of her. It practically crackled in the air, connecting her to the tower.

Jason couldn't use it.

He'd tried. He had failed.

But he wasn't an Arnson.

He wasn't a part of their family.

Janeya was.

"Use it," he whispered.

"I can feel something," she said, "though I don't know what it is."

"The tower. Draw on it."

Jessica glared at Jason and then turned to Janeya. "She won't be able to draw upon it. I have told you it requires the power of my family."

Janeya looked at Jason briefly as her eyes widened. Something shifted in her at that moment, as if she had come to a realization—and a decision. Her posture shifted, and she stood taller than she had before. "Are you sure?"

Jason nodded grimly. "I'm sure."

Then he could feel her attempting to.

At first, Jessica didn't recognize the threat Janeya posed, but the longer she worked, the more that she pulled upon power, the more certain Jason was that Jessica realized just what was happening.

There was a possession of the power within the tower, some connection to magic that seemed impossible for Jason to even fathom, let alone understand just how it existed. Jessica began to push, drawing upon even more power than before.

Janeya took a step back, though through the connection they shared, he recognized something else. There was more than just that power between them. There was their connection. The bond. And through it, he began to recognize her control over the power and how she asserted it.

Though Jessica attempted to gain control over it,

Janeya had familiarity with the dragon misfits, but it was more than that. Through the connection that she shared with Jason, she had access to something else.

She had access to the misfits.

The dragons wanted her to succeed. Wanted her to overpower it. Wanted for her to destroy Jessica. The dragons helped, and Janeya asserted her control.

He could feel it as she took control of the power in the tower.

It was enough that he wondered if *he* might be able to use it.

"What do I do?" she whispered.

"You have to push it back to the dragons," he said.

Jason didn't even know if such a thing were possible. At the same time, he suspected it would be. He suspected that whatever Jessica was doing, however she was summoning that power, there would have to be some way to reverse it.

That was what they needed to do.

Janeya started. The power flooded away from her.

It surged into him.

He took a deep breath. Connections to the dragons flared in his mind.

Jessica started toward them. "You won't—"

Jason slammed her with the wind.

She had enough power within her that she was able to fight back against what he did, but he continued to slam at her, using more and more of the wind to hold her back.

While doing so, Janeya continue to draw power from

all around her. She sent more and more flowing outward. Out. Toward the dragons.

Feeding *them*.

As she did, he knew it emptied the tower.

Which he thought needed to happen. The tower might have stored that power once, but it wasn't necessary any longer. The dragons should hold it.

"She shouldn't—"

Jason grinned. "You said your family. Unfortunately for you—and your family—*she* is your family."

Janeya continue to call on that power, and he could feel Jessica losing the upper hand. It gave Jason a moment to draw on power of his own. Janeya—through her connection to him—permitted it.

That was what he needed.

He summoned the energy, letting it fill him, and then he began to use all of it.

Everything within him began to crackle.

The northern wind and cold. The heat and anger deep beneath the ground. The wind through the trees. The chaos of the storm. The power of the earth. All of it mixed.

Jason summoned it together. He clapped his hands.

When he brought them together, everything burst into Jessica. All of the combined powers that he had begun feeling merged together. He was aware of the mingling of that power, and aware of how it flowed through him, and he focused it only on Jessica, pouring power into her. It was time that her rule of terror was over.

When he was done, she was gone. He hurried over to the tower's edge and looked down. There was no sign of her.

His blast had destroyed her.

He looked over at Janeya before sinking to his knees. "It's done."

26

"I'm not sure what to do with this energy," she said.

Jason focused on what she was doing with that power. "Keep pushing it back in the dragons, but don't destroy it."

"You *don't* want me to destroy this?"

He shook his head. "I'm not exactly sure why, but there's something about this that is old. Ancient. It's something the dragons gifted the people. We have to understand what it is, and then we can understand why. I think the tower held it to resurrect dragons, but we'll have to figure that out later."

She studied him for a moment before nodding.

He felt power beginning to seep back into him, and through his connection to the other dragons, he could feel it seeping into them as well.

It took a while. The power Jessica had been drawing was enormous, and it had very nearly drained all of the dragons of their power. Had they not intervened, Jessica would have done so.

He didn't want to damage the tower, or the power that came from it as he suspected it an ancient gift from the dragons. That would be a question for another time. As far as he knew, it was possible that the power within this tower prevented others from having a connection to the dragons.

Jason came to the edge of the tower.

Dragons circled high overhead. In the distance, he could feel as the dragons began to assert control over their energy again. He could feel that power flowing through them. There was something else out there. A different sense than what had been there before.

The females. They were guiding the dragons, giving them energy. They were doing something to them, and doing something for them. Jason had no idea what that was, only that something about them changed when the females were there.

"I can feel that," Janeya said.

Jason nodded. "I can feel that as well."

"It's… freeing."

Jason looked all around the city.

For the first time, he felt as if he were seeing it without illusion.

In addition to the tower, there were dozens of other buildings all made of the same white stone. The massive wall around it was a different stone, though he had a sense of heat from within that stone as well. People out in the streets looked up at the dragons, many of them stopping and staring.

Jason remembered what David had once told him, the way that he had warned him that people would fear the dragons. They would have to ensure otherwise. Somehow, they would have to make sure that the dragons were viewed as safe, not a danger. Not a threat.

"What now?" Janeya asked, joining him at the edge of the tower.

"Now we have to figure out what we will do next."

"What are *you* going to do?" she asked him.

"I haven't given it much thought. For a long time, I had wanted to simply end the fighting, but…" Now it seemed he had. Regardless of anything else, the fighting with the Dragon Souls, and with Lorach, could be over. "This is yours," he said to her. "All of this. You really can be the dragon queen."

She shook her head, turning away from the city. "That's never been what I wanted. I wanted to know the dragons. That was what Lorren taught me." Jason smiled, and she glared at him. "Why are you smiling? I thought you were going to want to make me stay here."

"I'm not going to make you stay anywhere that you don't want to be," he said. "You don't want to rule in Lorach, but someone needs to."

"They do," she said.

"And I suspect it needs to be somebody with ties to the ruling family."

He focused on the ice dragon. He could feel him out

there in the distance, high overhead, back in the north. Jason reached a hand out for Janeya, and she took it. While holding onto her, he called to the north energy and ice lightning caught him, carrying him up.

He landed on the ice dragon's back. From there, Jason tapped on his side. It didn't take long before they headed toward Dragon Haven. The illusion had long ago been shattered, leaving the city visible.

There was something beautiful about it, but he realized that something was not quite right. The ice dragon came to land and Jason hurried into the main building, Janeya at his side. She had been mostly quiet, and he expected her to be uncertain, though he wondered if she would agree to what he would suggest.

When he reached the main chamber, the throne room, he paused. There was a sense of energy within it. He pushed the door open and found Sarah alone within it. She looked up, her gaze darting from him to Janeya.

"It's done?" she asked. "She's gone?"

"It's done," he said.

Sarah looked over to Janeya. He couldn't read the expression on her face, but thought it might be fear. "Is she—"

Jason shook his head. "She doesn't want to rule in Lorach."

"She's one of their family."

"She is, but you are, as well."

"Distantly," Sarah said, turning away.

Jason crossed the chamber and touched her arm. It no

longer felt right to take her hand, though he wasn't sure if she would even agree to it if he were to try. "Not distantly. Close enough. Lorach will need leadership. They will need someone like yourself who knows how to rule, and knows how to do so peacefully. The rebellion can be over. Dragon Haven and Lorach can be united."

It seemed impossible to believe, but it felt true.

Sarah glanced over at Janeya. "Her claim is greater than mine."

"Only if she wanted to exert it," Jason said. He turned to Janeya. "Do you?"

Her face wrinkled in a deep frown. "No."

"See?"

"I don't know if I—"

This time, Jason did take her hand, squeezing it. "This is what you have been fighting for. This is your opportunity to work with the dragons. Work with those who have the power to reach the dragons. This is your chance."

She studied him. "What about you?"

"Lorach was never going to be my home."

"It could be. You have the same power. You could even lead there, if you were to want to."

There was an offer in that, but it was one Jason didn't think he fit. Sarah probably wouldn't understand. It had taken Jason a long time to understand.

"I can't. I'm not like that."

"But you are. You have the power of the dragons."

He shook his head sadly. "I don't know what power I have, but it's not the power of the dragons. I'm a misfit, just like the dragons I've been working with. It's time for me to understand what that means. It's time I find my real place."

Sarah watched him, and after a moment, she nodded. "It's really over."

"It's over. The dragons are safe. The rest of the Dragon Guard who came, along with the people of Dragon Haven who fought, are securing the Dragon Souls who remain. The other dragons are ensuring that the Dragon Souls aren't going to try to overpower them. And the city is waiting for you. It's waiting for its new leader. Its queen, if that's the title you would take."

Sarah wrinkled her face up in a frown. "I don't think that I want to be a queen."

"You can't be a king," Jason said.

"I don't know what I want to be. For now, I'll just be Sarah."

Jason smiled at her. "Maybe you're a bit of a misfit, too." He paused as Henry entered, his face bloodstained, the dragonskin stained. William joined him, standing a pace behind. Jason had felt them coming. "Did you find the rest of your people?"

Sarah flicked her gaze to Henry before nodding. "We found them. The dragons found them, really." She looked at Jason. "Your mother helped. The dragons could detect them. There were Dragon Souls that had surrounded them, but their power disappeared, and…" She shrugged. "Your mother led them back."

Jason breathed out in a soft sigh. They were safe.

And his mother had helped.

It was enough to make him smile.

Coming to Dragon Haven had been good for her. For Kayla.

It had given them a chance to be something else.

They could do that here.

Jason could not.

She laughed softly. "What will you do, then?"

Jason glanced over at Janeya. There was a bit of a hopeful expression in her eyes. "I think I'm going to visit with my sister, then my mother, and then I'm curious what's beyond the mountains. There's something more out there."

Far enough that it would be difficult for anyone here to reach him. But not so difficult for him to reach that other place. If Jessica had wanted to push the borders of Lorach, he wanted to know what was out there to ensure another threat wouldn't come.

He turned to Janeya. "What do you say, dragon queen? Would you like to explore with another misfit?"

She offered him a lopsided smile. "Queen? I saw how the dragons looked at you."

"And how was that?" Jason asked, ignoring the pointed way Sarah watched him.

Janeya laughed. "Let's just say I can't be the queen. But I would like to explore with you. And the dragons."

Jason squeezed her hands, but he didn't need the contact to feel their shared emotions: Trepidation. A hint of fear. But mostly excitement.

Maybe he would no longer have to be an outsider. Maybe with Janeya he could finally find where he belonged. Maybe he could find other misfits like them.

Janeya nodded, understanding and knowing him without him even needing to say the words.

Jason had finally found his place.

Looking for more dragon books?

The Dragon Thief series is set in the world of The Dragon Misfits. Book 1 is Lava Dragon.

It will take a Dragon Thief to find a Dragon Thief.

Tessa has found the key to funding her search for her parents. Dragon artifacts are valuable, and stealing them from the crown and selling them back has worked well for her. But when a dragon egg goes missing, and the king sends his most trusted Dragon Touched in search of the

Dragon Thief, Tessa suddenly finds herself chased for a job she didn't do.

She finds herself drawn into a dangerous plot against the king while fighting off her growing attraction to one of the men chasing her. To clear her name, and protect her friends, she has to figure out who took the egg, return it without anyone being the wiser, all while staying ahead of the dangerous Dragon Touched sent to find the egg.

I'm thrilled to reveal my first collaboration. Also set in the world of The Dragon Misfits, check out book 1 in Cycle of Dragons: The Caged Dragon.

A young man wanting to protect his family begins an epic journey.

Life on the farm at the edge of the kingdom is

anything but routine for Ashan. The plains around Berestal suffer from severe storms, making travel to the city difficult, with the threat of an attack from the people of Vard always looming. He long ago abandoned dreams of serving as a dragon rider, caring for his injured father and brother, but everything is about to change.

A Vard attack forces Ashan to risk everything to protect his sister. Doing so brings him closer to the dragons than he had ever imagined, but brings him into a war he never intended to join. Somehow, Ashan and his best friend might be the only ones able to prevent the Vard from reaching a prize they'd long sought, if only they can survive the dangers of the forest, the mysterious Djarn people, a terrifying creature chasing them, and the power of a dragon mage.

SERIES BY D.K. HOLMBERG

The Dragonwalkers Series

The Dragonwalker

The Dragon Misfits

Elemental Warrior Series:

Elemental Academy

The Elemental Warrior

The Cloud Warrior Saga

The Endless War

The Dark Ability Series

The Shadow Accords

The Collector Chronicles

The Dark Ability

The Sighted Assassin

The Elder Stones Saga

The Lost Prophecy Series

The Teralin Sword

The Lost Prophecy

The Book of Maladies Series

The Book of Maladies

The Lost Garden Series

The Lost Garden

Printed in Great Britain
by Amazon

59440742R10234